Michelle Larks

CRISIS MODE

Crisis Mode is a novella that any woman can identify with. Michelle Larks has written a unique novella about unplanned pregnancy, mental illness, infidelity, and old age that draw the reader into each character's world. Crisis Mode speaks to women across American that wishes to stand up and be heard.
The Literary Cafe
www.literarycafe.org

A How-To manual that teaches women across America to cope with problems, identifies fears, and become the victor. Michelle Larks has written a book for women across all racial boundaries.
Bella Online
www.bellaonline.com

"Crisis Mode is a brilliant series of unconditional love laden masterpieces! Larks dramatically captures the spirit and soul in an ingenious fashion."
Marc Lacy
The Looking Heart
www.marclacy.com

"Crisis Mode speaks of real life issues women face everyday. Michelle Larks doesn't just present the problems; she provides answers."
 Best Selling Author—Frederick James Preston
Do As I Say, Not As I Do

Crisis Mode

Michelle Larks

ISBN: 0-9762382-8-1

Edited by Kathleen Jackson
Layout and Design by Kim Williams

For more information and to order online,
www.michellelarks.com.

F&M Enterprises
P.O. Box 932
Boilingbrook, IL 60440

This book is dedicated
to the BMWs

Acknowledgements

Praises Be To My Father Above for continuing to guide my inner voice and hands at the keyboard. There are so many people I have to thank who've helped me along my writing journey; my mothers, daughters, sisters, brothers, other family members, and friends. Especially those who supported my first writing endeavor 'A Myriad of Emotions.' I'd like to give special thanks to my sisters, Sabrina, Donna, most of all Rolanda, and my D.C. pal Audrey for spreading the word and helping sell the book like you all were the author instead of me. I'd like to thank my publicist, Anita Shari Peterson of PCG Literary Marketing, for your assistance, support and constant enthusiasm. Special shouts out to Kathleen Jackson, my editor, for all your guidance and knowledge. Thank you Pittershawn Palmer for the book stunning cover design. You were on target.

Kudos to Sister Serious About Reading and Ya-Ya Mamas Book Clubs, your support and feedback has been invaluable. Many thanks to Mr. G's Super Club, Frugal Muse, African American Images, and Full Circle Bookstores for allowing me to sign books at your establishment. Thanks Raw Sistaz, The Literary Caf, Literary World, and Black Men in America websites for your great reviews. They are a source of inspiration. Winston Village, Thank You, Thank You, as well as Kid's Stop & Total Image Salon, Gardenia Florist, and Nicole's Beauty Supply, I appreciate your stocking the book in your places of business. Thank s to my co-workers, and everyone who purchased a copy of 'A Myriad of Emotions'.

Most of all I'd like to thank my husband Fredrick for your love and support as I worked feverously on both books. Without you neither book would have been possible.

Michelle Larks
2005

WHAT'S
a
Woman
to
do ?

One

Sharita Atkins stood in her small bathroom methodically washing her hands over and over as if in a trance. After rinsing and flickering off the excess water, she slowly dried them on a tattered pink towel hanging on the rack above the toilet. When she was done, she closed her eyes, recited the Lord's Prayer, uttered "Amen" and made the sign of the cross across her chest. Her eyes then homed in on the tube on the sink, which was a home pregnancy test kit. She turned and walked unsteadily out of the bathroom and into the living room, allowing the tiny tube time to process the specimen and deliver the final verdict. She sank heavily into the padded cushions of the couch, tucking her legs under her body. Trembling uncontrollably, she wrapped her arms around her upper body. *Lord, what if I'm pregnant again,* she thought, as a soft moan of anguish escaped from her lips. Sharita kept glancing at the old clock repeatedly to see if it was time to learn her fate.

She rose from the sofa, walked across the room and stared out the window. The scenery was depressing her, being a long-time resident of one of the many housing projects on the south side of Chicago. Like many of the surrounding structures, her building was scheduled for demolition next year. Bottles, papers and other debris cluttered the sidewalk and sparse grassy areas like polka dots. Children ran happily around the dilapidated playground shouting with glee. In the far recesses of the building, dealers milled about, waiting for the next opportunity to hawk their wares. In the dark corners of the buildings, teenage boys ran game on unsuspecting girls.

"How can I even think of bringing another child into something like this?" Sharita thought aloud.

Rita, as family and friends call her, is twenty-seven years old and the mother of three. She's a petite, attractive, Hershey chocolate woman of color, with a shapely build. Rita possesses a brilliant, twinkling smile, which lights her heart-shaped face. She keeps her coarse, short hair styled in twisties for low maintenance. Her only daughter Destiny is twelve years old and a miniature clone of her. The twins, Devan and Deante, are mischievous, hyperactive eight-year old boys, full of life. They favor their father in looks, as if he spit them out.

Her eyes gravitated to the clock again. Sighing softly, she thought to herself, *Finally, it's time.*

She walked back into the bathroom, her legs shaking as if the weight of her body was too ponderous for them to support. Her hands trembled as she lifted the tube off the sink. There were two lines, just as she'd known there would be. *Well, the verdict is in, I'm definitely pregnant.* She began wobbling and grabbed the sink for support.

"Lord, what am I going to do?" she said aloud to herself, letting go of the sink and sinking clumsily to the floor.

Beating the floor with her fists, she cried and then cried some more. After what seemed like an eternity, the tears finally stopped and she scurried into the bedroom to the closet, where her hands groped frantically on the top shelf until she came upon her stash. She sat lifelessly on the bed and rolled a joint. After firing it up, she suddenly changed her mind and stubbed it out. *Ugh, this is what got me into this mess in the first place.* She thought, grimacing as if the joint she held was pure poison.

A few months ago, her life was progressing nicely. At long last, Rita had begun making headway into breaking away from the stereotypical lifestyle she'd been accustomed to living. Step one was graduating from a trade school, which she completed a short while ago. She'd also begun setting attainable goals for herself at the recommendation of her caseworker, Ms. Jones. The philosophy was a difficult one for Rita to accept and grasp. However, as time went on, she began to make progress and bravely continued to forge ahead because of her love for her children.

Her Grandmother Millie, or Mah-Dear as family and friends affectionately call her, set Rita's project lifecycle in motion. She's definitely the matriarch of the Atkins family and rules with an iron fist. If you go up against her, you'd better have your stuff in order. Her tongue is razor sharp and capable of cutting a person to slivers.

In the fifties, she migrated to Chicago from Alabama and soon met the love of her life, Louis Smith. She'll tell you candidly that Louis was the coffee to her cream, he being very dark skinned in complexion and she being high yellow. They'd been together for more than three-fourths of their lives until pancreatic cancer claimed his life two years ago. Louis had begged Mah-Dear to marry him many times, but being the stubborn woman that she is, she would never grant his request, because putting one over on the government was too important to her. She bragged to all who passed her way about the government's money tree. Marriage to Louis was never a consideration, just like his feelings about many issues. Moving out of the projects and doing things *the right and legal way* was the root of many arguments between them, however, because of the deep love and children they shared, somehow they managed to co-exist happily most of the time.

In turn, Mah-Dear passed that same lifestyle along to two of her three daughters, Vonetta and Barbara Ann, Rita's mother. Angela, her middle daughter, managed to escape Mah-Dear's dubious legacy by winning a scholarship to Roosevelt University. She continued to excel in the academic world and achieved her goal of finishing college in three and half years. After that, the number one thing on her to do list was leave to Mah-Dear's house. Before the ink was dry on her degree, she hightailed it to Detroit, where she still resides with her husband, George and their daughter, Patricia Ann. Angela rarely comes back to Chicago to visit her relatives. In fact, the last time she was home was for her daddy's funeral.

Mah-Dear is getting up in age, close to seventy years old. She's a short, very light skinned woman with silver gray hair that she still wears in that old lady press and curl style. Her eyes are hazel in color and laugh lines have taken up permanent residence on her face. Mah-Dear wears focals, as she calls them, and has a peculiar way of peering over them when she looks at you.

Barbara Ann just celebrated her forty-fifth birthday, a honey brown skinned woman with big brown eyes like Rita's. She's taller than her mother and daughter, standing five feet five inches and she wears her thin reddish brown hair in a ponytail. She's slim, whereas Rita has the shape of an hourglass, just as Mah-Dear had back in the day. Barbara often bemoans her physical attributes of having no tits, little ass and skinny legs. To put it quite simply, Angela looks like Mah-Dear, Vonetta resembles Louis and Barbara is a combination of both of them.

When Louis died, Mah-Dear found God and a spiritual home at the Living Word Baptist Church, a small storefront edifice located near the projects. Since being saved, she's become even more opinionated as if she'd forgotten that Vonetta and Barbara Ann still experience life as she had instructed them for so long. Now, Mah-Dear fervently hopes that her granddaughters, particularly Rita, who is her first and favorite, won't repeat the same mistakes she made in life.

Mah-Dear's building was demolished nine months ago and Barbara's had come down a few months before. After that, they decided to pool their monies and move in together. The two are still adjusting to their new place of residence, which is a step up from the projects, that revered place Mah-Dear had idolized for so long.

So far, Barbara and Mah-Dear are doing okay. Rita comes over quite often to visit and can hardly wait until it's her turn to make that move. Even though she'd bought into the lifestyle, Mah-Dear had preached for so long that Rita was ready for a change and eagerly anticipated making a better life for her children. Now all of those dreams and plans appeared to be in jeopardy.

t W o

D amn, damn, damn!" Rita said, smacking her forehead, exasperated. "If only I hadn't gone to Lyn's party, smoking and drinking, I wouldn't be in this mess today. Going to Tone's afterwards was the biggest mistake of all," she mumbled.

Antone or Tone, is the father of her children. He also has the distinct honor of being her one and only, as well as her off and on lover. They've been arguing a lot lately, especially about Rita's change in lifestyle. His theory being, if life is good, why change it? If it ain't broke, then don't fix it.

Eight weeks prior, and almost to the exact day, Rita's best friend, Lyn, had thrown a birthday party celebrating her turning the big 30. Rita had been hitting the books hard and heavy in preparation for her upcoming finals. Since she'd started class, Lyn and Shirley had taken to calling her a hermit. A few days before the party, Rita and Lyn talked on the telephone.

"You've been staying in the house way too much. Come on Rita, it's time to take a break. You need to enjoy life, to stop and smell the coffee."

Laughing, Rita corrected her, "Isn't that stop and smell the roses?"

"Whatever, you know what I mean," Lyn fired back at her. "Don't be playing that school stuff with me girl. I knew you back when."

During the entire conversation, Lyn cajoled and begged until Rita gave in. The next step was convincing Barbara to keep the kids overnight, which was no small feat since her mother loved going out. Most Friday nights, Barbara could be found at her favorite local bar nursing a couple glasses of wine, and Saturday is bid whist night with childhood friends. They'd fry fish and chicken, cook a big pot of spaghetti, chop cabbage for coleslaw and Barbara would sip her wine and try to run as many bostons as humanly possible on the opposing teams. However, the weekend of Lyn's party, Rita was in luck and Barbara agreed to watch the kids.

On the night of the Lyn's party, Rita was clad in skintight black jeans and a burgundy low cut, silk shirt. Her hair shone brightly and nestled gently against her head. Standing in front of the bathroom mirror, Rita expertly applied lipstick to her pursed lips.

"Not too bad. Looking good, girl," she said, aloud to her reflection.

She dabbed her mouth with a tissue to blot off the excess lipstick, turned off the lights and left the apartment. She walked quickly along the winding concrete path to Lyn's building. Anticipation filled her body and Rita felt a rush of pure joy at the thought of spending time with friends, and possibly the night with Antone.

Since I haven't been out in a while, now is the time for me to kick back and let loose. Let's get this party started, she thought to herself.

The celebration was in full swing when she arrived. Smoke seemed to dance in the air and the acrid scent of marijuana assaulted her nostrils.

Antone hovered anxiously near the front door, waiting on her to make an appearance. As she stepped over the threshold, he wrapped her in his arms and planted a juicy kiss upon her lips.

"Hey, baby," Antone greeted her, smiling down at her uplifted face.

Taking her hand, he led her into the party. Friends and acquaintances shouted her name over the loud din of the music.

"Hey, Ree-Ree, what brings you out tonight?" Donna yelled. She's a childhood friend as well as a classmate of Lyn and Rita.

"Yeah, what brings you out stranger?" Marcus added. He's Donna's old man and Tone's cousin. "What's up, girl? We haven't seen you in ages."

"I've been studying," Rita answered, proudly. "You know I've been taking an LPN course and we had finals today. There's no doubt in my mind I aced that baby." Rita had been attending a local trade school for six months, training as a licensed practical nurse.

Shirley walked over to the group after getting her dance grove on and hugged Rita's shoulders tightly. "I'm proud of you, cuz."

"So I'm here celebrating that A+ that's coming my way, along with *Ms. Thang's* birthday," Rita explained, grinning at Lyn.

Congratulations were offered and a few catcalls of 'You Go Girl' resounded from friends. She walked to each of them, exchanging high-fives. After all the greetings and congratulations were expressed, Antone took her hand and led her to a secluded corner of the room. He lit a cigarette, the reddish yellow glow illuminating his face.

"You hungry, baby?" He asked. "Do you want anything to drink? How are the kids?"

"Tone, one question at a time," she scolded, playfully. "The kids are doing fine. Destiny got all A's on her report card this marking period. The twins, however, are another story altogether. Still, all in all, they did okay considering." She shrugged. "Devan is getting a little too mannish for me, but I can handle his little behind. As far as a drink, you can bring me a coke," she said, brushing her hair back off her forehead.

"I'll be right back," he promised.

Rita watched him maneuver his way through the crowd to the kitchen, his tight butt a synchronized symphony in motion. When he made it to the kitchen, a few of his boys were gathered there. While Tone stopped to holler at them, Rita stared at him mesmerized, her lips parted slightly. His six feet tall, slim muscular-built frame and creamy caramel complexion, topped with big expressive light brown eyes, was quite pleasing to her eyes. His big sensuous lips beaconed to Rita, seemingly saying 'kiss me'. His hair is styled neatly in locks, which curl and stop above his broad shoulders. As Barbara would say, he's fine as wine. Antone was the only man who could make her body sing. As she stood there looking at him, her body started tingling. He made her love jones come down instantly.

Since she'd started class, Antone complained bitterly that she was changing. Her response to that was that she had to change for the children. In her eyes, they should be the first consideration for the two of them. They'd been together since she was thirteen and he fourteen. They share an off and on relationship, but somehow they always seem to make their way back to each other. He promised her years ago he'd always have her back. So far, he hasn't failed her, not when it counted.

Antone makes his living selling drugs. He oversees a crew of runners, and that was all he'd ever really done as far as making a living. His father did the same before him, and unfortunately, his home is now a prison cell. Rita often prayed that the same fate wouldn't befall Tone.

During one of their many volatile fights, Rita calmly tried to reason with Tone about how they needed to break the cycle. She tried patiently to explain her thoughts to him wanting more for the children and that they deserved better than what they had. As the arguments grew in frequency, he stopped coming by as much.

"Anyway," she said, after Tone returned, sipping her coke, "I have good news. There's a chance I may be able to go to college. My caseworker has been checking into schools for me. It won't be a university, only a junior college to start, and she thinks she can find grants to offset the cost. If I do well, then who knows, maybe I'll go to a four-year university. Right now, Kennedy King College looks like a good bet. Maybe one day, I'll become a nurse."

Tone felt Rita had become unreasonable since she'd gotten her GED, you couldn't tell her anything anymore. It seemed she always had the answer to everything and was forever quoting Ms. Jones, her caseworker. If he thought she was unrealistic about the GED, he felt she was just plain ridiculous about the LPN certificate. At the same time, she'd been on his case for the longest for him to get his GED.

"Yeah, right," he'd sneer, contemptuously during one of their many fights, "all that for a minimum wage job?"

He didn't see how at his age, which was damn near thirty, a piece of paper would change the quality of his way of life. He still wouldn't have any marketable skills, just a piece of paper.

"You put in the time, get it and still barely have enough money for rent, more less a ride. Let's not forget to mention feeding the family, and don't even think about extras," he'd argue.

"Destiny is growing up, Tone," she'd counter back at him, "and do you know what they call girls who live in the projects? They call them hood rats and chicken heads. I don't want her labeled as such. She's my baby, a smart beautiful girl, and I want her out of here, out of the projects, out of this life. I want her to go to college like Aunt Angela, and who knows, maybe even like me."

Tone dropped out of high school when Rita was pregnant with Destiny. Shortly after that, he'd begun his illegal career. He'd stopped dealing a few times, but then money would become tight, tempers would flare and back into the streets he'd go. He was lucky in that he'd never been incarcerated.

Rita dropped out of school when she turned sixteen. By law in Illinois, one is not required to continue school after that age. She wanted to get away from Barbara, with her many rules and always being on her case about something, so she signed up for welfare, gotten her own two-bedroom apartment and had been on her own ever since then.

When welfare reformation came about, she had no choice but to rethink her future. With all her bragging of putting one over on the government, Mah-Dear never imagined the day when welfare would be no more.

Ms. Jones took the liberty of signing Rita up for Section 8 housing. She'd been on the waiting list for three months and hoped that within the next few months she would have her own place away from the project, just like Mah-Dear and Barbara.

While taking a sip of his coke that was spiked generously with rum, Antone noticed that Rita had that stubborn, 'ready to do battle' look on her face.

"Let's not fight, baby," he murmured, putting his middle finger gently on her lips. "How 'bout we just celebrate your grades, Lyn's birthday and enjoying each other's company."

When she finished her drink, he grabbed her by the waist and said, "Miss Rita, may I have this dance?"

Five hours later, the party was winding down. Most of the people had left in search of another set with more food, drink and smoke. Hot and sweaty, Antone and Rita stood in the corner, sipping their drinks and catching their breaths. As the soft strains of Maxwell's *"Fortunate"* began playing, Tone set both drinks on the table and pulled Rita onto the dance floor. He kissed her tenderly on the neck, his hands gently caressing her body, leaving flames of desire. Tone skillfully put the moves on her, and Rita feeling no pain, decided to go with the flow.

"Where are the kids tonight?" He whispered, huskily into her ear as the song was ending.

"Mommy has them," she answered, a wicked smirk on her face.

"How 'bout we go to my place then?" Desire was written on his face and his hands were driving her crazy, roaming over her body. "I've been missing you, Rita," he growled in her ear, sending shivers of desire up and down her spine. Her legs grew weak and she began to tremble.

"Tone, I really shouldn't. I need to…"

He kissed her deeply, silencing the words he knew she was about to say. Then taking her hand in his, he gently licked the middle of her hand and pressed it against his manhood, he felt rock hard. She moaned, swaying into his body.

"Baby," he said, smiling wickedly, "we've really been missing you."

After one last go-round on the dance floor, they left the party and headed to his place. When they entered the apartment, the strong scent of incense filled the air. Rita sat on the couch, unbuttoned the top of her blouse and slipped her shoes off while Tone put R. Kelly's *"12 Play"* into the CD player. Then he went to the kitchen and returned with a chilled bottle of Alize's Red Passion, a bottle of Hennessey and two long stemmed frosted glasses.

"You're mighty sure of yourself, aren't you?" she teased, gently.

He quickly rolled a joint, and poured generous portions of Red Passion into both the glasses, spiking his with Hennessey. Then he dimmed the lights.

"It's been a long time," he said, taking a seat next to her. "I know we don't always see eye to eye, but know that I love you, Sharita Annette Atkins. When I'm not right there beside you, close your eyes, see me, feel me and know that I'm there with you forever."

He sounded so corny that they burst out laughing. Still, she knew what he meant. He leaned over, pulled her onto his lap and kissed her deeply, wreaking havoc on her senses with his tongue. They smoke, drank, and the next thing you knew, clothes started flying. He led her into the bedroom and handled his business as masterfully as he had many times before.

"And now, here I am," Rita moaned, looking at the test tube with its two blue lines screaming, *"YOU'RE PREGNANT!"*

She knew in her heart that it was true. Tender breasts, bouts of nausea and a constant feeling of exhaustion had been her companion for the past couple of weeks. She just needed confirmation.

three

Rita's classes were held at a local catholic church. The grand structure was fascinating to her. Many times after class, she'd sit in the sanctuary and observe the priests and nuns in motion and watch as the people would come into the church to light candles and go to the confession booth. Soon, she began attending mass. After three months of study, she converted to Catholicism. When she told her family, they were mostly amused. Mah-Dear, on the other hand, was appalled.

"Girl, you crazy or sumptin? Black folks ain't got no business being Catholic. They are either Baptist or siddity Methodists. Next thing you know," Mah-Dear grumbled, "you'll be telling us that you're a republican. Ain't that the church where them priests been messing with children? How you gonna go to a place like that to worship God?"

Shirley, feigning innocence, added her two cents, "Rita converted because she doesn't want to go to hell. Didn't you know Mah-Dear, catholic people don't go to hell, they go to a place called purgatory. Do you know what else?" Her voice dropped to a whisper, "They don't believe in God, just saints."

Her comments definitely got Mah-Dear on a roll.

"How you gonna to go to a church with no God, girl? Saints my ass!" she screamed, in horror.

Finally she ran out of steam and looked imploringly around the room at anyone unlucky enough to witness the tirade.

"She's crazy, that girl done lost her mind," she said, shaking her head sadly.

Rita now regretted running off at the mouth, feeling it would come back to haunt her. She was well aware from her religious training that abortion is a mortal sin.

Damn, she thought, shivering, *why didn't he pull out? Hell, I should've stopped him.*

Glancing at the clock, she saw it was almost two-thirty. School was dismissed at two forty-five, therefore, the pity party would have to be postponed for now. Many years ago, Dantrell Davis, a seven-year-old boy, had been killed in the Cabrini Green housing projects while walking to school with his mother. The tragedy had such a profound effect on Rita that she made it her business to walk to school with her children in the morning and meet them afterwards. If she was unable to make it, or there was inclement weather, Tone had to step up to the plate. Since neither was the case that day, she got out of bed, grabbed her jacket and hurried out, slamming the door shut behind her.

She and the children met at the same location everyday. As her shoulders slumped forward, Rita stood there looking forlorn and lost in thought, with a dazed, *I don't believe this is happening to me* look on her face. The twins, who were dismissed earlier than Destiny, ran up to Rita clamoring for her attention with smudged graded papers clutched tightly in their little brown hands.

"Were you good in school today?" she asked Devan, smiling down at him.

He nodded yes.

"I'm always good," Deante bragged, grinning with missing teeth and all.

Just then, Destiny, wanting her share of attention, walked up and gave Rita a kiss, her braids swinging in rhythm.

"Mama," she said excitedly, "I got an A on my science test. Look." She thrust the paper into Rita's hand.

After giving Destiny praise for a job well done, the four walked back to the apartment, talking along the way. While Rita was at the stove preparing dinner, Destiny and the boys sat at the table doing homework assignments. From time to time, Rita would pause to help them when they became stuck on a problem.

After they finished having dinner, the boys sat in the living room watching television and Destiny lay in her bed with a book in her hand. With her evening chores done, Rita informed the kids that she was tired and going to lie down for a little while.

Upon entering the boys' room, Rita looked around and shook her head, astounded at the mess that had accumulated since that morning.

"I'll straighten up this room later." She thought, as she lay sprawled across their bed. Suddenly, tears filled the corner of her eyes. *I was so close to having it all*, she thought ruefully, wiping away tears. *I was trying to make a better life for my kids, now I could lose it all by having been stupid.* As she heard the doorknob turning, she quickly wiped away her tears and turned over in the bed.

"Mama, are you all right?" Destiny asked, standing at the door. "You never lay down this early unless you're sick. You're not sick, are you?"

"I'm fine, honey," she smiled, weakly, "just tired."

"Do you think you'll feel better by the weekend? Don't forget we're supposed to go look at houses. I can hardly wait to move so I can have my own bedroom," she said, spinning around the room. "The only bad part," she continued, "is that I'll have to change schools and I'll miss my friends."

"You'll be okay Des, you'll make new ones. Now go and finish your book. Let me rest."

"Okay, Mama. The book I'm reading is so good," she said, closing the door gently behind her.

Rita lay motionless on the bed, thoughts racing a mile a minute through her mind. After a while, she got up and walked into the kitchen. She picked up the telephone and dialed Antone's pager number. A few minutes later, the phone rang, but before she could pick it up, Devan snatched it up, beating her to the punch.

"Daddy! When are you coming over? We want to see you, we haven't seen you in a long time," he said, excitedly.

Then she heard Devan say, "I miss you, Daddy." After he finished talking, he handed the telephone to his sister.

"I want a new pair of jeans since I got an A on my science test," she informed Tone, in no uncertain terms. Then she yelled, "Mama, telephone!"

The boys began imitating her, exaggerating their voices and saying *"Mama"* in a girlish tone.

"Tell them to leave me alone." Destiny pouted, scowling at double trouble, as she called them.

"Leave your sister alone." Rita said, mechanically.

After she picked up the telephone, she could hear Destiny breathing heavily. "Hang up, I've got it."

"What's up, Rita?" Tone asked, casually. "The kids seem to be a'ight. Do you need something?"

"I need to talk to you," she said, hesitantly.

"Do you want me to come over tonight?" He asked, hopefully.

"No," she answered hastily, "tomorrow will be fine."

"How 'bout I pick the kids up from school, stop and get something to eat for dinner and head your way?"

"No, I need to see you before then. What about noon tomorrow?"

"This must be serious." He remarked.

"No, not really," she replied, half-heartedly.

"A'ight then, I'll see you tomorrow," he said, ending the call.

She left the kitchen, went into the bedroom that she and Destiny shared and began rummaging through the dresser drawer in search of the housing listing. Finally she located it and began reading, but her heart wasn't in it at all. *Good thing school is over,* she thought, *or I'd be in a world of trouble if I had to study now.*

Finally, she gave up after deciding the whole thing was an exercise in futility. She walked back into the kitchen, and once again, checked homework for the fiftieth time. Giving that up also, she decided to get the kids bathed and into bed.

After they were tucked in, Rita began preparing for the long night ahead. Sleep didn't come easy for her, cause she didn't have a clue as to what to do about her dilemma. Finally, she got out of bed, walked back into the living room and lit a cigarette. *This is truly a disaster,* she thought, *maybe I should call Mommy or Mah-Dear. On second thought, I'll talk to Tone first.*

After puffing on the cigarette a few more times, her stomach began heaving. She jumped up from the couch and made it to the bathroom just in time as her dinner flew into the toilet bowl, spewing from her mouth like an erupting volcano. Destiny came out of the tiny bedroom.

"Mama, you really sound sick. Are you okay?"

"Something I ate must have upset my stomach," she answered. "I'm okay now, just go back to bed."

Destiny reluctantly turned away from her mother and walked back into the bedroom.

four

After Antone got off the phone with Rita, he walked over to Marcus' apartment and rapped on the door. Marcus looked out the peephole, and after seeing that it was Tone, he opened the door.

"What's up, cuz?" He asked, holding out his hand.

"You got it, man." Tone answered, grasping Marcus' hand in return. Tone and Marcus are first cousins.

When Tone entered, Marcus' father, Michael, got up from the couch and pulled his cap on as if he was about to leave. Then he pulled Tone into a quick grasp. Michael was once one of Chicago's most powerful drug lords. He retired ten years ago, at which time, he began grooming Marcus to take his place when he turned sixteen.

For years, Marcus would say he was leaving the life, but like Mah-Dear, he too felt he was putting one over on the government. He loved the idea of never paying taxes. Forewarned before it became public that the projects were coming down, he began diversifying his monies. He'd also been scouting new territory to continue his lucrative drug trade.

"You want something to drink?" Marcus asked.

"Naw man, I'm straight."

"So what's up? What brings you out tonight, any problems?" Marcus asked, pointedly.

"No, it's all good. I just got off the phone with Rita and something's up with her."

"Any ideas what it might be?"

"Not really," Tone grunted, "I just know whatever it is, it's big."

"How you two been getting along?"

"Same as always." Tone said.

"Well, I guess you'll just have to wait until Miss Rita is ready to talk. I hear she's on the waiting list getting ready to move. How you dealing with that?"

"I'm cool. Personally, I think she has on these blinders or something. The woman really thinks her life is gonna change because of that nursing certificate."

"Well Tone," Marcus said, slowly nodding, "life is going to change. You got to remember that three generations of Atkins women have lived up in here. So, no doubt bro, it's going to be a radical change for her. You down with that?"

"Naw man, I ain't down with any of it." Tone answered, heatedly. "For real, what's a piece of paper gonna do? Shit is still gonna cost an arm and a leg no matter what address is on her mailbox. Poverty is always gonna be around, like it's always been. I feel like she's got her hopes up, thinking that certificate is gonna change something."

"Some of the things you said are true, no doubt," Marcus said, "but it's still a step."

"What do you mean by that?" Tone asked. "A step where?"

"Cuz, you seem to forget that these walls, the projects, are going to come tumbling down. You better be thinking about where you going. This has been the way of life, but everybody's going to have to leave here eventually. Rita is right in that she has to take care of the kids, especially since welfare is about to become a thing of the past. How are you going to take care of all of them? What's your plan dog?"

Marcus ran the drug activity in the hood and Tone worked for him. The fact that they were related gave Tone the luxury of leaving the business from time to time.

"Hell, I'm confused." Tone exclaimed, waving his hand about. "You've always pretty much talked against the government and politicians, hell even Mayor Daley, and let's not leave out the Chicago Housing Authority. So where is this coming from? You've always spouted off about how the white man kept us down. I don't get it."

"Times are changing and we've got to keep up with it. Once these walls come down, we've got to have a plan in place to keep the money coming in. Do you see where I'm coming from?" Marcus answered.

"Kind of, but I don't know man." Tone replied, at a lost. "Rita has been going on and on, now this coming from you. I don't know what's up with all that shit."

"Son," Michael said, nodding his head at Marcus, "I agree with you. You've got to have a backup plan to keep the dollars flowing. Hell, make sure you got a couple of plans. But I disagree with you on the paper trip, it don't mean a thing. You think the powers that be, aka the White Man, hasn't figured out that tearing down these walls is a double-edge sword. That's the city's politically correct way of dealing with drugs and the gangs all at the same time. The city also gets back prime real estate, particularly up Cabrini Green's way. It's too close to the lily white gold coast. Who's living in the projects? Us black folks. Ms. Chicago, courtesy of Mayor Daley and his flunkies, decided it was time for the land to come back to massuh, by any means necessary. So, who's gotta go, the poor, downtrodden black folks. You think the man really gives a shit about us down here in the projects? Open your eyes Marcus, the white man done held us down as a race, always have, always will."

Michael was in his element, preaching the word according to the illegal entrepreneur of the street.

"I don't care what you think a piece of paper says. Think about it, both of y'all!" He yelled, looking at Tone, his facial muscles twitching furiously as he spoke.

"Damn, here we go. He's on a roll now." Marcus thought, as a mild expression of distaste marred his face. Tone stared at Michael enthralled, always in total agreement with his uncle about most things. Uncle Mike was the closest thing he had to a father, he was also the only successful black man he knew other than Marcus.

"Affirmative action," Michael continued, "is almost gone. So now they're gonna limit who they let in their lily white schools, businesses, everything. Ever notice how the more elite the schools are, those are the very ones fighting to keep us outside of their doors. Them republicans think welfare was made just for us black folks anyway, even though statistics have proven that's not the case. You don't think it was an accident that the AIDS epidemic is higher in Africa and among blacks than in any other nation or racial group, do you? Hell, who can afford the treatment? Tearing down these walls is all about the almighty dollar, as everything is in life. Don't even get me started on minimum wage, which doesn't keep up with the cost of living. It's just another way of keeping a brother down. Let's see, you gotta work two or three jobs a day just to make in a week what we pull in over the course of a few hours."

"Hospital care is just plain ridiculous." Michael went on to say. "Medicine costs an arm and a leg. Hell, most old folks can't even afford it. Hmmm, I wonder why the newspaper never runs stories on how many old people die because they can't afford healthcare. Who controls all of that Marcus?" He roared, caught up in his own rhetoric, hands waving. "The white man, that's who. When those big boys were cooking them books at Enron and Arthur Anderson, they got little more than a slap on the wrist. You better believe most of 'em still have their money. It's always been a double standard for them and us. I can't no mo' tell this boy a piece of paper, GED, certificate or degree is gonna change his life. And you know why? Because he's right, it's a jungle out there and only the strong survive," he said angrily at Marcus. "What's wrong with you Marcus, you done gone soft on me?"

"I hear you, Dad." Marcus said in a bored tone, glancing down at his watch and hoping Michael would take the hint and leave.

The two men had different views on life. Marcus knew his father was old school, from a different time and a very different era. As far as Marcus was concerned, life never stays the same. His conclusion is that his father would always have his opinion and he his own. Marcus felt that his dad had done things his way and now it was his turn.

"So old man," he quickly interjected before Michael could continue, "don't you have something to do? I thought you said you had a hot date or something?"

"I can take a hint." Michael said, dignity intact. "I'ma blow like the wind. I'll holler at y'all later," he nodded at Marcus. "Tone, don't let my boy get to you by filling your head with that school bullshit. I didn't go to school and I turned out alright if I must say so myself," he laughed. "If you need someone to talk to, you know where to find me. I know the real deal. I'll see you both later." He zipped his black leather jacket, and with that said, he departed.

Marcus seemed to be deep in thought for a minute and then shook his head. "Man, I hate for him to even get started. So, what do you think is up with Rita?"

"I don't even have a clue." Tone said, dejectedly.

"When you find out, let me know. If you need help with anything, just say the word."

"I hear you. I'm outta here, later man."

"Okay, later bro."

Before heading back to his apartment, Tone made his rounds. Everything seemed to be in order. He told the guys he'd be back later for collections. After he returned home, his mind was stuck on Rita. He thought about calling her but changed his mind, tomorrow would be here soon enough.

five

As usual, bright sunlight flooded the room, nudging Rita awake a few minutes before the alarm sounded. She dragged herself out of bed, checked on the kids and then went into the kitchen, sat down at the table and lit a cigarette. When she was done, she put a pot of coffee on the stove. After showering and getting dressed, she roused the children. The day had officially begun. An hour later, they were out the door and walking to school.

Upon returning home, Rita sank into the sofa and cried, feeling drained. Her emotions were shaky and she was unable to concentrate on anything. *Did school just end a couple of months ago?* she mused, nervously twisting her hair. Somehow, it felt like years. She had given a lot of thought as to her options last night and reached some conclusions. None of which were really that good. She could (a) have the baby and talk Tone into moving in with her, (b) have an abortion, or (c) move in with Mommy and Mah-Dear, which was the worst-case scenario.

Rita's teen years were turbulent. She swore when she moved out of Barbara's house, wild horses couldn't drag her back. Barbara warned Rita repeatedly that she was headed for trouble. She'd tried hard to persuade Rita to hold off on sex and had even taken her to get birth control pills, but Rita was having none of that, feeling it was her life. The love and lust she felt for Tone was her first priority and nothing ever came in the way of that. As a result, she became very rebellious. She missed her curfew constantly and argued with Barbara just as much. Her grades slipped, she began smoking cigarettes and weed, then graduated to drinking liquor. Looking back on her life, she realized she'd been more than a handful. Eventually, Rita and Barbara mended their relationship.

Tone lived with Rita for a while when the twins were born. The crying, crazy feeding hours, the surreal feeling of non-stop noise, and the constant changing of the dirty diapers nearly drove him crazy. That was his only stab at being a supportive live-in lover and father. Rita vowed never to live with him again unless they were married. Presently, it seemed as though it would be much easier to have the abortion. Then, the move could go as scheduled and life would only get better.

At ten minutes to twelve, she heard a knock on the door and knew it was Tone. Walking over to the door, she pulled it opened. He stepped in, kissing and hugging her. She leaned heavily against him.

"Whatever you called me over here for must really be heavy," he remarked, as they walked to the couch. He studied her closely, seeing the despair on her face and the heaviness about her body that wasn't there a couple of months ago. "So, what is it Rita?" he asked tenderly, almost instinctively knowing what she was about to say.

"I don't know any other way to say it. I wish I didn't have to say this, but I'm pregnant." She walked across the room to the window, staring out with unseeing eyes.

Tone stood up and quickly walked over to her. Gently, he turned her face towards him.

"Say what?"

"Tone, I'm pregnant," she said, as tears began coursing down her face.

"You sure?" he asked.

"I'm positive, I took a home pregnancy test. Hell, I've been there before, I know the drill."

"So, what's the problem?" he asked, grinning broadly. "It's a good thing. Hell, maybe before we're through I'll have three sons," he said, proudly.

"Are you crazy? There's nothing good about any of this. I don't want another baby. Hell, I didn't really want the twins when I was pregnant with them. My life is just getting started. I'm finally doing things I should've done years ago." She took a deep breath, squared her shoulders and said, "I'm seriously thinking about having an abortion."

"Are you crazy woman?" he shouted, angrily. "Nobody is killing my child, I mean that Sharita!"

She knew he was very angry. He only called her by her given name when he was upset.

"It's my body!" she yelled back at him, hands waving and her body quaking with righteous indignation. "I call the shots!"

"Rita," he said coldly, a murderous look in his eyes, "what you seem to have forgotten is the baby is my child too. I knew you shouldn't have taken that damn class," he said, disgustedly. "It's enough you getting on your high horse about the GED, what you want for the kids and where you're even going to live, but to make a decision like that, or even think about doing something like that without considering my feelings, is madness. Mah-Dear is right, you've lost it."

"I don't know what else to do!" she shrieked, voice cracking. She looked at him beseechingly, pleading for understanding. "I have to think about me and the kids that are already here."

"I can't believe you're saying this," he whispered. "I thought abortion is a sin in your new church. What's up with that?"

"I need you to understand," she begged. "The kids are growing up, I don't want to be held back because I was stupid enough to get pregnant with another baby."

"Oh, so now making a new life with me is stupid?"

"No!" she hollered. "That's not what I mean. I don't want the responsibility of a newborn baby. I just don't want to start over, not now when I'm so close to changing my life. Do you understand what I'm saying?" Tears gushed from her eyes.

"Oh, I understand alright. It's about you and your feelings only. I don't count, ain't got no say so about this at all."

"It's not that exactly," she said, floundering. "Well maybe, we've been over this before," her expression hardened. "I want more, I want the kids to have nice things and visit places. I want to expose them to better things, I don't want them just to live the life we had. I know this is hard for you to understand."

"You're not hearing me," Tone quietly, said. "My opinion don't fucking count anyway. Why bother to tell me this in the first place? What do you want from me? If you think I'm going to say I'm down with this abortion shit, then you're just fooling yourself."

"I don't know what I want from you!" she screamed, stomping her foot. "I'm still trying to sort it out. I just haven't gotten it together yet." She shrugged her shoulders helplessly.

"Tell you what," he said, with a look of revulsion on his face, "I'm outta here. When you think you have a plan and feel I should be included in it, give me a call. Okay?"

He looked down at her, sad resignation on his face. Suddenly, the look turned to anger and regret, as if to say, *how did it come to this?*

"Don't kill my baby, Rita," he said, changing his tone. "I don't think I could stand it." Then he left, slamming the door behind him.

Rita ran into the bedroom, threw herself on the bed and wept. She lay there a long time, replaying the scene in her mind. Realizing for the first time that she wouldn't be able to please everybody, her spirits sank even lower. *I obviously made a mistake talking to Tone this soon,* she thought. *Maybe I just wanted him to talk me out of it. I don't know what the hell I want to do.* She moaned helplessly and then screamed aloud. Her face contorted as a gut-wrenching primordial cry of anguish escaped from her mouth. All of the frustration she felt was reflected in that sound. After she stopped crying, she felt drained.

The telephone rang and she quickly picked it up, hoping it was Tone. Instead, it was Barbara.

"Hello?"

"Hi Rita, how's my favorite daughter?"

"Hi Mommy, I'm okay. How are you today?"

"I'm doing fine. I'm calling to see how all my babies are doing."

For the millionth time that day, Rita's eyes filled with tears. "We're okay."

"You don't sound like it," Barbara said.

"I had a little fight with Tone, but really, I'm fine."

"What did you two fight about?"

"Nothing really." Her voice rose an octave. "Say Mommy, I need to talk to you about something."

"What's up?"

"I really don't want to go into it over the phone. Maybe when the kids get out of school we'll come over to your house."

"Okay," Barbara answered, slowly. "I should be home from work by four."

After the conversation ended, Rita turned over in the bed and went to sleep.

SIX

At her job, Barbara hung up the phone, frowning and immediately began worrying.

"Rita didn't sound good at all. I hope nothing is wrong with the children," she thought aloud. "No," she corrected herself, "she would've told me that. What could she and Tone be fighting about? They get along fairly well for the most part. I don't like this, not at all." She quickly dialed her own telephone number.

"Hello?" Mah-Dear screamed into the phone.

"It's me. Have you talked to Rita today?"

"No chile, I ain't talked to her. Why, is something wrong?"

"I don't know," Barbara admitted. "I talked to her a few minutes ago and she didn't sound right."

"What did she say?"

"I don't know Dear, but it had something to do with her and Tone having a fight."

"Barbie, that would explain it," she said.

"Yeah, I guess so, but she still didn't sound right. She and the kids are coming over this afternoon, maybe we'll get something out of her then. She did say she wanted to talk to me but didn't want to get into it over the phone."

"Good," Mah-Dear said, "I'll take some fish out the freezer and fry that for dinner. Rita's a good child, she'll talk to one of us. Try not to worry. I'll see you when you get home."

"Okay, Dear," Barbara sighed, not happy at all about the wait.

A short time later, Rita awakened reflecting on happier times, like her graduation from the LPN class. *It was one of the proudest days of my life,* she thought, contritely. *One of the few times I started something and finished it.* She remembered the pride and love her family showered upon her that day.

Someone must've told Tone to bring flowers, since he'd bought a dozen roses with him. The kids waved colorful balloons with the words *Congratulations Grad* emblazed upon them. Mah-Dear and Barbara cried silently when Rita's name was called.

Mah-Dear sniffled, saying to Barbara, "I sure wish Louis was here with us today, I know he'd be so proud of Rita."

The family didn't boast many graduates. Angela had been the sole recipient for a long time. However, Rita and her cousins, Shirley and Sheila, planned to change all of that in time.

Marcus and Donna had even graced the family with their presence. Ms. Jones had even attended and promised to join them for dinner. When Rita's name was announced, she strutted proudly across the stage. The happiness she felt was apparent to all by the look of pride upon her face. *This is a new beginning, the start of a change for the better,* she thought, smiling.

After the ceremony, Mah-Dear insisted on walking through the church. "So, this is what a Catholic church looks like. Um hum, it's too much for me, chile. Give me my little church any day," she kept saying.

She talked to Father Pat, questioning him with the relentless intensity of a detective. It was a nervous moment for all when she asked about the molestations. His answer was that most of them occurred years ago. He did his best to reassure her they did a better job of monitoring those situations today. Rita thought she would die of embarrassment as she listened to the conversation.

All the while, Barbara kept alternating between patting Rita's back and hugging her tightly, while saying, "I'm so proud of you, baby." Her face beamed rays of happiness.

After leaving the church, everyone headed to the proud mother and grandmother's house for dinner. As usual, Mah-Dear outdid herself in the kitchen. The meal was a feast of soul food: turkey and stuffing, a pink glazed ham dotted with cloves, mixed greens, string beans, macaroni and cheese, candied yams, cornbread and homemade rolls. Vonnie baked cakes and pies. Uncle Johnny Man, Vonetta's companion, contributed his specialty, homemade ice cream. Tone and Marcus supplied the champagne.

After everyone was stuffed, the older adults played bid whist in the kitchen, while the younger ones listened to music and sipped champagne in the living room. From time to time, Barbara came in bopping along with them and asking them to show her the latest dances. That day was truly a joyous occasion for the family. Rita and Tone's children were simply happy that the whole family was together. They liked nothing better than dinner at Mah-Dear's with their parents, grandparent, great-grandmother and the rest of the family together.

I was just on cloud nine not so long ago, Rita thought. *Now, look what happened. I fucked up, no ifs, ands, or buts about it. I just knew that day was the beginning of a new life for me and I surely didn't mean that literally.*

She later got up, picked the kids up from school and came back home. Rita felt tightly strung, like a yo-yo going up and down on a string.

After the children changed clothes, they took the bus to Barbara's house. The kids, as if sensing Rita's mood, didn't say much. The twins, who were usually little chatterboxes, were unnaturally quiet. They didn't even indulge in their favorite pastime of teasing Destiny, who'd gaze uneasily at her mother periodically, trying to gauge her mood. Like Barbara, she knew something wasn't quite right with her mother.

Before long, they stood at the door. Devan rang the doorbell.

"Mah-Dear!" he shouted, hugging her tightly about the waist when she opened the door.

"You got something for us to eat?" Deante asked, with a grin on his face.

"Well, don't just stand there, come on in. Didn't your mama feed you today?" she asked, smiling at them.

"How are you, Miss Destiny?"

"I'm okay, Dear," she replied, woodenly.

"How 'bout you, Miss Rita?"

"Just fine, Mah-Dear."

"You don't look fine, chile. What's wrong with you?"

"Nothing." Rita answered, gesturing towards the kids and shaking her head.

Destiny, who caught the exchange, glanced quickly at her mother with a worried look upon her face.

"Nothing, everything's great. We'll talk later when Mommy gets home," Rita said, with a catch in her throat.

"Okay, come on twins, and you too Miss Destiny. Take those jackets off." Mah-Dear clapped her hands together loudly. "Oh no, we're not leaving clothing lying on the furniture," she announced, while watching the boys fling them carelessly about. "That will never do. Deante, hang your coat up. Give them boys some hangers," she told Destiny. "Then help them hang their jackets in the closet."

After the task was completed, Mah-Dear smiled at them. "Let's go see what Mah-Dear has in the kitchen for her great-grandbabies to eat."

Rita walked into the living room, stopping in front of The Family Wall. There were so many pictures displayed, it was almost covered. Shirley often joked that soon they'd need a bigger place just to put up new ones. Some were taken at portrait studios, others just snapshots. Along the top left side of the wall was an 11x14 picture of Mah-Dear. Grandpa's matching picture graced the right side. Not liking to take pictures, Grandpa's face was a study of seriousness. Beneath their pictures were photos of their own relatives, and underneath those were photographs of their three daughters at various stages of their lives, celebrating many occasions. All those beautiful multicolored smiling faces made up the Atkins/Smith family. The past and present commingled, commemorating happy times.

Rita could hear Mah-Dear and the kids talking in the kitchen. She quizzed them about what they'd been doing lately and how school was coming along. She admonished Destiny to stay away from them nasty boys since they're nothing but trouble. Being from the south, Mah-Dear was a firm believer in feeding guests. She took cookies out of the cabinet and poured milk for the children.

"Mah-Dear," Rita yelled from the living room, "they don't need sweets, especially the boys!"

"Girl, I know you ain't telling me what to feed my own babies, is you?" she yelled back.

"No," Rita replied, meekly, "I'm not."

Before long, Barbara arrived home from work, her face drawn as she walked into the house. Her expression softened as she exchanged hugs and kisses with her grandchildren. As she pulled her shoes off to get comfortable, the kids brought her up-to-date on the new events in their lives, with their favorite topic being the move.

"We might have a backyard. Won't that be great, Grandmama?" Devan proudly informed her.

"It sure would baby," she smiled at him.

"Grandmama, can I ask you something?" Destiny whispered to Barbara.

"Sure baby, you know you can talk to me about anything."

"I think something is wrong with my mama."

"Why do you think that, baby?" Barbara asked, gently.

"She's been crying a lot. She thinks I don't see her, but I do. Grandmama, I think she's sick. I'm worried about her," she said, sadly.

"Now I don't want you worrying. Mah-Dear and I will fix whatever is wrong with your mama. You know that, don't you?" she said, reassuringly.

"Please help Mama, I'm so scared." Destiny begged, her eyes filling with tears.

"Don't worry, little one, I promise we'll make it alright," she vowed grimly, hugging Destiny tightly.

Mah-Dear had prepared dinner, which consisted of her Friday night special of fried catfish, potato salad and macaroni and cheese. After Barbara finished talking with Destiny, she took her into the bathroom, moistened a towel and wiped her face. She then sent her into the kitchen to see if Mah-Dear needed help with dinner.

Barbara walked into the dining room and grimly told Rita they needed to talk after dinner. After the meal was consumed, the kids trekked into Mah-Dear's room and settled down in front of the television to watch videos. The three women sat solemnly at the kitchen table.

"So Rita, what's up?" Barbara asked.

"Yeah, Rita." Mah-Dear asked matter-of-factly, chomping on a fish tail. "Looks like you gained some weight there. You ain't pregnant, is you, girl?" she asked.

Barbara gasped, staring sharply at her daughter. "You aren't Rita, are you?"

"I wish I wasn't, but I am." Rita moaned. "I took a home pregnancy test and it came out positive."

"My God." Mah-Dear murmured, sitting up in her seat frowning. "Girl, what you gonna do now?"

"I don't know what to do. I was so close to having it all," Rita said, holding up two shaking fingers. "I know that I don't want another baby, Lord help me," she moaned.

"Humph," Mah-Dear snorted, "I'll tell you like I tell Destiny, you shoulda kept them legs closed."

"Dear, that's uncalled for," Barbara said, frowning. "It's a little too late for that now. Saying something like that at a time like this doesn't help the situation."

"I talked to Tone this morning." Rita continued, her voice cracking. "You called after he left and he was so upset."

"Upset about what, girl?" Mah-Dear asked. "Y'all been here before, he ain't got nothing to be upset about. Hell, the nigga should've kept it in his pants," she sniffed.

Rita took a deep breath, trying desperately to compose herself. "I'm thinking about having an abortion," she blurted out.

"I know you didn't say what I thought I heard you say." Mah-Dear recoiled in horror. "I know you ain't even thinking about that, girl. How could you even say something like that? Kill yo' own baby?"

Barbara walked back to her chair and dropped her head into her hands. She looked up and said, "An abortion is a hard thing to go through and you really need to think about it carefully. Once you go there, you can't undo it. It's not an easy thing to live with afterwards. I know, you see, I had one myself."

"Mommy!" Rita shouted, her eyes growing wide as saucers, "did you say what I think you said? No, I can't believe you just said you had an abortion!" Rita looked at Barbara as if she had just spoken to her in Spanish.

Mah-Dear stared at Barbara and Rita, a disappointed look on her face, hazel eyes bucking and rolling. "I can't believe both of y'all." Her fork clattered to her plate, fish tails forgotten for the moment. "I think that's something you should've kept to yourself, Barbie," she said, shaking her head. "No, there's no need to bring that old stuff up."

Suddenly, there was a loud thud from Mah-Dear's bedroom. Mah-Dear quickly stood up and then paused to look at the two women.

"I'ma go check on the children," Mah-Dear said, "y'all stay here and talk. I don't think you should get rid of the baby. I know you didn't ask my opinion, but I'm giving it anyway. I'm begging you Rita, don't do it, please don't do it."

"Mommy," Rita said, falling back into her chair, "I 'm shocked, I can't believe it."

Her eyes were drawn to Barbara and her mouth dropped open. There was complete silence in the room for a few minutes.

"Did it hurt? Was it hard for you to do?" Rita asked Barbara.

Barbara sighed, saying, "It was one of the most difficult things I've done in my entire life. I never wanted a lot of children like Vonnie. Actually, I had thought about having an abortion when I was pregnant with you. Somehow, Mah-Dear caught wind of my plan and talked me out of it, same as she's going to do with you."

Rita felt like she'd been punched in the stomach, her muscles contracting spasmodically. Her mouth opened and then closed. *"Damn,"* she thought, *"I almost didn't make it here."*

"I know what you're thinking," Barbara said, soberly. "But I did have you and I've never regretted it, only maybe during your teen years." She smiled, weakly. "But when all is said and done, I'm glad I did have you and I'm so grateful for all my grandchildren. So, don't go getting our situations mixed up, the two are totally different. Tell me, what do you really want to do? What does Tone think about this?"

"I finally have things going the way I want." Rita began earnestly, voice still shaky. "I've just finished my class and I'm even thinking about going to college. I've gone on a couple of job interviews and have more lined up. The sad thing is I really don't know what I want to do. I can probably go through with the abortion, but I don't know if I could live with myself afterwards."

"I know exactly what you mean," Barbara said, patting her hand. "But baby, this is one decision you're going to have to make for yourself. You've got to weigh the facts. I caution you to give it time and not rush into anything."

"That's the problem," Rita sobbed, "I want to rush, like a dog chasing a cat. I feel like I have to in order for my life to get back on track. Tone wants me to have the baby, but he hasn't said a word about what his plans are for the future of him, the kids and me. In fact, he hasn't said much period. It seems lately whenever we're together, we argue constantly. All he does is criticize me about how I plan to change my life."

"Honey," Barbara said, softly caressing her face, "trust me, he's just scared. I'm sure he feels threatened by all the changes. He may never admit it, but the man is terrified. Your roles in life have changed, with you moving, starting a job and all. Have you thought about marrying him?"

"He asked me once and I turned him down. That was damn near ten years ago though."

"I don't have to ask you if you love him, I already know the answer to that," Barbara said. "You two have been together for so long. In all my infinite wisdom, I do know one thing Rita, and that is he loves you. He'll stand by you and do the right thing, no matter how angry he seems right now."

"I don't know about that. I've never seen him act that way. You know what Mommy? You would've thought Tone was the Catholic and not me. When he called me *Sharita*," Rita said, imitating his deep voice, "I knew he was hot and that I was definitely in trouble." She unsuccessfully attempted to smile.

"So what else are you thinking? I've heard you say that you don't want another baby, but do you really think you could go through with an abortion?" Barbara asked.

"I don't know," she replied, candidly. "I feel like I could because then life would be easier. However, when it comes down to it, I really don't know if I could go through with it. Hell, I'm still tripping over you having one." Rita glared at her balefully.

"Back in the day, I loved me some Marvin McCall. As Mah-Dear would say, I loved his dirty drawers," Barbara said, with a faraway look in her eyes. "The problem was he just wasn't no good. I thought the sun rose and set on that man, nobody could tell me he wasn't the one. But you know what, he wasn't. He was more like an itch, a rash or poison ivy. I stumbled into that bush and couldn't stop scratching and that old rash would flare up from time to time. When I got pregnant with you, he wasn't ready for a child."

Barbara continued, "No, he wasn't happy at all, so I knew the burden of raising you would fall on me. He'd come by occasionally with a little money, but not as often as I would've liked. So, like Mah-Dear and Vonnie, I had you and got on welfare, we were the original welfare queens. Vonnie's thing was having more children, cause more babies equaled more money and that was her thing. I guess that worked for her, since she has five. One thing I can give Johnny Man credit for, like Daddy, he stayed and did right by her. Vonnie, like Mah-Dear, didn't want to marry and give up the money tree."

"That's why I was so hard on you," Barbara said, earnestly. "It was like watching an instant replay of my own life and I wanted better for you. I thought about going to college but got too comfortable with my lifestyle. One thing I can say about us Atkins women, we are truly one-man women. When I got pregnant the second time, I thought about how I'd get more money from Mr. Welfare, but truthfully, I didn't want to be bothered with another baby. I never told Mah-Dear, although I'm sure she suspected something."

Rita listened to her mother talking, enthralled as if she were listening to a Grimm fairy tale that was bewitching and repulsive at the same time. Her facial expressions changed with each new revelation, running a gamut of emotions. *Life is something else. You think you know someone really well, like your mother, then you hear something like this and find out you don't know jack,* she thought, ruefully.

"Did you tell my daddy about the baby?" Rita asked, curiously.

"No, just Vonnie. She went to the clinic with me."

"Did it hurt? Were you scared?" Rita asked, shivering.

"It was more of a mental hurt. My soul ached and I hadn't taken that into account. Physically, it was no worse than cramps. I was torn apart by doubts and not sure if I was really doing the right thing. It took me a long time to get to the point where I could function. I still think about that day from time to time. I knew Vonnie disapproved but she still went to the clinic with me and stayed by my side the whole time, not judging or condemning me. Afterwards, I stayed at her house a couple of days to recuperate. I cried that night, Rita, like a motherless child. Vonnie just sat with me holding my hand and rubbing my back. I wasn't crying so much because of the abortion, but because I knew my relationship with Bobby was over. I have regrets cause you can't do something like that and not feel anything. However, in the end I know I did the right thing. I wasn't emotionally equipped to handle another baby. When I had the abortion, I also got my tubes tied."

"Damn," Rita said, deeply moved by what she'd just heard. "I don't know what to say, except that's some deep shit."

"Now tell me, Ree-Ree, what can I do to help?" Barbara asked caringly, holding her hand. "You know I try not to judge anybody. If I can do anything to make it better, just tell me. I do want you to be sure about the abortion though, Rita."

"Mommy, I want to start working more than anything," Rita answered. "I've never had a job a day in my life. I did go on two interviews last week, which Ms. Jones was very helpful in setting up. However, she warned me that it might take some time to find a job and not to get discouraged. You know what else? Most of the time, I want Tone being with me, living with me and loving me. I love that man and always will. I can sense some of what he's feeling," Rita said, nodding her head. "He's got to step to me correctly and tell me what he wants, let me know if he sees a future for us. I'm not going to run behind his ass questioning him."

"In view of your condition, I think you have every right to question him about his intentions," Barbara said bluntly, looking at Rita's midsection.

"Most of all," Rita said plaintively, hands waving and her face flushed, "I want a house. The kids need their own bedrooms, especially Destiny. I'd like to get them a computer. Their little minds need to be opened and exposed to other things in life besides the five-mile radius of the projects. That's one of the reasons I was considering putting them in Catholic school, the obvious being their school system is better than the public schools. Sometimes Devan is hard for me to handle and I believe the discipline of a Catholic school will help. If Tone were around more that would help too. Those are the things that I want, with or without him. I guess it sounds like a lot, doesn't it?" she sighed.

"Hmm," Barbara said, reflectively, "it's all good and possible but only if you're willing to work hard to get those things you want. I regret sometimes that I didn't leave the projects sooner, but we knew Mah-Dear would never leave except strapped to a gurney, in a body bag, or in our case, the building was torn down. When Daddy passed, I knew I had to be the one to live with her. Vonnie has Johnny Man and her family not that she doesn't do her share. And

Angela, I don't think she'd ever take her in. Daddy, bless his heart, wanted out of the projects too, still he stayed there because he knew Mah-Dear wouldn't leave. Her problem is she only sees them for what they used to be and they're nothing like that today. It's pretty bad there and has been for some time. At least Marcus and his crew made life a little easier for us. Not too many people bothered us, and using his own money, he made sure the buildings stayed fairly clean and functional. Still, on a daily basis, we had those hotheaded, trigger-happy thugs that had little regard for life to deal with."

"I hear you, it's definitely not easy living there. You know what? I'm glad we talked," Rita said, getting up from her chair and giving Barbara a big hug and kiss. "I still don't know what I'm going to do but it's good we talked. I'm still tripping, I can't believe my own mother had an abortion."

"I'm glad we talked too and you actually heard what I was saying. You're looking a lot better than you did earlier," Barbara said. "You scared me when I talked to you on the phone earlier. I just never imagined it would be about another baby. Now dry those tears, let's so see if your boys left any food for us to snack on."

They walked together into Mah-Dear's room. She sat in her rocking chair, head lolling on her neck, snoring and fast asleep. Her glasses had slipped down her face. The boys were lying on the floor, their faces propped up by their hands, hypnotically glued to the television screen. They'd finished watching movies and were now laughing at the antics of a character on a sitcom program. During commercial breaks, they'd point to Mah-Dear and laugh at the nocturnal noises coming from her mouth. Suspecting she wore false teeth, the boys snuck over to her and peered into her open mouth.

As usual, Destiny had a book in her face. She looked up as her mother and grandmother came into the room. Her heart felt light at seeing a semblance of peace on her mother's face. She giggled to herself, thinking, *Grandmama was right, she did make it better.* Barbara suggested they all spend the night since it was so late.

"We're going to look at houses tomorrow, so we have to get up early," Destiny reminded her.

"That's no problem, baby," Barbara replied. "Let's go into the living room, you can help me set up pallets. I think there's some popcorn in the kitchen with Devan, Deante and Destiny's names written on it just waiting to be popped."

Mah-Dear awakened and said, "Y'all get out of here now, I'm an old lady and I needs my sleep. Rita, I'd like to talk to you before you leave tomorrow."

"Yes, Ma'am," Rita said, saluting her pertly.

"Don't get smart with me, girl," Mah-Dear said, sharply.

"Sorry Mah-Dear, I promise we'll talk in the morning."

Rita and the children settled down in the living room, while Barbara prepared a snack consisting of popcorn, pop and juice. After devouring the snacks, they watched television until television watched them back.

Rita tossed and turned as she tried to get comfortable on the old couch, but sleep seemed to be impossible. Her mind raced at the revelations from earlier that day. Although Barbara warned her not to confuse their situations, it seemed to add more fuel to the fire as far as her own decision was concerned. She knew deep in her heart the situation Barbara painted with her father didn't apply to her and Tone. Her father still lived in the projects and she saw him from time to time. When she was younger, he'd give her money on her birthday and sometimes for

Christmas. After she had her children, he'd ask about them and that was the extent of the father-daughter relationship.

However, there was love between her and Tone. He hadn't exactly played an active role during their children's infancy because of immaturity, and she acknowledged that she probably should've married him years ago.

She rose from the couch, went to the kitchen and poured a glass of milk. She took a seat at the table and soon became lost in thought. *Some decisions can really change the course of your life,* popped into her mind. *If I have the abortion, how will that affect me and Tone's relationship? Would he ever be able to look at it as a step towards improving our lives? God knows, I still don't know if I can myself. He made his thoughts clear on how he feels about abortion, which means realistically he won't be able to see things my way. How am I going to deal with it myself? Mommy's a much stronger person than I am, and she even had a hard time dealing with it.*

Those questions and other thoughts swirled around in her mind. Finally, she gave up trying to figure it out, walked back into the living room and lay on the couch. Tomorrow would be here soon enough, she'd deal with all of it then. Glancing at the clock as she laid back on the couch, she noticed it was two o'clock in the morning.

seven

With cell phone clutched in his hand, Tone angrily paced the rooms of his apartment like a caged animal in the zoo. He'd called Rita numerous times and the phone just rang. He sat on the couch and lit a cigarette, his mind jumping from one thought to the next. He still couldn't believe Rita would even think about getting rid of their baby without considering his feelings. *I've been with this woman over half my life and she can't even talk to me about something this important.*

He rolled a joint, smoked it and felt himself calming down. Then he picked up his cell phone and tried calling Rita again, still no answer. He punched in Marcus' number and he answered on the first ring.

"What's up, cuz?"

"Man, you got some time? I need to talk to you right away, like now!"

"Come on over," Marcus urged, "I'll make the time."

Tone hurried out his apartment and was soon knocking at Marcus' door. Marcus opened the door quickly, peering at his cousin intently. While Tone pulled off his jacket and sat on the couch, Marcus made a detour to the kitchen, bringing back with him a six-pack of beer.

"What's up, man?" Marcus asked, upon returning to the room.

"It's Rita," he growled, "she's pregnant."

"Damn, you two are more potent than rabbits," he laughed. "Four kids, you're the man."

"Ain't nothing funny about this shit," Tone snarled, hotly. "She's talking about getting rid of the baby."

"No shit?" Marcus replied, as the smile disappeared from his face.

"As real as the projects coming down, dawg."

"Shit, that's tough," Marcus replied, running his hand through his hair. "Obviously you have a problem with it."

"You damn right I do. She ain't even bother to ask me what I wanted, she just started tripping about what she wanted."

"Did she say she's definitely going to get rid of it?"

"Not really, she just said she was seriously considering it," he said, mimicking her.

"So what you gonna do?"

"I don't know Marcus. You and I both know Rita is stubborn as a mule. When she says 'seriously considering', that means it's pretty much a done deal."

"So what do you want to do?" Marcus asked.

"Hell, I want her to have the baby. What in the hell do you think I want? I want her and the kids with me, that's all I've ever wanted in this life."

"Did you mention that to her knucklehead?" Marcus asked, reverting to Tone's childhood nickname.

"Naw, not really," Tone answered, clearly embarrassed. "I just kinda lost it. She snapped and the next thing I knew, I was snapping too. I had to leave before I did or said something I'd regret. I've been trying to call her all evening, but she's not home, I guess she's at her moms."

"Tell her what you just told me man. I know Rita loves you, she may be waiting for you to say something. Man, you need to declare your intentions. What else did she say?" Marcus asked.

"A whole bunch of stuff about exposing the kids to things. All she talked about was things like vacations, computers, Destiny going to college … yadda, yadda, yadda. She basically wants out of the hood."

"As I was telling you last night," Marcus said, seriously, "life is going to change bro, whether you're ready for it or not. Since you're not telling her anything, she's taken it upon herself to do what she has to for the family. I agree with you, though, she should've talked to you first about getting rid of the baby."

"You know what burns me up?" Tone said, stormily. "I've been with that woman since I was fourteen. I knew that she was the one for me back when she used to stick her tongue out at me, cross her eyes, make faces at me and hit me in the back and run away. Hell, she's still the one." Tone paused for a moment, as if trying to collect his thoughts. "And get this, I ain't told nobody but my moms that I bought Rita a ring. When she finished her class, I was gonna take her out to dinner and lay it on her. But she was always busy with interviews, among other things. Then I was gonna take her out to dinner, the whole shebang after Lyn's party, but we got so messed up. Damn, I bet that's when she, what's the word Marcus?"

"Conceived," he supplied, trying not to laugh.

"Yeah, that's the word. Damn man, I bet that's when she conceived," he said, with a goofy grin on his face. "I asked her to marry me when I was nineteen, you remember? She turned me down and I decided I wasn't going to ask her again. I thought maybe I'd wait for her to ask me."

"You tripping man," Marcus laughed, "Rita ain't hardly gonna ask you to marry her. Women always want to be asked, not do the asking."

"Yeah, like you know."

"Whoa, I've been thinking about doing the wedding thang with Donna," Marcus said. "She's a good woman and took her chances with me. I may just go ahead and make that move. But back to you, how you set for cash? You were always a cheap bastard, so I know you got a little something put away."

"Fo' sho', I got a little sumpin, sumpin."

"So, what you gonna do?" Marcus asked, again.

"Talk to her, I guess. See if we can work this out," Tone said, sheepishly.

"If that's what you want then go for it man. We're not getting any younger, plus your boys are getting older. They're what eight now? You don't want them to get out of hand," Marcus advised.

"I hear you," Tone replied, pensively. "You know what? Sometimes I wonder if I'm good enough for Rita."

"Where is this coming from?" Marcus frowned. "Why would you think something like that?"

"She just finished her class and she's already talking about college. I was never that good in school. Hell, I never even finished high school or got my GED. What if I ain't enough for her? What if I can't cut it? I already feel like she's getting above herself. If she goes on to college, I see nothing good ahead for us."

Marcus went back into the kitchen, returning with another six-pack. "I guess it's time to let you in on a little secret, cuz."

"What's up?" Tone asked.

"I have a college degree."

"Say what!" Tone said, as beer sprayed from his mouth. He wiped his chin on his shirtsleeve. "I swear Marcus, you never quit, you're always full of surprises." He said, shaking his head from side to side.

"I have a degree in finance."

"Like I know what that means," Tone replied.

"To put it plain and simple, it's learning about money. The whole education thing wasn't too bad for me, I was always more into school than you were. You were too busy chasing Ms. Atkins. All of that is to say, I'll help you. You need the paper man, it can't hurt in the long run. Maybe that will ease some of your fears about Rita. Give it some thought."

"I sure will," Tone shook his head in amazement.

"We've had a good run with the business," Marcus said. "Hell, I'll just put it out there, we've been lucky. Donna's been on me to get out and I've been seriously thinking about it. I've been grooming my cousin Tony to take over certain areas of the business. That's one of the advantages of being the boss. In fact, I've started implementing Plan A."

"What's Plan A? What do you mean by that?"

"So far, I've purchased carwashes, Laundromats, nail and beauty salons. My sister, Tina, is running the salons. I've also bought some commercial and residential property, and I'm checking into franchises now. Tell you what bro, you get that GED and maybe I can hook a cousin up. I know your heart was never really in the business, it was just a means to justify the ends for you. You gave it your all, but I could tell your heart wasn't really in it."

"I don't know what to say," Tone replied, touched by his cousin's offer. "I'm blown away, but I'll think about all this. Thanks for the advice and for listening to a brother. Well, I'm outta here," he said, standing and heading toward the door. "I'll let you know what happens with Rita. Peace out."

eight

Rita awoke early Saturday morning, her body sore and aching from sleeping on the lumpy couch. She decided to leave the kids with Barbara while she and Shirley looked at the houses. Since Rita always kept a set of clothing at Barbara's house for her and the kids, she could dress for the day there. But she still needed to go home since she didn't have the listing with her. She got up, put a pot of coffee on the stove, hopped in the shower and got dressed.

By the time she finished dressing, the coffee was perking and the kitchen was filled with its strong aroma. Rita heard Mah-Dear shuffle out of her bedroom and into the bathroom. A short time later, Mah-Dear sat at the table, her pink curlers half in her head. She was clad in a pink flowered housedress and had yet to put her false teeth in her mouth.

"Good Morning Rita, how are you this morning?" she asked.

"I'm fine, Dear. How are you?"

"So-so, I didn't sleep a wink thinking about you, other than that, I'm okay."

"So what's on your mind?" Rita decided to take the offense and be ready for anything.

"I know you came over to talk to your mama and that's good. Girls should talk to and listen to they mamas. I know you girls think I'm always in your business, sticking my nose where it don't belong. I only do it because I care," she said, thumping her finger hard on the table. "I don't beat around the bush, I call it the way I see it. If you go ahead with this abortion thing, you're gonna be making a terrible mistake. I don't speak from that firsthand, but hearing what I did from your mother last night and you know me, I listened," she admitted, unashamed. "I know she wants you to make your own decision without any of us putting in our two cents. Still, I have to tell you how I feel. In my heart, I know it would be a mistake for you to do this. I was thinking last night 'bout when Barbie got rid of her baby. Yo' mama was a terrible sight to behold and it broke my heart. I kept asking her what was wrong and she just smiled sadly and said she didn't feel good. She lost weight and stayed in her room for weeks on end. I pestered Vonnie until she told me the truth," Mah-Dear sighed.

"I couldn't fault her, she was just being loyal to her sister. I 'member right around that time she'd caught your daddy with another woman, that just 'bout killed her. She hated your daddy after that. You and Barbie were possessions to Marvin but I can tell Tone loves you and the kids. Marvin was just plain selfish, ain't no doubt about that. He didn't have it in him to love nobody but himself. Barbie was never the same after catching him with that hussy and getting rid of that baby. I kept waiting for her to come and talk to me but she never did. To this day, she don't know that Vonnie told me what happened. I felt her pain like it was my own and it hurt me so," Mah-Dear whispered, sadly.

"I wanted to say something to comfort her but I just couldn't find the right words. Yo' mama suffered badly." Rita stared at her mesmerized. "I don't know if doing that messed her up but I do know she ain't never had no mo' babies. I just figured that whatever happened when she confronted Marvin messed her up bad. Please think hard about this Rita, it's something you gonna have to carry with you the rest of yo' life, just like yo' mama."

"I know you kids laugh at me sometimes," Mah-Dear sighed, peering over her focals. "I know y'all talk about me, saying I'm a mean old lady and that I think I know everything. I hear y'all saying you wonder how Mah-Dear came to be like that. Thing is, y'all never asked me. I thought you or Shirley would ask, but y'all never did. Humph, seems like my modern granddaughters would want to know something about they Mah-Dear's life before she came to Chicago."

Overwhelmed by what she'd just heard, Rita could only manage to croak out, "Why Dear, why are you like you are? Tell me what happened to you." She stroked her wrinkled grandmother's withered hand.

"You know, our peoples are from a little town near Selma, Alabama. I had me two sisters, Myrtle and Mayleen and one brother, Joseph. We were lucky in that we owned our own farmland. Our Papa worked the land and our Mama took in washing for some of the white ladies. Still in all, life was good. Then the droughts came. Two years in a row we couldn't grow nothing no matter how hard we tried, the farm stopped producing. Mama had a green thumb and could grow enough in her garden for us to eat on. Our crop was cotton and that's how Papa made his money but when them droughts came the cotton dried up and the money with it. We hardly had enough money to buy seeds or keep and feed our animals. Then, by and by, Papa had to sell them off before they got too skinny.

Mama's brother, Uncle Luther, worked for the railroad and got Papa a job and things got better. Then there was a terrible accident, a train crash. Papa got hurt and couldn't work no more. The railroad didn't give him nothing, not one red cent." Mah-Dear cried. "And it was they fault, the accident was the railroad's fault. Mama took in more washing and took care of Papa. We helped her as best we could but my dear Papa's health failed and he got worse.

Chile, our life got hard. We'd get up, try to work the land, and help Mama with the washing and ironing. We managed to finish the sixth grade. Time went by slowly it seemed. We had less money, less food, less heat, less everything and Papa got worse and went down quickly.

Papa died about a little over a year after he got hurt. Mama did what she could to keep things going but it was too late. We found out later Papa didn't pay the taxes so we lost everything, the land and the house." Mah-Dear's eyes brimmed with tears. "Papa used to say that land was all he had in the world, except for his family. I'll never forget when the government man came to put us out our place. Mama musta cried a river of tears. I started hating the government ever since then. Rita, I know now that hate didn't do me a bit of good.

We went to stay on Uncle Luther's farm. He had a little shack that he fixed up and we lived there. Then when we all got older, we came up north, all except for Joseph and Mama who stayed behind. She was never really right after Papa died, Mama changed and became very quiet. She never talked too much after all that, as if the light in her went out. I guess everything that happened was too much for her. I always felt the government broke up my family and stole my home and I swore I was going to get back at them if it was the last thing I did.

When I came up here and they started welfare, I signed up for it. I was at the front of the line. When I met Louis, I knew he was a good man. We started courting and he asked me to marry him. He asked many times but I wasn't feelin' him, as you young people say. I was stuck on getting back at the government and that decision caused me a lot of heartache," Mah-Dear said, sadly.

She got up from her chair, walked over to the stove and poured herself another cup of coffee. Her veined, callused hands shook slightly. She came back to her seat and plopped down heavily.

"Oh, I knew better was out there, I just didn't want to face up to it cause I was greedy. I wanted the money, no matter what it took, I was willing to pay." Mah-Dear continued, her eyes downcast. "To me, it was a good deal, all the colored people putting one over on the government. Angela used to fuss at me about that all the time. That's the reason she never comes home, she felt I was just content raising a bunch of bastards, as she called them. When Vonnie and your mama had kids, she said I wasn't teaching them right. She thought I should've preached more school and less welfare. She believed school could change a person's way of life. She told me I was starting a cycle that would have dire consequences for the family. I didn't understand what she meant at the time. I feel bad that Angie has such a low opinion of me, but at the time, I was just stuck on revenge.

She would tell Louis that he should just leave me, and how the projects were going to hold us down, but Louis loved me and he stayed with me all those years. He was hoping I would change but I never did. You don't know how I regret that now," she said, tears dripping down her face. She sniffed and wiped them off quickly with the back of her hand.

"He was such a good man and I miss him so much today. I hate I never told him that he was right and I wish he could see how I've changed. Most of all, I regret not marrying him. Louis worked in the same factory all his life till he couldn't no mo'. He often said he had benefits and could take care of all of us. He'd say he'd have a pension one day and if something happened to him, we'd be okay. At the time of his death, he had life insurance. To put it simply, in the past, we might not have been able to help you, but we can now. We got us some resources, as yo' mama calls it."

Rita sat stunned, thinking these Atkins women were too much. They held so many secrets and so much heartache. Just then, Barbara walked into the room and put her arms around her mother, kissing her loudly on her cheek.

"You know I was listening to you, Dear. I'm glad you talked to Rita. I disagree with some of the things you did in the past but we're family. Sometimes talking about things that happened in the past can help the future. Maybe I should've talked to you about being pregnant but we were all welfare queens back then. I don't think it would've made a difference anyway." Barbara continued, looking toward Rita. "I've been telling Dear that she needs to call Angie and talk to her, tell her everything she just told you." Then, she turned back to Mah-Dear. "Angie needs to know about you from your mouth. I think it might make a difference in her feelings towards you, Dear. I think Daddy planned on telling her but he got sick."

"Mommy is right," Rita exclaimed. "Dear, I think you should talk to her."

"Listen to you," Mah-Dear sniffed, "trying to tell your old grandmother what do."

The three generations of women looked at each other and laughed.

"I realize now, that I made some big mistakes, I don't want you to do the same. I know Tone be selling drugs and I don't like it one bit, not at all," she said harshly. Then her tone softened. "But because I saw what happened with Papa firsthand, it made me understand how hard it is sometimes to provide for your family the right way. Him selling drugs is not good, but a man gotta feel like he the man. A man *should* provide for his family. Marvin didn't love yo' mama the right way, but Tone does love you and the kids, I can feel it. So talk to him Rita, before you do something you might regret."

"Know this too," Mah-Dear said, nodding, "nothing is more important than family. We can't pick our family and sometimes they can make you mad as all hell," she bristled. "But you just remember baby, nothing before family and you'll be fine. I don't care how mad you get or what happens, family is still family. We gotta love the family God gave us."

"Mah-Dear is right," Barbara added. "Marvin messed me up. My power to love and forgive was non-existent, but with the passage of time, I've learned and I'm getting better."

"You know what, Mommy?" Rita said, thoughtfully. "I don't remember you ever having a boyfriend when I was growing up."

"Oh I had friends," Barbara laughed, "just nobody I wanted to bring around you or the family."

"How did you two get so wise?" Rita asked.

"Life baby," they said in unison, laughing.

nine

The telephone rang. "I'll get it," Rita said, jumping up from her seat.

"Tone, what's up? You do? I guess so. I need to stop at home first. Tell you what, pick me up in an hour."

"Tell him to come over in half an hour and I'll have breakfast ready," Mah-Dear said, in the background.

Rita repeated the information back to him and he answered that he was on his way. Mah-Dear got up and began putting pots and pans on the stove.

"What did Tone want?" Barbara asked.

"Something about wanting to talk to me and going with me to look at the houses. I'm sure he's going to want to know what I'm going to do about the baby. Hmm, this is the first time I've called it a baby."

"Alright," Barbara cried, "that could be a good sign."

Pouring eggs into the skillet, Mah-Dear couldn't resist getting in the last word.

"Keep yo' baby, Rita."

Twenty minutes later, the doorbell rang. It was Tone. He eyed Rita anxiously and came into the kitchen, kissing Mah-Dear and Barbara. He sat down at the table and stared at Rita while she poured him a cup of coffee. Mah-Dear took a stack of pancakes out of the skillet, reached into the cabinet and handed plates to he and Rita.

"I wasn't sure if you wanted me coming over here," Tone said, awkwardly.

"Don't talk foolish boy," Mah-Dear replied, tartly. "Last time I checked you was still my great-grandbabies' father."

"She's right," Barbara added. "We were just talking about the importance of family. Let's try to sit down and see what we can come up with."

"We'll have to do it later," Rita said. "Right now, I've got to go home and pick up my house listings."

"You know Destiny and the boys wanted to go with you," Barbara remarked.

"I know, but they'll just have to wait until next time," Rita replied.

"Sounds like a plan then," Mah-Dear said, winking at Tone.

Tone smiled, sensing Mah-Dear was on his side. He noted Rita looked better than she did the day before.

"So, it looks like Rita staying the night was a good idea," he said, winking back at Mah-Dear.

The kids, hearing their father's voice, stirred and came running into the kitchen. "Daddy!" they screamed, showering him with hugs and kisses.

"Daddy, are you coming with us to look at houses?" Destiny asked.

"Time out guys, change of plans," Rita said. "You're not going this time, I'm going to look first. If I see something I like, we can all go back."

"That's not fair," Destiny pouted.

"Yeah," Devan piped in, "that's not fair. You promised we were all going."

"I know you kids ain't talking to yo' Mama like that, is you?" Mah-Dear said, sternly.

"No Mah-Dear," they chanted.

"How about spending the day with us?" Barbara asked. "Let's get you bathed and dressed. Then after breakfast, we'll figure out what we're going to do today. If you act like the good little people I know you can be, we'll go to the arcade in the mall."

"Cool!" Devan shouted.

"We want to go with you Grandmama," Deante said.

"Okay, settle down," Tone said, leading the boys in the bathroom. "Let's wash up and get you dressed."

Rita and Tone left after the kids were dressed and eating breakfast. Both sat quietly in the car, each lost in thought. Tone turned on the radio.

Rita glanced at him warily, saying, "I'm surprised you came to Mommy's. After we talked yesterday, I didn't think I'd see you anytime soon."

"Don't give me that bullshit, Rita. *We* didn't talk yesterday," Tone ranted. "It was more like you informed me of what you may or may not do with your body. We've been together most of our lives," he said, glancing at her quickly. "You could've at least let me have my say. I've let you do your thing most of the time in this relationship."

"Say what?" Rita said incredulously, eyes rolling, "You let me what?"

"You heard me, I let you have your way for too long. Hell, I've spoiled your ass rotten. Whatever you asked me for I've pretty much done so. It stops here. We're both adults, damn near thirty. This is real life, not some fucking fairytale. As I said over the phone, I want to go with you to check out the houses and make sure you settle in the right territory. When we're done with that, we'll come back to my place or yours, sit down calmly and discuss what we should do. You'll have your say and I'll have mine. Got it?"

"Yes sir," she answered, mockingly.

He cut his eyes over at her glaringly.

"Okay Tone, I hear you," she said, holding up her hands conceding the point.

Before long, they were at the projects to pick up Shirley. As soon as she stepped into the car, she sensed the tension that was thick as fog. Tone drove to the first house on the list and they began the momentous task of finding the right house.

ten

Barbara and Mah-Dear sat on a bench outside the arcade. The kids were in seventh heaven, Barbara had given them a handful of change and set them loose.

"Barbie, what do you think?" Mah-Dear sighed.

"I think we need to just stay out of it for now," she replied. "Let's give them a chance to come up with a solution." Barbara glanced at her mother. "What do you think about all of us living together if they can't come up with anything?"

"We don't have enough room."

"That's true, not where we are now. But she has to get a place anyway and she's going to need help. Maybe we should all live together."

"Hmm," Mah-Dear said, thoughtfully peering at her, "I was thinking the same thing."

There was a pause and then they looked at each other and laughed.

"That's assuming she's going to have the baby and that we don't know yet," Barbara said.

"Oh she is," Mah-Dear nodded, sagely. "Trust me, I have a feeling about this."

Tone, Rita and Shirley were now at the second house. Tone disliked the first one, saying that it was a little too run-down for his taste. The second one looked a little better, it was a two-story frame, with three bedrooms and an unfinished basement.

"This one has my vote," Shirley said, enthusiastically. "What do you think Tone?"

"Not bad, but let's keep looking," he replied.

As luck would have it, house number three didn't meet Tone's approval either. Forty-five minutes later, they were checking out the fourth and final house. It had basically the same layout as the second house, however, the bedrooms were a little larger and the kitchen a little bit smaller.

"What do you think?" Tone asked, looking at Rita.

"Actually, I liked all of them," she replied, tiredly. "The second house was a little closer to the bus line, but there are more stores near this one. The public school is within walking distance and there's a Catholic school not too far away. Tone?"

"As far as I'm concerned, either this one or number two will do. Is that it for today? Are there others to look at?" he asked.

"Not today we don't, we're done."

"I'm hungry," Shirley exclaimed, rubbing her stomach, "Tone, can we go to Jew Town and get some polish sausages?"

"Sounds good to me," Rita remarked.

"Let's go ladies," Tone said.

An hour later, they were dropping Shirley off at home. As she exited the car, she whispered to Rita, "I'll talk to you later."

When she got to the door of her building, she looked back at them with a puzzled look on her face, shaking her head.

"So where to lady?" Tone asked.

"Let's go to my place," she answered, ominously.

They entered the apartment in a matter of minutes.

"I'm drained," Rita remarked, as they both sat heavily on the couch.

"So how did it go with your moms and Mah-Dear?" Tone asked, curiously. "I know you talked to them about the baby."

"Yes, I talked to them and they were very supportive, at least Mommy was. Dear just came flat out told me not to have an abortion. I found out Mommy had one herself. Can you believe it?" she said, amazed. "I'm still tripping over that."

"I bet you are," Tone said.

"I guess we should talk." They both said at the same time.

Rita laughed nervously, running her fingers through her hair and said, "You go first, Tone."

He took a deep breath, stared deeply at her, and said, "First of all, I wanna say that I agree with Mah-Dear, no abortion. You're right Rita," he said, holding up his hands, "it's your body and I can't stop you from having one, but I want you to have the baby."

"Why?" she asked, quietly.

"Because it's my baby too and I don't believe in abortions," he answered.

"That's not a good enough reason Tone." Rita said, plaintively. "You can do better than that."

"Because I love you and that baby is a part of both of us."

"You're getting warmer," she said, the chill in her voice diminishing somewhat.

"I asked you a long time ago to marry me and you turned me down. Hell, I figured when you were ready to settle down you'd propose to me."

"Whatever gave you the crazy idea that I'd propose to you?"

"Anyway, I've been talking to Marcus." Tone went on seriously. "I've got some money saved, but I know the projects coming down will affect my money. However, Marcus says he's on top of things and has a plan. By the way, I learned that he has a college degree."

"No kidding," Rita said. Her nose wrinkled and her eyebrow arched as she listened attentively.

"He said that if I go back to school and get my GED, then I could manage one of his companies. Marcus is going to go legit and hinted it would be a good time for us to get out of certain parts of 'the business'."

"Marcus might have told you that," Rita said, shaking her head, "but he'll always have his hands in the pie."

"Yeah, you're probably right about that," Tone agreed. "Anyway, he says he'll help me study for the GED."

Hell, I'll help you myself, she thought.

"I know if you keep the baby, you won't be able to work, at least not right now, but you could still go to school. By the time you're done with that the baby would be born, then you could start working. I'll do my part and step up to the plate. Whatever it takes to convince you to keep the baby, just say the word and I'll do it."

"Oh baby!" Rita cried, jumping up and embracing him. "That's all I wanted to hear, that you'd help me. I still don't really want another baby. I let too many years go by before

I started getting my shit together. Things have just started falling in place," she said, reticently. "I remember when the twins were babies, you were no help at all," she said, poking him in his chest.

"Back then I was trying to do the right thing, and since it didn't go too well, I didn't know how you'd feel about trying it again. This time though, I'll do a better job," he said.

"I can't do this alone Tone, I need your help," she warned. "Mommy has her own life and I didn't want to invade her space with three children and a new baby. She's still somewhat young and likes to go out and have a good time. Mah-Dear is not used to living with boys and I have doubts as to how all of that would work out."

"I think we should at least try living together, Rita. Hell, we should get married."

"Say what?" Rita's mouth dropped, and then she flashed him that brilliant smile. The one that made him fall in love with her many years ago. "Did you say what I thought you said? Did you just ask me to marry you?"

"Yeah, I guess I did," he said, as he stood up and pulled a little velvet box out of his pocket. He sat down next to her, removed the ring from the box, placed her hand to his chest and then slid a diamond ring on her finger. "What do you say Rita Atkins, will you marry me?"

"Yes, of course I will," she squealed, with delight.

He pulled her into his chest, kissing her with steamy passion. Sparks started flying. They sat for a while just holding each other, Rita crying happy tears. She instantly thought of five people that would be ecstatic by the news.

"Know what I'm thinking?" Tone said.

"What?" Rita asked.

"Destiny is a year younger than we were when we started kicking it."

"Like I don't know," she replied. "You're right though, our little girl is growing up.
I see boys and men looking at her with their tongues wagging, drooling at her curvy little butt and fear comes into my heart. I worry many a day about living in the projects."

"Excuse me," Tone said, snippily. "Last time I checked," he said, looking down at his body, "I was a project boy."

"True baby, but you're an old school project boy, an exception to the rule," she said, kissing his cheek. "Let's face it, the boys today are nothing like the boys were back in the day. I won't say they're all bad, but a majority of them are nothing but trouble."

"Well, maybe the projects would be the best place for her. Between me and Marcus, nobody would dare lay a hand on her."

"You can't control everybody Tone and there are some crazy people in this world. It's best that she has her father around, where he can keep an eye on her out of the projects," she said.

"Yeah, you're right about that," he agreed. "By the way, I have money saved to buy a house," Tone casually informed her.

"I'm shocked," Rita laughed, "as tight as you are with money."

"Shut up," he teased her.

She scooted closer to him as he put his arms around her, and the love started flowing.

"Um Rita," he paused, then continued, "you wanna call your moms and ask her if she can keep the kids tonight?"

She smiled mischievously and replied, "Let me see what I can do."

"At least we don't have to worry about you getting pregnant," he added, a wicked gleam shining in his eyes.

A little later, Rita called Barbara and she agreed to keep the kids for the night. Rita assured her that she and Tone would pick them up in the morning.

While Rita was talking to Barbara, Tone called Marcus on his cell phone.

"Hey dawg, I just wanted to tell you it's all going to work out."

"I told it would, bro," Marcus said, laughing. "So when's the wedding? And I know I'm the best man."

"True dat and of course you're the best man," Tone exclaimed. "I expect the same honors when you and Donna do that thang."

"You got it," Marcus said. "Handle your business, I'll holla at you later."

After declining Tone's offer to dine out, Rita prepared a tasty but simple meal of burgers and fries. They sat comfortably in the bed, eating and feeding each other. Oldies blared from the radio as they lay laughing and reminiscing about the old days. There were slight disagreements as to who chased whom, each swearing it was the other. Tone boasted about being the best dancer, hands down.

"I beg to differ," Rita said, "I'll dance your ass off the floor on any given night."

She confessed to being glad he was finally getting out the business. He admitted he never felt comfortable with it, but it was his only way to make a living at that time. He felt bad when he couldn't do better providing for his family when he worked legitimate jobs. Most of all, he told her about how ashamed he was of not having a high school diploma.

"I always knew in the back of my mind that not having one held me back," he said. "I know my Moms will be happy that we're finally getting married. She's been on my case for the longest."

Rita gave him further details about her conversation with Barbara and Mah-Dear.

"Now Rita, I want you to answer one question for me. How were you going to have an abortion by telling your Moms, Mah-Dear and me?" he asked her, teasingly. "I thought women just snuck out and did that kind of thing."

"Deep down inside I was hoping that one of you would talk me out of it," Rita confessed.

They laughed, then got up from the bed and danced to one of their favorite oldies. It was a sexy dance, full of promise of the showdown to come later. When the song ended, Tone picked her up gracefully and laid her gently on the bed, kissing her deeply and passionately. He lovingly removed her clothes, slipping her tee shirt and blue jeans off her body. When he was done, she slid his jeans over his slender but hard hips and removed the rest of his clothing. He gently caressed her swollen, firm breasts. He tenderly kissed her erect nipples and she shivered in anticipation. His manhood saluted her passageway to love. Tone smoothly turned her onto her back, knelt alongside her and kissed her navel.

He looked up at her and said, "That's my little homey in there, my son."

He tenderly stroked the round curve of her belly. Rita's stomach muscles clenched and unclenched fitfully, then Tone held her in his arms, savoring the essence and aroma of *his woman*. She inhaled deeply, reveling in his hard masculine form enveloping and filling her body with unbearable heat. Tears of joy filled her eyes. Then it was on, they made love, demonstrating tenderness and a sense of urgency, matching each other stroke for stroke. Their lovemaking hit an all-time high that night because declarations of love and commitments had been made.

Before she fell asleep with a satisfied smile on her luminous face, Rita's last thought was that she'd been right after all. This was a new beginning.

The next morning as they lounged in bed, there was much laughter and giggling, as if they'd reverted back to teenagers. Rita couldn't stop looking at him, she was afraid that after all was said and done, last night would turn out to be just a dream. She grabbed hold of his hand and wouldn't let it go, while at the same time admiring her ring.

After a while they got up, dressed and headed over to Barbara's. When they arrived, the two women were sitting in the kitchen drinking coffee, and they just smiled at Rita and Tone. Seeing so much love in their eyes, made them remember their own sweet love promises from long ago.

Mah-Dear's eyes became moist and Barbara playfully said, "I guess you two came up with a plan, huh?"

"That we did," Rita said smugly, slyly holding her left hand behind her back and out of sight.

"When is the wedding?" Mah-Dear asked, innocently.

Rita's mouth dropped. "How did you know Dear?"

"Because I'm your grandmother and I know these things," she answered, sassily.

"Well, we haven't set a date but will soon," she said, holding up her left hand.

"Before the baby gets here I hope," Mah-Dear said, directly.

"Yes Mah-Dear, we'll do it before then," they answered in unison.

"Amen," she said happily, as she and Barbara got up to hug them.

FAMILY
secrets

O n e

Two Months Prior...

In a state of nervous apprehension, Jeanine Meyers sat inside her dark blue Ford Fiesta in the parking lot of Jackson Park Hospital, located on the southeast side of Chicago. Unbeknownst to Jeanine, Liana, her favorite cousin and best friend, sat in her own car several car lengths and a few rows away from Jeanine. Liana's face knotted with worry as she kept a vigilant eye on her troubled cousin. Her presence at the hospital came at the request of Jeanine's parents, afraid some unfortunate mishap would befall their youngest child.

Over the objections of her family, Jeanine chose to make the first leg of her painful journey to recovery alone. Liana's eyes overflowed with tears as she watched her cousin struggle mightily with the decision of taking the first step towards bettering her life. She stuffed a fist to her mouth, trying hard to muffle the sob that threatened to escape her mouth as she watched Jeanine's body jerk spasmodically, as if she were in the middle of a blizzard without outer clothing.

As Jeanine continued to sit in her car, the tears flowed from her eyes like the Mississippi River. When the tears stopped flowing and her vision cleared, Jeanine glanced towards the building. Her expression conveyed a combination of fright with a tinge hope, as if making a silent appeal for divine intervention from the Lord above. She bowed her head and prayed silently that maybe, just maybe, the hospital would contain a magical potion that would infuse her body and soul with much needed strength in order for her to take that first baby step of removing herself from the car. Then cross the threshold into the building to begin treatment for the much-needed help she'd been unable and unwilling to seek in the past. According to her family, minister and therapist, salvation awaited her through the revolving doors. All she had to do was gather the strength to put one foot ahead of the other, enter the structure and begin the healing process. This may have been easy enough for some people, but not Jeanine, whose face was a snapshot of sadness and devastation caused by horrific events a few months ago.

Her left foot began impatiently tapping a beat only she could hear. Her face, a portrait of ruin, the center dominated by two deadened orbs, dark and unseeing, looked like she no longer physically or mentally inhabited this world. Her olive colored face still bore a few fading telltale marks of bruises, which she'd made a half-hearted attempt to mask with makeup caked on her face like dots of flour. She looked and felt so beaten down and her face and body reflected it literally and figuratively. Jeanine's life had been thrown for a loop, turned upside down like a roller coaster ride careening out of control at Six Flags. Oh, what a high degree of turmoil she'd gone through. Most people, if they're lucky, will never experience in their lifetime the waking nightmare that inhabits her life, which began almost two months ago, leaving her in this bizarre environment. Normalcy is a state of mind that she won't be returning to anytime soon. Her biggest challenge is coping with life, making it through the ensuing days one day at a time.

Suicidal thoughts, like a ticking bomb, intrude in and out of her mind throughout portions of her waking hours. Her worried family keeps watch over her night and day. Someone is always with her, patiently standing guard. Her mother, Rose, her sister, Medora or Meme, as her family called her, cousin Liana and even her Daddy, Isaac, sit with her sometimes.

It was an infamous day that changed life for Jeanine and her entire family. After a series of unpleasant events and poor decision-making, James, her husband of ten years, started exhibiting violent tendencies and spiraled out of control. On that evening, in the haze of a drunken rage, he struck their only child. Albeit an accident, James hit the child with so much force, that he'd nearly died. Yes, seven-year-old Jamal, her precious baby boy's only mistake in all of this was trying to protect his Mama from a beating inflicted by his Daddy. That single act had thrown her life off course, derailed like an Amtrak train and there was no turning back. How could she allow her child to be in a situation that caused him nearly to be murdered by his own father?

The press had a field day with that story and the subsequent ones that followed. Pictures of her, Jamal and James occupied the headlines and articles in the Chicago Sun Times, Tribune and Defender newspapers for a long time. Co-workers, neighbors, friends, even relatives were interviewed by the press and local television stations. With horror-stricken looks on their faces, they stood expressing their disbelief that something like that could happen, saying how the Meyers' seemed like such a nice family. James and Jeanine experienced their fifteen minutes of fame, although it was more so infamy in their case.

"It was just a blessing from God that Jeanine wasn't charged as an accessory to the crime. Society can be so rigid sometimes," Medora often remarked.

When thinking back on the events of that day, Jeanine wavers between being out of control like a spinning coin going round and round until it finally drops, or else she shuts down and refuses to eat or communicate for days on end. She has yet to recover mentally or physically.

Coming to this crisis center and participating in an intervention program is the first prescribed step towards recovery, or so that's what they all told her. So, here she is now, sitting in the parking lot trying to summon the courage to get out the car, begin the healing process and try to come to terms with all that had transpired in her life a short time ago. Her initial diagnosis is a debilitating malaise of the body and soul. She kept glancing at the clock on the dashboard and then to the doors of the hospital, like the hands of a metronome sitting on top of a piano. The meeting was scheduled to begin in a few minutes, and a part of Jeanine wanted to enter the building, knowing somewhere in the unburied part of her heart where she could still feel and react, this would eventually help her cope with all that had happened.

Lord knows I want to go in there, she thought, *but I don't know if I can bear to tell another person aloud the details of Jamal's accident and the part that I played in it, at least without literally falling apart.*

Her sole reason for living, or so she says, is the thought of her child someday coming out of his coma. Still, she refused to go to the hospital and visit him. A part of her wants to stay in that place in her head where life hadn't changed and Jamal was still a part of her daily life. In her dreams and sometimes during waking hours, she talks to him. Her baby is still with her in the flesh, grinning mischievously at her with those two missing front teeth. Then, other times, when she closes her eyes, his perfect dimpled smile haunts her. Yes, being in that happy place is sometimes preferable than the travesty that her life has become. No, there was just no way possible she could talk to other people about any of that. *My shame is too great*, she thought, sadly. The wound left on her psyche is a red, bleeding canker sore that she knows will never heal, but that which will remain to fester the rest of her days on this earth.

Jeanine didn't think she could explain the events to anyone else, they hardly made any sense when she tried to put the pieces together herself. It's so confusing, like trying to put together the pieces of a giant, intricate jigsaw puzzle whose pieces just don't fit no matter which way you turn them cause of a manufacturer's error.

Last night when they talked on the telephone, Medora offered to come along with her to the meeting for moral support saying, "Jeanine, you don't have to do it alone, we're here for you, all of us."

But she knew she had to go it alone, take that step into the hospital and claim her life back.

Once upon a time, in another lifetime, she was a nice looking woman, a little on the plump side, but still pleasing to the eye. She had soft light brown hair that she'd worn in a flip style. Now her hair, like her soul, has dried out. Weight loss over the past two months has left her with a gaunt and fragile appearance, as if a strong gale of wind could knock her over. Dimples framed her tightly clenched mouth like parenthesis, since she'd hardly smiled in months.

Since that day, Jeanine has more or less just been a person existing, going through the motions of the day, but not really there in mind. Her clothes no longer match anymore or fit her body. Most of the time she just wears an old raggedy terry bathrobe, which she keeps clutched tightly about her body. Her hair is an untidy mess that she gathers in a rubber band on the top of head and the band has broken off strands of her hair. It dawned on the family that Jeanine is fighting a battle for her mortal soul and they're willing to do whatever it takes to bring her back. The person with them looks like Jeanine, sounds like Jeanine, but is only a shell of her. Their precious daughter, sister and cousin has left them and escaped to a place where it doesn't hurt anymore and where her Jamal is in perfectly good physical condition, up and running about, a happy child with his mama.

Jeanine's large brown eyes project myriad emotions, when she's able to focus on the person speaking to her. Hurtful pain, indignation, resentment and shame, smolder to the core of her very being. Rev. Bowen, the family minister, has been counseling her since that night. He's tried to do his best to help her come to grips with her situation, ease the hurt and keep the demons at bay with his deep melodic voice, but Jeanine couldn't hear the words. Yes, she could hear his voice, but the words didn't make sense. They translated to something resembling gibberish, as if someone was speaking a foreign language. Sadly, Rev. Bowen felt they weren't making progress, and to her horror, he'd actually talked to her family about the lack of improvement in her condition. Medora, with Jeanine in tow, trekked down to Dr. Johnson, her physician's office. Upon hearing Rev. Bowen's findings, Dr. Johnson suggested that perhaps participating in the intervention program at the hospital might be the jolt needed to bring Jeanine back to herself.

two

Still sitting in her car, and with shaking hands, Jeanine lit a cigarette. She promptly coughed, inhaling too much smoke. Much to her family's dismay, this was another habit she'd acquired since that night, and her parents were afraid she'd carelessly burn the house down.

After pulling on it a couple more times and exhaling, she quickly stubbed it out. Jeanine pushed the car door open and swung her legs onto the ground. She stood up slowly, feeling somewhat lightheaded, and slammed the car door shut. She stood there a minute and stared at the entrance of the hospital. The entrance seemed so far away and the distance seemed like miles instead of feet.

All sounds ceased as she began walking unsteadily towards the door. Her stomach muscles twitched uncontrollably and she felt nauseated. Finally, after what seemed like an eternity, she stood at the front of the hospital and weakly pushed at the door, it didn't move. Exerting more strength with her second attempt, the door swung around. Having forgotten her glasses, she squinted at the numbers posted on the wall. As she approached the meeting place, low murmuring voices greeted her ears. Jeanine picked up her pace a bit and walked into the room.

A group of people sat in a circle of chairs in the front of the small room, while others huddled around a coffeemaker. Jeanine slid quietly into the first vacant seat she came upon. Tiny beads of sweat dotted her forehead, while perspiration trickled coldly down her armpits. A smiling African-American woman wearing a white coat sat in the middle of the small group, she gazed compassionately at Jeanine.

"The meeting will begin in five minutes," the woman in the white coat announced. She then rose from her seat, walked over to Jeanine and asked, "Would you like a cup of coffee or something before we get started?"

Jeanine began trembling again and shook her head no.

The woman gazed down at her again, the corners of her mouth curved into a kind, motherly smile. A few people openly stared curiously at Jeanine, causing her to panic, thinking they probably recalled her picture strewn across the headlines of the newspaper the past few months.

The woman called the meeting to order, and those not seated headed to the chairs and sat down.

The woman stated, "I'd like everyone to introduce yourselves to the group, and if you feel like sharing the circumstances that brought you to the meeting, by all means, please do so. For those of you who don't know me, my name is Dr. Selma White."

Round the circle they went, everyone giving their names, some speaking briefly about the incident that brought them to the hospital that afternoon. Finally, it was Jeanine's turn. She sat hunched over the seat, hands clasped about her upper arms, like a drowning person grabbing at a lifeline.

"My name is Jeanine Meyers," she whispered in a timid voice. Then she choked up and couldn't utter another word.

With the introductions concluded, Dr. White remarked, "I know this method of coping or coming to terms with the death, trauma or illness of a loved one is probably unfamiliar to most of you. Still, it'll help you over the course of time if you stick with it."

Some people listened intently to her words. Eyes seemed to stray curiously at Jeanine, as if trying to gauge her story. The group was composed of ten people total: seven women, consisting of three Caucasians, two African-Americans and two Hispanics, and three men, Caucasian, African-American and Asian.

After Dr. White gave a summary of the upcoming schedule, she informed the group of her credentials in which she'd studied at the University of Chicago, her major being general medicine. She told of how later she'd returned to school to study for a master's degree in psychology and had been practicing in that field for ten years now. It became her life's work to help people cope with fatal tragedies and traumas in their lives. Her plan today was that everyone would become comfortable with one another as a group. She told them how each person would help the other's recovery one way or another. It might not seem apparent now, but her methods had been proven and worked. The key was giving it time.

One member of the group, Mr. Graham, asked, "If I'm not being too forward Dr. White, can I ask what made you decide to specialize in this type of work?"

"With tragedies occurring as frequently as they do, whether it be accident victims or those afflicted with the HIV virus, along with the high rate of violence that has hit our nation and cities, I felt an overwhelming need to form support groups, especially here in the inner city," she answered. "It's a method to assist people with coping with the expected, as well as the unexpected. It's my way of helping our people put their lives back together."

Another participant, Mrs. Brown, raised her hand. "Dr. White, do you speak from a personal experience?"

"Yes I do. With that said, hopefully you, along with everyone in the group, will be able to assist each other with coping and perhaps overcoming the adversity you're currently facing. Obviously, everyone in this room has faced the loss of a loved one in some form or another and a lot of people tend to blame themselves." Jeanine felt herself blush as Dr. White continued. "You have to be able to move beyond those thoughts of blaming yourself or trying to figure out what you could've been done differently. That's the only way you can resume productive lives. This is where the group as a whole and I come into play. I would caution you to give it time, at least four sessions, to see if this method is effective for you. I've worked with many people facing diverse situations much like you all." She nodded. "I would like to add, my success rate is fairly good, but only if you are willing to open up, share and believe you are someone worth saving."

Several people looked downward, considering her comments. Jeanine felt skeptical and doubted that anyone there would be admitting their child was in a coma at this very minute, lying in a hospital bed because of the mother's inability to rid herself of a bad marital situation.

As if sensing her thoughts, Dr. White said, "I've heard it all, so don't hold back. Group, we're not here to be judgmental, we're all in this together." She added, "Mrs. Wong, why don't you start us off?"

An hour later, Jeanine falsely told Dr. White that she'd be back next week. During most of the hour, Jeanine sat quietly and didn't contribute much, deciding she really didn't want to continue with the sessions. A hopeless melancholy invaded her being like a virus, feeling no one could help her. But she could hear her parents and Medora in the back of her mind, giving her fifty reasons why she should continue with the sessions.

Dr. White peered at her intently, touching her arm. "Jeanine, I truly hope you'll come back. I can help you, I promise," she said.

Keeping a safe distance behind a couple of members of her support group, she walked out the building and into the parking lot. As she reached her car, Jeanine got in, sat quietly for a moment and re-lit the cigarette she had stubbed out earlier. Then she fumbled in her purse for the car keys, which she finally located, and started the car. She initially headed towards her parents' house, with Liana trailing a few car lengths behind her. Suddenly, she swerved and made a detour, driving to the house that her family had once resided in. She quickly pulled into an open parking spot outside the house, turned the car off and stared at the place she used to call home.

Jeanine, it's not healthy for you to be there. Come home right away. Her sister's voice came unbidden into her mind.

But home is right here, she thought. *For me, James and Jamal. I shouldn't be going to Momma and Daddy's house, I want to be right here with my own family.*

She could hear Jamal calling her in his high-pitched voice and a single tear trickled down her face. She wiped it away with the heel of her hand. Then Jeanine started the car up again, put it into gear and drove north to her parents' house.

Upon entering the house, Jeanine greeted her mother.

"Hi Mama, I'm tired. I think I'll go upstairs and take a nap."

She plodded slowly up the stairs to the bedroom she once shared with Meme and laid on the bed, suffused with exhaustion. A few minutes later, she rose from the bed, went into the bathroom, picked up a cup and filled it with water from the faucet. After placing two tiny pills in her mouth, she swallowed the water. Dr. Johnson had prescribed a mild sedative to help her relax. Mercifully, they kicked into her system quickly and soon she lay in her bed fast asleep.

Rose stood in the kitchen preparing dinner, while Meme sat at the kitchen table cutting vegetables for a tossed salad.

"How did she seem when she came back from the meeting?" Meme asked Rose.

"Tired, just plain tired," she sighed.

"Mama, you know these things take time," said Meme. "And I think it's going to take a long time for Jeanine to return to her old self, that's assuming she ever will."

"Of course my baby will return to her old self," said Rose, indignantly. "Jeanine is just going through a bad spell, but she'll be back."

"Oh Mama," sighed Meme, "don't you think all those years that she spent with James and the beatings have taken a toll on her. Not to mention all that she has on her plate right now with Jamal."

"Time heals all wounds," Rose remarked, strongly. "She has our prayers and the church's. The Lord will hear and answer our cries."

"I hear you," Meme said, rising from the table chair and walking over to the stove to hug her mother. "I know this is rough on you and Daddy and I'll do whatever I can to help."

"We know child," smiled Rose. "I'm just worried about Jeanine. She's been through so much, but I know in time my girl will be fine."

"I hope you're right," Meme intoned.

"Why don't you go up and check on her for me?" Rose asked. "You know how nervous I get when she's by herself for too long."

"Mama, she's probably asleep. I think we should leave her alone." Meme chided her mother gently, as she expertly and quickly peeled white potatoes to go with the pot roast baking in the oven.

"Please," Rose said, cajolingly, "indulge your old mother. I just don't think I can bear anything happening to her after Jamal."

"Okay, I'm going," she said, rising from the chair again.

She squeezed her mother's arm as she brushed past her, went up the stairway and into the bedroom. Meme stood motionlessly in the doorway, watching the rise and fall of Jeanine's chest as she inhaled and exhaled. Then she turned around and went down the stairs, sat back down at the kitchen table and resumed peeling potatoes.

"She's still asleep," Meme said.

The backdoor opened suddenly and Isaac stepped into the room, rubbing his hands together. He shut and locked the door behind him.

"How are you, honey?" he asked Rose after kissing her on the cheek. Then he strolled to the table, bent down and kissed Meme on the forehead. "How is Jeannie, did she go to the meeting?"

"She's asleep," answered Rose, stirring a pot of greens. "And yes, she did go to the meeting."

"Did she say how it went?"

"She didn't say much about it, other than she did go. I didn't ask her too many questions, I didn't want her to feel pressured," Rose said.

Isaac removed a tall glass from the cabinet over the sink, walked over to the refrigerator and poured himself a generous helping of water. He's a heavyset, sixty-eight year old, mahogany colored man, projecting an old school demeanor. His thick coarse gray hair, or what's left of it, sticks out like tuffs of cotton along the back of his head and his brow looks curiously unfinished, as if something is missing because of his receding hairline. He's worn a look of bafflement for the past few months, not quite understanding why these misfortunes have befallen his family, and particularly to his baby girl, Jeanine. His mind is unable to comprehend why she'd stay with James under the circumstances she did. His grandson's injury hit him especially hard since he and Rose had only managed to produce two girls, much to his consternation. He'd wanted a son badly and his first and only grandson, Jamal, filled his sonless void and brought him joy. The two share a special bond and he feels lost without him. His facial expression displays a melancholy expression when his thoughts stray to Jamal and Jeanine.

They all simultaneously turned towards the stairwell upon hearing Jeanine walk slowly and laboriously down the creaky staircase, like an old arthritic woman. It seemed to take her twice as long as it used to for her to complete anything these days. She shuffled into the kitchen, her mouth agape, yawning and stood motionlessly next to her mother.

"Hi honey, are you hungry?" asked Rose.

Meme just stared at her sister and began choking up, not trusting herself to say anything.

"Jeanine," said Isaac, motioning to her, "come on over and sit down by your Daddy." He sat patting the empty chair next to him. "How did the session go today?"

Jeanine sank into the chair and dropped her eyes down at the table, not wanting to look at any of them.

"I guess it went okay. We introduced ourselves and the doctor, her name is Dr. White, explained how the program works."

"That sounds good," said Isaac, with false bravado in his voice, clearly out of his element and embarrassed that Dr. Johnson had suggested Jeanine see a headshrinker, as he called them.

"Dinner is just about ready, we can eat in a moment," Rose announced, opening the oven door and removing the pan of pot roast.

As she opened the cover to make sure the meat was done, an appetizing aroma filled the kitchen.

"Meme, are you staying for dinner?"

"Yes count me in. Marcel picked the girls up from school and he's taking them out to dinner," Meme answered.

Marcel is her husband and they're the parents of two daughters: Stacy, a ten-year-old, plump mischievous girl, who looks a lot like Jeanine did at the same age, and Tatiana, six years of age, a small thin, hyperactive child, who favors her father in looks.

"Today is treat day," Meme continued, "so he's taking them to McDonald's for dinner."

Then she shrugged her shoulders helplessly, wondering if she should've mentioned that at all, considering Jeanine's plight. However, so much had changed and sometimes, being tactful slipped her mind.

"I'm sorry," she said, apologetically to Jeanine. "I'm going to call and make sure everything is all right," she said, quickly excusing herself and walking into the living room.

Jeanine's already depressed mood plummeted at her sister's words. *At least she has children and a husband to go home to. I'd give my life if things could just go back to that day.*

Lord, I wish I could turn back the hands of time, she thought, sighing audibly.

Seeing her daughter's shoulders slump, Rose knew her daughter was experiencing a rough moment.

"Why don't you set the table for me, Jeanine?" she asked, trying to ease the tension that gathered like clouds in the air.

A few minutes later, Meme walked back into the kitchen and said, "I'll put the food into bowls and on the table."

Soon, they were seated at the table with their heads downcast as Isaac offered thanks for the food prepared. They ate quietly for the most part. Isaac, Rose and Meme tried hard to keep routines as normal as possible.

Isaac, a retired bus driver, now works in the yard in a maintenance position. Isaac laughingly relayed a couple of amusing stories that occurred during the course of his day. Meme mentioned that the lawyer she worked for had just made partner, so there was a possibility her workload might increase.

"Mr. Taylor might bring another girl on part-time to assist me," she added.

After Jamal was injured, Rose had taken a leave of absence from her job as a cook in a high school cafeteria.

After dinner was concluded, Jeanine sat in the living room with Isaac as he watched the evening news, leaving Meme and Rose in the kitchen to put up the leftover food and wash dishes. Shortly after joining Jeanine and Isaac in the living room. Meme glanced at her watch.

"Well guys, if there's nothing else to do, I need to head home. Marcel and the girls should be home by now," she remarked. "Hopefully, Stace and Tiana are busy with homework." She walked over to the closet and removed her coat, quickly putting it on. "What's up with you tomorrow Jeanine, do you want me to go to the hospital with you when I get off work?"

"No, I'm not going tomorrow."

"Come on," Rose pleaded, "don't you want to see Jamal? After all, you haven't been to see him one single time."

"I can't Mama, not yet."

Meme cut her eyes at her mother, rolling them to the top of her head. Isaac nervously rubbed his forehead. Meme knew that Jeanine's reluctance to see Jamal hurt her parents and she didn't understand it herself. If Jeanine loved Jamal so much, how could she not go to the hospital to see him? That kind of reasoning she couldn't comprehend. Sometimes she wanted to go off on, snap at and then shake some sense into her sister. Maybe that would bring her out of the stupor she seemed to inhabit.

"I've been doing some reading on Jamal's injuries and comas in general," Meme remarked. "Studies show if someone close to the patient, usually a parent, talk to them, it can help to bring them out of it. He's your child, your baby, I don't understand how you wouldn't want to see him."

"You're right Meme, you can't understand," murmured Jeanine, tensely. "No one can understand what I'm feeling."

"Why don't you enlighten me then," Meme said, folding her arms across her chest, her tone a little harsher than she intended it to be.

"Now, don't you go upsetting your sister, Meme," said Isaac, eyes flashing with anger. "I won't have it, she has to do this her own way."

Rose nodded in agreement with her husband. "We can't force her to go, Meme. Jeanine will know when it's time and then she'll go, right?" she asked, turning toward Jeanine.

"Of course, Mama," said Jeanine, listlessly. "I'm going to see him soon, I just don't know when."

Isaac's head dropped into his big hands, massaging his closed eyes, as if he couldn't bear what he was seeing and hearing.

"Okay, okay, I'm sorry," said Meme, holding her hands up in surrender.

She'd gone round and round on this subject with her parents time and time again. She felt her parents enabled Jeanine to stay in her fantasy world. Aware that only two months had elapsed since that night, she still felt that Jeanine should at least be at the point where she was visiting her child.

Jamal is a patient of La Rabida Children's Hospital situated on the south side of Chicago in the community of Hyde Park. The doctors on staff specialize in children diseases and ailments and it's considered one of the top facilities in the nation. Meme is a paralegal at a law firm in close proximity to the hospital. She visits Jamal at least three times a week during her lunch break. His condition is a shock that she's still trying to come to terms with. A sense of bereavement pierced the very core of her system when she laid eyes on him the first time in the hospital. His little head seemed so fragile in those bandages, and there were so many tubes attached to his body that lay twisted in a fetal position. Now his vital signs seemed to be improving, but his brain activity was not good.

The doctors hadn't given up hope on Jamal. They were cautious regarding his condition and wouldn't predict one way or another what the outcome of his situation might be when, or if, he woke up. Being of Christian faith, the family remained hopeful that Jamal would one day recover, probably not to the normal child that he'd been, but in time, close to it.

Wanting nothing less than the best medical care for Jamal, Rose and Isaac took out a loan against their home, which they owned free and clean. The entire family resides in Avalon Park, a community on the southeast side of Chicago. Meme, after conferring with Marcel, co-signed the loan along with her parents but with strong reservations about their actions. She loathed putting that kind of financial burden on her parents, given their ages. But with James incarcerated, God only knows when Jeanine would return to work, so there was no other choice. A loan was the only option available for them to pay the ever-surmounting medical bills.

Meme surfed the net and called city and state agencies for funding, even welfare, waiting for whatever came through. She'd broached Jeanine with the idea of selling her house, but her sister was adamantly against that suggestion. Although deep in her heart, Meme knew it was unlikely that Jeanine would ever return there to live, she didn't give up on that plan. She hoped in time the therapy would kick in and Jeanine would be able to make some of the decisions that she was now forced to deal with.

Her parents started their family late in life, and with Meme being the oldest, she felt the brunch of the burden. She didn't mind it ninety percent of the time, but sometimes she got tired, especially with having her own family to contend with.

Another thing unfathomable to Meme was that not only did Jeanine refuse to visit Jamal, but it also seemed James didn't exist to her anymore. She never spoke of him, to him and refused to have any contact with his family. Meme sometimes ran into his mother, Loretta, at the hospital visiting Jamal. Like Isaac and Rose, she wore that same perpetual bewildered expression on her face.

The sound of Rose's voice snapped Meme back to the present. "Why don't you go on home, we'll talk about this later," urged Rose.

"You always say later, but later never seems to happen."

"I know it seems that way, but it'll all work out in the end, we just have trust God."

"Okay, I'll see you tomorrow." She walked over to Isaac, kissed him goodnight and patted Jeanine on the arm.

After Meme left, Rose yawned and said, "I'm tired, I think I'll turn in now." She got up from the couch and went into the kitchen to make sure all was in order.

Isaac glanced at Jeanine. "Are you tired baby?"

"Yeah Daddy, I am. I'm ready to go to bed," she sighed.

"Give me a minute," said Rose, checking the lock on the back door. "Everything looks fine in here, let's go up to bed now."

After Rose and Isaac had retired upstairs, Jeanine sat on the couch unmoving as if paralyzed by inertia. Finally, she pulled herself up and slowly trudged up the stairs. The low buzz of voices could be heard from her parents' room, and she knew the topic of the conversation was of none other than her. After turning the television set on with the sound low, she lay stretched across the bed. A pang of agony hit her so hard that she rolled over and tears gushed down her face. She stuffed the end of the bedspread in her mouth to muffle the screams that threatened to explode.

"Jamal, I'm so sorry," she sobbed.

When the crying jag ended, she leaned across the bed and reached under it, pulling out a shoebox full of sedatives. Jeanine lay in the bed, staring at the shadows moving like an African dance troupe on her bedroom wall, patiently waiting for her parents to fall asleep. They were creatures of habit and she knew there wasn't much time before one of them came to check on her. She poured the pills out of the bottles and played with them for a time, rearranging them on the coverlet.

"You okay in there?" Isaac asked, loudly from their bedroom.

"Uh hum, yeah Daddy," she replied. "I'm going to sleep now."

She sat upright on the bed, holding her knees with her arms. Finally, Isaac's snores permeated the upper part of the house. Jeanine tiptoed to the door, quickly twisting and locking it. She stole back to the bed, picked up the pills and walked into the attached bathroom. She washed them down with a cup of water, then walked back into the room and fell on top of the bed.

"Forgive me Jamal, I'm so sorry. Mommy couldn't protect you," she repeated over and over, as her body relaxed and her eyes became heavy.

A short time later, Rose suddenly sat up in bed and shivered as an eerie chill snaked down her spine. The loud sounds of her husband's snoring assaulted her ears. Uneasily, she poked Isaac in his back. He turned towards her, yawning, eyes red and bleary.

"What's wrong, Ro?"

"When was the last time you checked on Jeanine?"

"I don't know, I had planned on getting up but fell back to sleep."

"Well, get up man. One of us need to check on her right now," Rose insisted.

"I'll do it," he grumbled, half-asleep. "You stay here."

He got up, stuck his feet into his slippers and walked down the hall. He tried opening the door and it wouldn't bulge.

"Oh my God!" he shouted, twisting the knob again and then he began banging loudly on the door.

"Isaac, what's going on out there!" Rose yelled, upon hearing the commotion.

"The door is locked, I can't open it."

"Father in heaven," Rose moaned, jumping out of bed and running down the hall. "Knock it down!" she shouted, frantically.

Using his shoulder as a battering ram, Isaac managed to get the door open and spied Jeanine lying limply on the bed.

"Call 911 Rose!" he screamed, in terror.

"I am!" she yelled, running back into their bedroom.

Isaac gathered Jeanine in his arms and began performing CPR.

"Oh dear Lord," said Rose, upon returning to the room. Her body weakened as she looked on. "Is she…?" Her voice trailed off sobbing, as she stood sagging.

Then her legs gave way and she fell to her knees, never taking her eyes off them. Soon the wailing sounds of the ambulance's siren could be heard in the distance.

Isaac, continuing to hold Jeanine in his arms, prayed aloud, "Lord, please don't take our baby girl from us, not now. I don't think we could take it. Come on baby girl, please hold on," he pleaded. "I promise you, everything's gonna be alright."

three

Six months later...

Jeanine was back at her parent's house after a five-month stay in the psychiatric ward of Jackson Park Hospital. She's been instructed to attend counseling twice a week on an outpatient basis. Her appearance has improved, although traces of the calamity she endured are still evident on her face. She's managed to gain a little weight and has started combing her hair and bathing more frequently. The attempt to end her life, or parts of it, is a clear recollection, one she'll never forget. It seemed she stepped out of her body and could see the events as they unfolded. To this day, she can still hear Rose and Isaac's frantic cries of terror after he broke down the bedroom door and held her tenderly like a baby. All the time, he kept repeating over and over for Jeanine to hold on, his teardrops plopped onto her face.

Jeanine could feel the paramedics administering drugs into her body. She also recalled being placed into the ambulance, but then her memory failed. She didn't remember the ride to the hospital. Later, she recalled Meme looking tragic but angry, like somebody had died. Once the pills had been pumped from her system and she was stabilized, there were many conversations with Dr. Johnson, as well as Dr. White, about admitting her into the hospital. They explained she wasn't well enough to stay home yet. Then the painstaking intense sessions began as Dr. White worked hard to bring her back from the brink of insanity.

"I can't sugarcoat it no matter how hard I try, I lost my mind," she told her family.

She's even begun visiting Jamal and there was even talk of taking him off the respirator in the near future. Though the doctors don't predict a full recovery, they think he can become a somewhat functioning adult if things continue to go well.

Jeanine still hasn't visited James. He faces a stiff sentence at Joliet's Statesville Correctional Center. He's begun attending group sessions and is receiving much needed counseling. Maybe in time Jeanine will be able to take that trip and talk to him. She finally realizes the life they'd shared as a family is over.

One evening Jeanine called Meme and Liana on the telephone, requesting they come over to their parents' house for dinner. She finally wanted to talk to those closest to her about what happened that fateful night. They all gathered in the living room of Rose and Isaac's bungalow house, the sunshine casting shadows on the walls.

"Meme and Lili, I asked you over tonight," said Jeanine, sitting on the sofa between her parents, "because I want to share with you what happened that night at my house." Her eyes were luminous with unshed tears. "I also want to say thank you for being there for me. This is probably the toughest situation I've ever experienced in my life. Mama and Daddy, you've been there for me, as well," she said. "The words 'thank you' seem so inadequate because I know your lives have been turned upside down by all of this too. I know you begged me to leave James, Meme." She continued, looking at her sister. "God knows I wish I had now. I just never imagined anything happening to Mal, I always thought it would be me."

"Aw baby," said Isaac, pulling her into his arms, "we're your family, we love you."

"I know, Daddy," she whispered, grabbing his and Rose's hands.

"Should you be talking to us at all?" asked Meme, pointedly. "Perhaps it would be better if you waited until the doctors say it's okay."

Meme felt bitterness towards her sister. It took quite a few sessions with Rev. Bowen for Meme to somehow come to terms with the empty space left by Jamal's accident and not lash out at her sister. Every now and then those feelings would spill over and she'd experience a deep loathing. She was unable to come to terms with how someone, especially her little sister, let that monster do something so repugnant to her only child. She'd known things were not right in Jeanine's house and had begged her many times to leave James before something happened to her or Jamal and how Jeanine would stubbornly defend James.

"You just don't understand him, he's had a hard life, or, I can handle the situation." Were some of the excuses Jeanine would make.

"Yeah, she handled it alright," Meme thought, as the image of Jamal's unmoving body flitted through her mind, causing a pang of sorrow to skewer her heart.

As if sensing her mood, Isaac quickly interjected. "If Jeanine wants to talk to us, I don't see anything wrong with it."

"I agree," said Rose.

Jeanine's voice took on a dreamy, almost singsong, quality as she explained the events leading up to the tragedy at the Meyers' house nearly eight months ago.

"It was a day almost like any other day of my life. I didn't go to work that day because I was just dog-tired and had a bruise on my face," she admitted, as her head dropped, her hair fanning over her face. She inhaled deeply and continued. "I took Jamal to school even though he wanted to stay home with me. I felt school might take his mind off what had happened at home the night before. Unfortunately, he knew James and I had been fighting because he heard us. I dropped him off at school, came back home and called my job."

Wringing her hands tensely, she continued speaking. "Dave, my manager, had been very understanding in the past about my problem or my clumsy problem, as he would call it. You see, up until that point, I would tell him I fell, bumped into the door or tripped on the stairs and he'd always suggest I stay home until my wounds healed. In the beginning, James wouldn't hit me in the face much, only every now and then because he knew I had to work, so the blows were usually to my body."

"When I called Dave that morning," Jeanine continued, "the understanding he usually showed in the past was gone." She paused to look out the window. "He suggested that I take the rest of the week off and give some thought as to how to get out of my situation. I was embarrassed and mortified. He'd never made mention of anything like that before. He said at the rate I was going, I would end up dead..." Her voice trailed off again.

"Jeanine, he told me, do what you have to do but get out of that situation now. Listening to him talk was almost like a premonition of things to come. He added that most men that abuse women continue to do so unless they want help and seek it out for themselves. He informed me I was over the limit as far as taking days off. He said he could cover for me to a certain extent but that it was time for me to take steps to save my life.

After I got off the telephone with Dave, I cried like a baby. It seemed everyone knew my business or had their opinion as to what was going on in my house. But I knew he was right in his assessment of the situation and simply cared about me as a person. I've always liked Dave, he's good people and a great manager. He's gone to bat for me time and time again when I was too bruised or sore to go to work."

Rose held her hand over her mouth, eyes widening and teary. She had no inkling of the horrors her daughter had endured. Just listening to that weak little pitiful voice trying to explain the madness she'd withstood was almost too much for her to stand. Rev. Bowen had advised her and Isaac to be patient and that Jeanine would talk to them when she was ready. In the meantime, they should keep an eye on her and be supportive.

Isaac felt numb and leaden. How in God's name did it come to this, his baby girl used as a punching bag by that scum James? He rued the day he walked her down the aisle and given her hand in marriage to James.

Meme just listened impassively. She of the five people present was the one most knowledgeable of the travails Jeanine endured repeatedly, or so she thought. With their parents up in age, neither sister confided in them about what was going on Meyers' house. Both sisters felt a pang of guilt, realizing now maybe one of them should've gone to their parents with information years ago. Perhaps they may have helped in persuading Jeanine to leave James. Rose and Isaac were torn apart but handling things in their own way. Jamal in a coma, with no guarantee that he might awaken, was indeed a low blow for the two elderly people.

Jeanine went on, "James hadn't been in a good mood for a couple of weeks. Over the past couple of years, he'd become extremely controlling, offering his opinion on everything. No, let me correct that, telling me what I could and couldn't do, even to the point of what clothes I could wear. He inspected my clothing each morning before I went to work to make sure they weren't too revealing. When I bought my new car, he picked it out although I was the one who'd saved for the down payment. Then he started telling me what meals to prepare for dinner. I couldn't do anything on my own without him telling me when and how to do it. Things got really bad when his job started downsizing and they started letting employees go. He had a feeling he was going to be in the next group released and his mood became ugly. The rumor mill had it that another round of men would receive pink slips in their pay envelopes that coming Friday.

After I talked to Dave, I got to thinking maybe it was time to leave James. I went upstairs and packed clothes for Jamal and myself. When I was done with that, I put the suitcase in the trunk of my car. I then decided to clean up the house and fix what I wanted for dinner for a change. I had even considered poisoning James."

Rose and Isaac were simply aghast. No, this couldn't be their daughter talking about murdering her husband.

"This wasn't a situation that I could just walk away from," Jeanine said, glancing at Meme, as her nails dug into her parents' hands. "James would tell me I couldn't ever leave him. He said that he'd kill me first, then Mama and Daddy and I believed him," said Jeanine, pleadingly. "In fact, he threatened to do the same to you and your family," she said, as her eyes darted to Meme. "But he never talked about hurting Jamal, that's one reason I stayed with him. I really didn't know what to do at that point. Then I realized it was just a matter of time before he'd seriously hurt or kill me and that finally it was time to go.

I did file a complaint with the police a couple of years ago and got an emergency restraining order. When they released him from jail though he went upside my head so fast that by the time he was done, I saw stars and it was still daylight. I had a few cracked ribs too, and all of that happened before they actually served him with the papers, so I dropped the whole thing. I was so scared of him and a feeling of dread filled my very being whenever he'd go on a binge. My life became a living nightmare, one that I could never seem to wake up from."

She coughed nervously. "Don't get me wrong, he wasn't like that all of the time, but when he was, all I could do was remain alert and try not to make him angrier. Sometimes I couldn't gauge his mood correctly. When I didn't, I paid dearly for the lapse. When he drank liquor it was like he was another person, a Dr. Jekyll and Mr. Hyde," she said, shaking her head from side to side.

"You know I always said James was like a big cuddly teddy bear to me when I met him, a tall heavyset, cinnamon colored man, muscular in build, with dark brooding eyes, a baldhead, keen nose and a goatee beard. Well, right before my eyes, my teddy bear would transform into a raging Kodiak bear with a lust for blood. I didn't fear for Jamal, not then because I knew he loved him and had never laid a hand on him, except to discipline him. Even during those times, it was never excessive. At first, he rarely got angry enough to hit me in Jamal's presence, but when they started laying the men off at his job, his mood swings got worse and he would occasionally backhand me in front of him."

Taking a deep breath, she said, "So, there I was stuck in hell. I would talk to Lili and Meme sometimes, but never you and Daddy. I didn't want you to think less of me and I didn't want to put that burden on you, considering your ages. I know now I should've done things differently, and if I had…," her voice faltered, "Jamal would be here today. My own stupidity nearly killed him."

"Oh my poor baby." Rose sobbed, visibly distraught, tears streaming from her eyes. "Jeanine, it was an accident, please don't blame yourself."

"I have no one to blame except myself," she said, shaking her head sadly. "I cleaned the house and changed my mind about fixing what I wanted to for dinner, deciding to fix James' favorite meal since I was leaving. I logged onto the Internet, looking for jobs and apartments in other nearby states. You see, in my head I was going to take Jamal and move to Kansas. After I finished searching the net, I went back to the school and picked Jamal up. We came home, I fixed him a snack and he did his homework.

James was late coming home from work that evening and didn't bother to call to inform me of that fact, so Jamal and I ate dinner alone. Afterwards, Jamal watched television for a while and then got ready for bed. As I tucked him under the covers, I told him that he and I were going on an adventure, a trip, just the two of us and for him not to tell anyone."

'How come I can't tell anybody? Why not my Daddy?' he asked me.

"I remember his little face looking up at me quizzically and then understanding dawned on his face."

Jeanine's voice choked up again and she paused for a minute as tears streamed down her face. "As I kissed him goodnight, I told him that sometimes mommies and their favorite sons do things together and go places without the daddies. Then I asked him if he could keep a secret."

He nodded and whispered, 'Yes Mommy, I can keep a secret.'

"I hugged him tightly to me and pulled the comforter up around his shoulders. As I sat on the side of his bed, I could hear James fumbling at the front door. I left Jamal's room and went downstairs to the foyer. He finally made it into the house, reeking of alcohol, barely able to stand or walk. The first thing out of his mouth was, *'Stupid bitch, why did you move the furniture?'* I didn't, I tried to explain. Then BAP, he slapped me across my face, near my ear and it started ringing. I knew enough not to say anything more, so I backed away from him and asked, *'Are you hungry?'*"

He said, 'Are you crazy or something? Of course I am. You need to take your ass into the kitchen and fix me a plate.'

"I did just that, running into the kitchen and rubbing my ear at the same time. I prepared a plate for him and said a silent prayer at the same time. God help me, I hated him something awful, and at that moment, I felt a strong urge to hurt him. It took all my strength not to go into the drawer, get a knife and kill him. As I waited for his food to warm up in the microwave oven, a thought like a red alert ran through my mind. Get Jamal out of the house! LEAVE! I wanted to go so bad that I could taste it. My mouth was actually watering at the thought of escaping. I felt an overwhelming urge to get my baby to a safe place."

"James," Jeanine spat, "almost fell out of the chair after he finally managed to sit down. Immediately, he began complaining the food wasn't warm enough, even though I knew it was. There was nothing wrong with it, that was just the impetus he needed to commence to beating me."

Jeanine stopped again as if the memories were too painful for her to recall. Her family sensed that she was literally reliving that night over again. Her body began shaking and she kept rubbing her arms, as if trying to draw inner reserves so she could continue. She shook her head silently, still in that dreamy state.

"Jeanine," said Meme, quietly, "you don't have to do this. If it's too hard for you, we can always do this at another time." She walked over to the couch, bent down and stroked her sister's hand.

Isaac just sat there leaden, with the same look of dread and horror mirrored on everyone else's face on his. He and Rose both looked as though they'd aged ten years since Jeanine began talking.

"No," said Jeanine, "I've got to get this out in the open because I've held it in for to long. Usually, I'd let James rant and rave, hit me a couple of times and get it out of his system. But that night, he was out of control, in a way I've never seen before. And God willing, I'll never have to again," she vowed.

"As we sat at the kitchen table, I asked him casually, *'how did your day go?'*

'How the hell do you think my day went? It was shitty. Management finally got around to informing me that I'm next on the chopping board and that I can expect a pink slip in my pay envelope next Friday.' He replied, looking at me incredulously, his eyes bulging in their sockets.

"As soon as those words left his mouth and I saw the expression on his face, I knew I was in serious trouble. In my gut, I felt there was a good possibility that I might not make it out of there alive. I told him that I was sorry and who knows maybe they might reconsider the decision and keep him on. I tried to take the pressure off him by saying that I contributed to the household expenses too, so it wouldn't be like there wasn't any income coming into the house.

I guess it was foolish of me to continue talking to him, I should've dropped it. I think I wanted to put off the inevitable, but I knew what lie ahead for me. Then I made the mistake of telling him, *why worry about something you can't control.*

He looked at me like I was stupid, a look I'd come to recognize frequently. His eyes flattened into slits and his nostrils flared out like a horse running a race, he was simply enraged with anger. The next thing I knew, I was flying across the kitchen, and I do mean flying, my feet literally left the floor. He knocked me out of the chair so hard that I ended up hitting my head against the wall. James started to walk over to where I lay and I tried crawling away from him. Then he jerked me upright and started punching me. Every time he hit me, his mouth opened and closed with each blow, like a pez candy container. He cursed and swore at me, the words spewing from his mouth like water from a faucet. James looked like a monster to me, blows from his hands and kicks from his feet rained all over my face and body. I tried not to cry out because I didn't want Jamal to hear me.

Soon my body just felt liquid hot, like when you got your ears pierced in the olden days with a needle. Blood started trickling down my face, and I could feel my nose and lips swelling. When I inhaled or exhaled, it hurt so bad that I figured he had re-injured or broken one of my ribs."

Everyone in the room stared at her in abject horror. Her story sounded like something you'd see on a television movie or read in the newspapers. They couldn't imagine something that terrible happening to anyone in their family. Isaac's eyes were closed and he kept rubbing them nervously. Rose, Meme and Lili just sobbed in their seats.

"I could feel myself slipping into unconsciousness," Jeanine said, mechanically. "With my good ear, I could hear the pitter-patter of Jamal's feet as he ran down the hall toward the kitchen. I tried to scream at him to go back to his room, lock his door and not to come in the kitchen. But my lips were so swollen at that point that my mouth wouldn't allow the words to escape. I don't know if he would've listened to me anyway. He raced into the kitchen and came to an abrupt halt, slipping in my blood and staring at James like he was a creature out of a scary movie.

Jamal started crying and screaming, *Daddy, what are you doing? Leave my Mommy alone!* He tried to pull James off me and began hitting him with his little fists. James was still in a frenzied state and just kept kicking and smacking me. All I could hear was James talking about me, raging harshly about how I was a stupid moron who couldn't do anything right and didn't understand anything. He was breathing heavily, panting like a dog. Then Jamal bent down and bit him on his leg. I can see it all over again in my mind, like slow motion," Jeanine said, rocking back and forth in her seat, her eyes closed.

"James turned away from me and tried to push Jamal off him. I don't think he knows how strong he becomes when he gets like that and he turned around and pushed Jamal harder a second time. His little body sailed across the kitchen and his head smacked the radiator. I heard a plopping sound as his head connected with the radiator," She said, dully.

"Then it got quiet, James had stopped hitting me and I never heard Jamal say another word. James started crying hysterically and fell on the floor next to me. I tried to crawl over to Jamal but my body just wouldn't cooperate, I couldn't move. With what little voice I could muster, I kept telling James to check on Jamal, but he just sat catatonically on the floor next to me, staring at his bloody hands. I kept begging and pleading with him to make sure Jamal was all right.

'He's not moving!' I cried to James. *'Please go see about him.'* My body and my face ached so badly, I wanted to close my eyes, go to sleep and then wake up and find out all of it was only a dream.

Then a short time later, although it seemed like hours at the time, James walked over to Jamal and pulled him into his arms. He began crying, *'Oh God Jean, Jamal isn't breathing, I think I killed my own son!'* He sat stunned, as if he couldn't believe all the havoc he'd wreaked upon us.

I fought hard not to black out again and croaked out, *'James call 911, maybe he's all right, he can't be dead.'* I didn't want to believe that, I couldn't go there. *'Please just call 911.'* I whispered, over and over again. I could see where the blood had pooled before James picked Jamal up, so I knew his injury had to be pretty severe.

Then I heard banging at the back door. It was my neighbor, Freda. She kept yelling repeatedly, *'Jeanine, are you all right? Answer me, open the door!'* I took a deep breath and managed to call out as loud as I could, *'Freda, call the police and an ambulance, Jamal has been hurt!'* she yelled back, *'I'm going back home and make the calls, I'll come back to let them in!'* I had given her a spare key to our house a while back in the case of an emergency.

I must have fainted because when I woke up, the paramedics and the police were there. They were working on Jamal, he looked so little and still and was barely breathing. I called to him, *'Jamal, talk to me baby.'* And as you know, he didn't. The paramedics explained they were taking us to Jackson Park Hospital. The police began questioning me, asking me what had happened, saying over and over, *'Did your husband do this to you and your child?'* I could see revulsion on their faces because I'd actually allowed my son to be hurt by his father and gotten myself beaten in the process. I just turned my head from them, not wanting to see the looks on their faces. I was consumed with fear about Jamal."

Jeanine stopped talking for a minute, swallowing hard. Then she continued on, her voice hoarse. "When I woke up, I was in the hospital. You all were there and Jamal was in intensive care. Daddy, I could see the pain you were feeling on your face and Mama, your face looked so sad, as if you couldn't believe this was happening. Meme, I saw that same disgusted look on your face that the policemen had on theirs. James had been arrested and all of our business was splashed across the newspapers.

I know my eyes were blackened, my nose and a couple of ribs were broken and that I suffered a mild concussion. I think they said my spleen had ruptured and that I shouldn't be moved. Still, I begged a nursing assistant to get a wheelchair and take me to where Jamal was. When I got there, he was hooked up to a respirator. I knew he was hurt bad, worse than I could ever imagine. It scared me out of my wits, seeing that big tube inserted in his mouth and his head so swollen. Before the assistant took me down to his room, I remember asking you how he was doing and if he was okay and you told me that he was. I knew something was wrong though, I could see it in your faces.

Seeing him lying there so helpless broke my heart. I swear I could literally feel it separate. Somehow I knew my baby wasn't going to live to see his next birthday, his first date, go to his prom, get married or have children. I sat in that wheelchair next to his bed and cried for so long and talked to him. *'I'm so sorry, Jamal. Grownups mess up badly sometimes. I was so wrong for not getting us away from Daddy before it was too late,'* I begged Jamal to forgive me. I wanted to be the one in that bed instead of him but it was not to be. The doctors talked to me later and told me he had sustained severe brain injuries and they didn't think he'd ever come out of the coma.

I yelled at them hysterically that I was a Christian, and that I had hope and they couldn't predict everything. God was in charge and there's always hope. My mouth was saying those words but I knew my baby was not coming back, at least not the way he left. James called me tearfully from jail the next day, and like a fool, I took the call. He begged me to forgive him, but I couldn't, not yet anyway. Truthfully, I don't know if I'll ever be able to. It took almost losing a child for him to realize that he has a serious problem. He said remorsefully, *'Jean, you know I wouldn't do anything, not intentionally anyway, to hurt you or our son. I was out of my mind. The pressures of the job were heavy upon me and I could feel you slipping away from me. I couldn't handle it Jean, please don't leave me,'* he pleaded. I told James that his price was too high and I never wanted to talk to him again in this lifetime. Rev. Bowen counseled me that in time I'll be able to forgive him, but I can't, not right now," she said, licking her lips.

"I also swore to stay away from Jamal myself. I was so sickened with myself that I couldn't face him, I thought he'd be better off without me in his life. After all, I'm the cause of his being hurt and all I could feel was shame.

The Lord left Jamal in this world for over five months on life-support. After the first month passed, I knew the doctors were right. The injuries that affected his brain were critical, to the point where he was never coming back. I thought hard about taking him off life-support because I didn't want him to suffer, but I didn't have the guts to do that, just like I didn't have the guts to leave James. Since that night that landed him in the hospital, Jamal has never regained consciousness," she wailed, swaying back and forth faster now.

"My initial plan was to have Jamal removed from the respirator and then kill myself, but you never left me alone for too long," she complained. "Therefore, I had to rethink my plan. I had those pills stashed away and I had even bought a pack of razor blades."

Rose interrupted, her voice trembling as she stroked Jeanine's hair. "I know it's been hard for you Jeanine, but it wasn't your time to go or Jamal's. I know Rev. Bowen has explained all of that to you. We don't understand why things happen, but even that night, as terrible and horrible as it was, it still wasn't your time. God left you and Jamal here with us for a reason."

"See Mama, that's where I struggle with all of this. Why would God allow something like that to happen to an innocent child? Me, I can understand, I know I deserved everything that happened to me for staying with James, but my baby, I don't get it," she said plaintively, as if begging someone to help her to understand how her life had been turned upside.

You dummy, shrieked Meme, in her mind, *all of this happened because you didn't leave James, and these are the consequences of staying with that deranged man.* She tightened her lips as if trying to stifle the words before they could escape.

"You know what else?" said Jeanine, shaking her head from side to side. "It has taken many sessions with Dr. White for me to finally realize that I deserved better. I'm starting to feel good about myself as a person and understand that my lack of self-esteem caused me to stay in the situation for as long as I did. As part of my illness, I was totally convinced that Jamal was going to die and nothing could change my mind about that."

"Now, now, Jeanine," said Isaac soothingly, patting her shoulder. "I just hate that you went through all that suffering alone and didn't talk to your mother and me about it."

"Daddy, my shame was too great, I couldn't even look you all in the eye," whimpered Jeanine.

"Ours is not to reason why," said Rose, getting up from the couch, walking into the bathroom and returning with a box of tissue. She handed one to everyone in the room.

Meme stood up also, saying, "I need a break, I'm going to fix us some coffee."

Liana sat slumped in the chair, her head bowed down, sniffling, stunned as everyone else was by the story Jeanine had just told them.

Isaac feeling helpless, his heart heavily laden, quickly brushed away tears from his eyes and gathered Jeanine into his arms. He began murmuring soothingly to her, trying his best to comfort his youngest daughter.

four

Meme returned to the living room shortly, carrying a tray with cups of coffee for everyone. Her hands shook slightly as she set the tray on the table and her red eyes were a dead giveaway that she'd been crying.

Jeanine sat on the couch between her parents, propped up like a limp rag doll that had been washed and gone through the rinse cycle in the washing machine. Her head drooped forward, afraid to look up and see the looks of abhorrence that she was sure were on her family's faces. She still hated herself sometimes, so how could her family not feel the same. Rose turned to Jeanine and took her face gently in her hand, lifting her chin.

"Jeanine, look at me," she said quietly. "Your father, Meme, Liana and I, we love you. It's not our place to judge you, baby girl. We'll always love you unconditionally. I don't think any of us could take it if something happened to you too. We're always going to be here for you."

Meme just shook her head, twisting her mouth into an angry slash. "You should've left him a long time ago Jeanine," she said, pityingly. "You can't reason with drunks, gamblers or drug addicts. You stayed in it too long."

"We don't need to be pointing fingers here," said Isaac, sharply.

"I'm sorry," said Meme, quietly. "I don't mean to come off critical, but I feel we should be honest with her." She looked dispassionately at her parents. "I begged her over and over to leave him, I told her that I'd help her. Every time I told her that she should leave him, she'd tell me she loved him and had faith things would get better. And she's paid a high price for that love, just like she said."

"You're right," Jeanine sighed, "the price was too high and now I've got to live with the results of being passive the rest of my life. Dr. White tells me all the time that I'll feel better about myself one day, I just have to give it time. For the longest, I didn't believe her. It would've been much easier to just give up and die, but I can now move forward because she didn't give up on me. Also, I need to be here for Jamal. Most days, I wonder where I'm going to get the strength to get through all this."

Rose interjected as she held Jeanine's hand. "You've got to dig deep baby. That same faith you had regarding James and his problem, use that to get better and take care of your baby."

"I just didn't have any idea James was so violent," mused Isaac. "If I'd known, I would've gotten both of you out that house myself."

"It doesn't do any good to harp on shoulda, coulda, woulda," said Rose. "What's done is done, we can't turn back the hands of time. We now need to stay focused on helping Jeanine and Jamal."

"It's just that the whole thing has been so ugly," murmured Meme. "All the publicity and James' trial, I swear I didn't know how we were going to cope with all of that."

"We can always cope with any adversity thrown our way. The Lord is with us all the time," said Rose, her faith unshaken. "God will always see us through."

"Your mother is right," said Isaac, nodding his head, "our lives are in our Father's hands."

"Do you think it was His will for Jamal to end up like he has?" Meme lashed out angrily.

Liana gasped with dismay at Meme's words, her hands fluttering and covering her mouth.

"I'm so sorry, Jeanine, I was out of line," Meme said.

Jeanine looked ashen, as if the life force had been sucked from her. She stared sadly at her sister.

"Please forgive me, it's just been such a trying time for all of us," Meme begged, sorrowfully.

"Liana," said Rose, "why don't you take Jeanine up to her room and keep her company for a little while? Isaac and I would like to talk to Meme alone."

"Sure Aunt Rose," said Liana, grateful someone had given her a way to escape the heavy scene. She could only guess what else was lurking over the horizon. "Come on cuz," she urged Jeanine, trying unsuccessfully to smile. Then she led Jeanine, who was now weeping, up the stairs. Rose prayed that Liana would close the door to the bedroom and she did.

"Meme," Rose said, turning to her oldest child, "I know this has been hardest on you and how much it's upset your life. You've carried so much of the burden by yourself and your Daddy and I love you for it, but we'll not have you bullying or expressing negative thoughts to your sister right now. Slowly but surely, she's coming back to the Jeanine we used to know. I don't want anyone blaming or judging anyone in this family for any shortcomings. Drs. White and Johnson told us to be firm but gentle with her, she's still in a fragile state of mind."

"I know my little girl," Isaac said, "and a wrong word, especially from any one of us, could push her back over the edge." His voice took on a saddened tone. "You don't know how bad I felt when I pushed that door open and saw her lying there like she was dead. When we finally came home from the hospital, I asked Rose over and over where we failed, how did this happen? She was never outgoing but we thought she was okay. She was raised in the church with both parents in the household. All I could think of was how people say, whenever something bad happens to a child that it always comes back to the parents."

"Mama, Daddy," cried Meme, moving to the couch to sit between them, "don't feel that way, you two are the best parents in the world."

"How do you know? Maybe we didn't do something correctly raising Jeanine," Rose said, quietly. "Maybe we missed something when she was a child, or we should've spanked her more or not even spanked her at all, it could be a number of things."

"I see what you're saying," said Meme, sitting back, her anger deflating like a beach ball whose air plug had been pulled out.

"Come on over here Meme, sit close to your daddy," Isaac gestured. She slid towards him and he put his arms lovingly about her shoulders. "We just don't know what went wrong with James or Jeanine and we can't dwell on that too much right now. Our job is to get your sister back to a functioning adult so she can take care of her son. He can't remain in La Rabida forever and there are still decisions to be made in regards to his care. She's not capable of that responsibility right now. Maybe one day when your sister's life resembles something more normal, we can go into that, but right now we feel she shouldn't be upset because she's getting better and we don't want her to relapse."

"According to Dr. White," Rose added, "her progress has been good under the circumstances."

"I still can't help my feelings," said Meme. "I feel such anger towards her sometimes."

"Hush now," murmured Rose. "She's mentally ill, God knows that's the truth."

"I'm disappointed in you," Isaac said, sternly. "Your sister can't help it, she has some mighty powerful troubles on her right now."

"I'm sorry, I can't help how I feel…" Her words trickled off.

"In that case, I think you need to continue your visits with Rev. Bowen and learn to have some tolerance!" Isaac roared, pounding his fist on the cocktail table.

"I will," Meme said, crying. "I wish to God I didn't feel this way about Jeanine, but God help me, I do."

Rose picked up a tissue from the table and began dabbing at her eyes. She handed another one to Meme. "You know, we've been talking to Dr. White on a daily basis almost since Jeanine took the overdose of pills."

"She tried to kill herself Mama, why can't you and Daddy see that? Isn't that what she just told us?"

"Medora Rose Clark," said Isaac, loudly, "I'm asking you to respect our feelings while you're in our house. Would you just be quiet, listen to your mother and let her talk? Can you do that?"

"Okay, I'm sorry," Meme said.

"Like I was saying," Rose went on, "Dr. White told us your sister suffers from low self-esteem and clinical depression. She's been carrying around those feelings deep inside for a long time. Part of the reason is because she felt in competition with you, or at least that's what the doctor told us."

"Me? How could she think something like that?"

"It's the illness," said Isaac. "Her reasoning was off, but not to the point where she couldn't function. Most of the time she suppressed those feelings, however, they still surfaced from time to time. When she met James, she was past twenty-five years old, living here at home with us and had pretty much given up on marrying ever. She viewed herself as a spinster."

"So, she was ripe for the picking for James. Is that what you're saying?"

"Yes, that's what Dr. White said in so many words," said Rose. "James loves Jeanine in his own twisted way. He saw in her a submissive woman who would do his biding without question. The doctor also feels that had she not had Jamal, she and James would've continued the way he wanted. Having a child caused her to re-think her position and that more than likely started the problems in their relationship. The attention that James felt belonged to him was now bestowed on Jamal. You know when Dr. White explained all that stuff to us at first, none of it made any sense, but your daddy and I put our heads together and agreed with her. Even though the two of you have always been close, she still felt a rivalry for you in her head."

"Man," Meme said, smacking her forehead, "I never suspected anything like that."

"Umm, we didn't either," Isaac mumbled, "until we started family counseling. I admit I wasn't pleased with the idea. I always felt the church and minister had a solution to any of life's problems, but when I held Jeanine in my arms after she took those pills, it hit me hard that my baby girl is sick. She's thirty-two years old and I never knew." Isaac said, struggling to hold back a sob.

"But why me?" asked Meme, holding her hand to her chest with a puzzled look on her face. "We're four years apart, didn't attend high school together and never dated the same guys, I don't get it."

"For those same reasons we mentioned before," Rose supplied. "It had to do with her inability to reason and her low self-esteem. She felt you were the prettiest and our favorite child. Your job at the law firm overshadowed her working as a telephone operator in a hospital. You completed college and then went back to school for paralegal training. She never attended college or a trade school, her aspirations were never as high as yours."

"Man," Meme said, shaking her head, "I swear I never had a clue."

Rose went on to say, "Dr. White says her self-esteem was almost non-existent. You don't know how much hearing that hurt us. We thought we treated both of you the same, but Jeanine, because of her illness, thought she saw something else. We also talked to Liana after we'd talk to Dr. White and she confirmed some of the things Jeanine had told the doctor."

"How could Liana know something like that and not say anything to us?" Meme asked, with a perplexed look on her face.

"I can't answer that," murmured Rose. "Remember, most of this stuff happened years ago. I think perhaps she thought Jeanine had gotten beyond all that."

 All three heads swiveled towards the staircase at the sound of approaching footsteps. Liana walked in and sat back down tensely into the chair she'd occupied before going upstairs with Jeanine.

"I'm sorry," she said, apologetically, "I couldn't help but overhear you talking and I want to say that I feel just as bad as everyone else that I missed the signs too. What you said is true Meme, Jeanine did confide in me about many things, one being her feelings about you, James was another matter altogether. She was very secretive about her life with him, especially the last few years. I'd try to get her to meet me after work for drinks sometimes or go shopping and she'd refuse. Her excuses would be that she had to go home to James or they'd made other plans. We became closer after she had Jamal because we were pregnant at the same time, so becoming mothers drew us together. Then when Duane and I moved to the suburbs, we sort of lost that sister/cousin relationship we shared. I'd drop by her house sometimes to visit and see bruises or marks on her arms and legs. She'd tell me like she told everyone else that she injured herself. I wouldn't say I saw signs every time I was there, not with enough frequency for me to become overly alarmed. I guess when things got unbearable for her, she just didn't feel comfortable talking to me about it. I assumed if anything was terribly wrong, I would hear about it from one of you."

They sat silently for a while lost in thought, taking in Liana's revelations. The sun was just beginning to set outside the brown colored draped picture window, allowing a view of the passing traffic. Various plants were lovingly placed around the window, on the hardwood floor and positioned on planters. There were pictures of both daughters, from kindergarten through high school and Meme's graduation from college. Baby and school pictures of the grandchildren were lovingly displayed on the fireplace mantle.

"I guess you're right," Meme sighed, "I'm going to have to give Jeanine the space and time she needs to get through this and not become impatient when she isn't progressing as I think she should."

Rose and Isaac nodded their heads in satisfaction, tiny smiles on their faces.

"Please do," Liana interjected, seriously. "She really can't help her feelings. You've been popular and outgoing all of your life, and you have lots of friends and attended tons of parties from grade school on. If you'd stop to think about it, Jeanine never had many friends and only one or two boyfriends throughout high school. She's basically a shy, quiet person and a homebody. I had to badger and beg her to go on trips before we both got married. I know for sure she had given up on love or marriage at the age of twenty-one, and the sad thing about that was she never experienced life, at least not the way you and I had."

"When I look at it that way, I know you're right," Meme whispered, softly. "I guess sometimes we just never know what a person is feeling, even if it's your own sister."

"Right," Liana nodded. "I also feel that her lack of life experiences had a lot to do with her putting up with James' mess. With her self-esteem already low, she was just grateful to have a husband and then a son."

Rose and Isaac just sat there, shaking their heads.

"We've got to come up with a way, something that will help her boost her self-worth without James," said Rose. "She's been married to him for ten years and that's a long time to be in that kind of situation. It's almost like she has to unlearn all that unhealthy behavior and replace it with newly learned ones."

"Another thing Jeanine would harp on almost obsessively," Liana added, hesitantly, "was the fact that she thought she was adopted and you never told her the truth."

Rose sagged forward and Isaac caught her in his arms.

"Well that's ridiculous, there's no way she was adopted, right Mama and Daddy?" Meme asked, not missing the play of emotions on their faces.

Neither said anything for a minute. Liana heard talk on the subject years ago from her mother Violet, Rose's older sister. Sensing this to be another touchy subject, Liana stood up and looked at her watch.

"It's time for me to go home. Tell Jeanine I'll give her a call tomorrow." She kissed her aunt and uncle goodbye, squeezed Meme's hand and closed the front door softly behind her.

"That was certainly strange," Meme said thoughtfully, staring intently at her parents. "Where in the world would Jeanine get a strange idea like that? Anyone can tell we're sisters, we look alike, just like Mama."

"You know..." Rose's voice faltered. "Sometimes things come out that wouldn't under normal circumstances. We had a discussion with Dr. White about Jeanine's suspicions. That was the next thing we'd planned to tell you.

"Tell me what?" she asked, desperately.

"Well," Isaac began, sighing heavily, "Jeanine isn't adopted in the legal sense, but she isn't my biological child."

"What do you mean she's not your child?" Meme shrieked. "How could she not be yours and we so much look alike? Does that mean you're not my father either?"

"The truth of the matter," Isaac said, matter-of-factly, "is that she's your mother's child but not mine."

"Say what, I know Mama wasn't creeping on you?" Meme asked, incredulously.

"No, it wasn't anything like that," Rose answered, eyes dropping, clearly abashed. "Your daddy and I were having some marital problems at the time and we separated for about a year. I took you, went back home and stayed with my parents. One night, I went out with an old boyfriend. The only thing I can say in my defense is that I wasn't thinking clearly. On the way home, we had a few drinks, and being as though I'm not really much of a drinker, I got drunk and passed out. A few months later, I found myself with child. I went through a very bad time, much like your sister." She went on, eyes tearing up. "I was miserable, my Mama got in touch with your daddy, he came down to see me and we talked. I even thought about getting rid of the baby but Isaac talked me out of that idea, saying nothing living that came out of my body was going to be killed. He said he'd give Jeanine his name and raise her as his own, and that's what he's done."

"I don't believe it," Meme said, shaking her head from side to side. "Well, that at least explains her feelings for me. She must've felt something and it affected her."

"That's pretty much it, other than the fact that because we never told her the truth and not knowing ate at her. I'm so sorry that I did that to her," Rose said.

"One thing I know for sure is you and Daddy didn't make any differences in raising us, as far as how you treated us. So, what made Jeanine suspect that?" Meme asked.

"She told Dr. White and us that she felt there was something different about her. She couldn't put her finger on it, but she felt a difference. She also overheard someone talking at a family reunion," Isaac answered.

"Damn," said Meme, cursing softly. "Oops I'm sorry, that slipped out. I just can't believe all this. It's too mind boggling for me to comprehend right now. One thing is for sure," she added gently, grabbing Rose's hand, "none of it was your fault, Mama."

"I've only been telling her that for the past thirty something years," said Isaac. "I also told her that she should tell you girls the truth. With family members aware of that information, it was only a matter of time before someone spilled the beans."

"I was guilty of bad judgment and it cost me dearly, just like Jeanine," said Rose, blowing her nose.

"At least you can see now why we won't have you upset or judge her harshly. Most folks, if they're honest, have something in their past that they're ashamed of or wished had never happened."

"I swear you two have blown me away," said Meme, shaking her head from side to side again. "Do you think Liana knows?" she asked.

"There's no doubt in my mind that she does," nodded Rose. "That's more than likely her reason for bringing the subject up before she left."

"Please don't tell me everyone knows except me and Jeanine," Meme groaned.

"I wouldn't say the whole family knows," commented Rose. "Vi knows, of course, and no doubt some other family members know."

"God, this is just so unbelievable," Meme moaned. "I always thought our family was open and honest about things and there were no skeletons in our closet."

"Everybody's got them," Isaac said, nodding his head. "I think most people think they can stay buried but they always seem to come back to haunt you one way or another. Your mother thought we were doing the right thing by not telling her."

"Just like Jeanine thought she was doing the right thing by staying with James," said Rose, sagely. "One thing we've learned from this family counseling stuff is that we've got to be honest with those we love or everybody will get hurt in the long run. I think, and this is just me talking, that she stayed with James to have the family she felt was missing with us."

"My name's on her birth certificate, and in my heart and mind, she'll always be my baby girl, because like you, she's a part of my Rose," Isaac said, a loving expression shining on his face as he looked down at his tiny wife.

"So, if all of this hadn't happened, you two never would've said anything?" asked Meme.

"I can't rightly say," Isaac said. "That decision was always left up to your mother."

"I don't know either," Rose admitted. "A part of me knew that it was the right thing to tell you both, and then another part of me wanted to keep that secret forever. I now realize how selfish I was to do so. Your sister has a long way to go as far as therapy is concerned according to Dr. White. At some point, she's got to face James too. The doctor was very insistent about that. It's like she has to close doors to get to the open ones that will determine her new path in life. I ask Jeanine maybe once a week if she's ready to go to Joliet to see him, so far her answer has been no. Dr. White says she will in her own time."

"I suspect she will one day," Meme nodded. "After all, she's started seeing Jamal now and talking to James' parents."

"I know it's hard for you to comprehend, Meme," said Rose, "but she wasn't thinking clearly with all that was going on. Her thoughts and actions wasn't even close to what we'd do in a similar situation. Jeanine can now deal with Jamal's getting hurt and get beyond it. It was her wake-up call and that's truly a blessing. When people are sick like she is, they can't make changes easily unless something catastrophic happens. Jeanine said when Liana stopped calling and coming by as much as she used to, it made her feel abandoned. Liana said she doesn't want Jeanine to feel that way again on account of anything she's done, so she promised that she'll call and visit her more often."

"What a night, I feel so drained," Meme said, exhausted.

"If you think you feel drained, imagine what your sister feels like and what it has been like for her these past six months," said Rose.

"I know you're right, and like Liana, it's time for me to head home and check on my girls. I promise to do better with Jeanine," she said, kissing them and standing up. "I'm going upstairs to tell Jeanine good night."

"Okay," they both said, in unison.

Meme walked up the stairs, opened the closed bedroom door and paused for a moment. She watched as Jeanine sat at her old school desk writing furiously in an open book.

"Hey little sister, what you doing?" asked Meme, standing next to the desk, hands on her hips.

"Dr. White suggested I keep a journal of my thoughts and activities on a daily basis, so I'm making my entries for today."

"I'm getting ready to go home and wanted to tell you goodnight."

"Okay," said Jeanine, standing up and closing the book. "Will I see you tomorrow?"

"You'd better believe it. Do you want me to drive you to see Jamal?"

"Believe it or not, no I don't. Loretta is coming over here tomorrow and she's going to take me."

"Okay, that's great. I'm sorry about what I said Jeanine, I guess I can be so dense sometimes."

"You were just being your usual honest self, I'll see you tomorrow," Jeanine said. The two sisters hugged each other tightly.

When Meme departed, Jeanine she sat back down at the desk and resumed writing.

f i v e

Epilogue or Three Months Later...

One mild spring Sunday afternoon, after attending church service, the family traveled along Illinois' Route 53. Isaac drove his old, but perfectly tuned, Lincoln Continental to Joliet's Statesville Prison. Jeanine had finally consented to seeing James after filing divorce papers a month before. James agreed to sign the papers but insisted on talking to Jeanine first. Meme felt he was still in control freak mode, but Dr. White advised Jeanine to do so for her own closure and peace of mind.

"Are you sure you're okay with this?" Meme asked her sister.

"I'm fine Meme, stop fussing," she answered, with a nervous look on her face. "This is something I should've done a long time ago."

"Okay then," said Isaac, "let's get this show on the road."

Forty-five minutes later, they were processed and sitting inside the prison's visitor area. Isaac, Rose and Meme whispered to each other nervously, huddled on folding chairs along the back wall of the room. Jeanine sat nervously, hands fidgeting, at a table within their eyesight, waiting for James to make his appearance. Not long afterwards, James strode into the room looking around for his soon to be ex-wife. He had lost weight and the menacing look that had become his normal expression for so long was gone, now replaced with a grim look. He sat down across from Jeanine.

"How have you been doing, Jean?" he asked hesitantly, looking like a stranger.

Jeanine flinched a little and began shaking. Her eyes bucked at him like he was crazy for even asking the question.

"I'm doing about as well as can be expected under the circumstances."

"Hmm, let's just cut to the chase and make this easier for both of us," he said, quickly. "First, I want to apologize for my actions. How's Jamal doing? Believe me, I never imagined our lives would turn out the way they have."

"He's out of the coma and has started physical therapy," she answered, flatly.

"What do the doctors say about his recovery?"

"He'll never lead a normal life, but they feel in time he'll be able to take care of himself to a small extent."

"That's good," he sighed. "I guess I fucked up pretty bad, huh?"

"Yes James, I would say you did."

"Alcohol cost me my wife, my son and most of all my life. I'll be here for at least another four to ten years, so my lawyer says."

"James, what is it you want from me?" Jeanine asked edgily, taping her fingers on the table, not comfortable being there. "You could've signed the divorce papers without seeing or talking to me. I don't feel this face-to-face meeting was really necessary."

"I guess I just wanted to see you and apologize face-to-face for what happened," James answered. "That day still haunts me and will for the rest of my life."

"James, don't you dare call me baby," Jeanine said huffily, as her breathing became labored and heavy.

"Sorry, that slipped out. Really, I have no ulterior motives," he said, holding his hands up. "I just pray that one day you and Jamal will be able to forgive me."

"I hear you," Jeanine said, waving her hand impatiently. "Now, if that's all you have to say, please sign the divorce papers, although I can get it without your signature."

"Thanks for seeing me Jean, I know this is hard for you. I was messed up in the head and that's the God honest truth. Drinking brought out the worst in me and I couldn't stop no matter how hard I tried. When it seemed I had nothing else in this world, wife, parents and job, Mr. Jack Daniels was always there for me. When I was feeling low, he bolstered me up so I could make it through another day and not have to face how truly messed up I was. He helped me stay in denial, or that's what I thought."

Jeanine sat with a skeptical expression on her face, staring at him trying to recall why Dr. White felt it was important she make this visit.

"I knew I was headed for a fall before the layoffs started at work. I just didn't know what to do about it, except turn to my buddy Jack. The more I drank, I know the meaner I became. However, there's no excuse for the way I treated you and Jamal. I hope in time you'll forgive me. Do you think you can?" His eyes pleaded with her for forgiveness.

"Right now I can't do that. Every time I look at Jamal struggling with therapy, it's a reminder of what you did to both of us. Did Loretta tell you I tried to kill myself?" she murmured.

He looked at her appalled and shook his head no.

"Yes I did, I planned it carefully and methodically. I was finally going to consent to taking Jamal off the respirator and then kill myself after he died. The Lord intervened, Mama woke up and Daddy saved my life, otherwise we wouldn't be having this conversation today. It took me a long time to pull myself together. I'm glad my parents saved my life so I can be here for my son. Lord knows he needs one of his parents fully functional. I don't know how in the world I'm going to explain to him what happened and how his injuries are a result of his daddy's actions."

"Maybe I should be the one to tell him."

"If you think I'm ever going to allow him to come to this place or have anything to do with you, then you're sadly mistaken," Jeanine said, harshly.

"I'd like to write to him. At some point, he's got to know the truth. I'm not going to be in here forever. Financially, I won't be much help for a while, that's assuming I can even find a job with my criminal record. Still, would you please revise the divorce papers to say that when I start working again, I be allowed to contribute to Jamal's upbringing."

"If I had my way," she hissed, "I wouldn't take one red cent from you, but considering that his medical bills are astronomical, I'll take whatever you give me. Mama and Daddy took out a loan on their house just to help me. You should know that Meme put a note in the divorce papers that states our house is being sold because we need the money. When Jamal gets to the point where he can leave La Rabida, we'll be staying with my folks. Meme is also looking into some grants I may qualify to get, because not only will Jamal need physical therapy, but he's going to need counseling too. You know what James? None of this would've happened had you not been out of control!"

"Jean, I don't know what to say except I wish to God I could take that night back."

"You literally terrorized me and there's no doubt in my mind that Jamal would've been next. I hate you, and it's going to take some time, if ever, for me to get over what you did to me. You beat and stripped me of my self-esteem over and over again for years. I can't stop you from seeing your son when the doctors give the okay. However, I prefer not to see or talk to you ever again. Realistically, I know I have to deal with you at some point, but the contact will be minimal. I hope, James, you're getting the help you need while you're here, because if you aren't, you'll never see Jamal again, I promise you that. If I have to start over and leave the state, I'll do that, because my child will not be hurt like he was ever again in this life."

"Jean, I'm getting help. I attend counseling sessions, and my Moms come out here to help me. Bless her soul. She hasn't given up on me. I promised her I'd agree to anything you asked for. I have always loved you, but because of the drinking, I became weak and took all my frustrations out on you in the worst way. I know it's over between us, and it should be. Too much has happened for us to overcome all of that. All I can say is that I'm getting the help I need and I'm a better man for it. I hope in time you'll forgive me and let me see my son so that I can explain to him what happened."

"I can't make any promises, James. All I can say is that I'll cross that bridge when I get to it." She tried to stand, but her legs were too shaky. "I've got to go now, I feel claustrophobic in here. Please sign the papers, James and return them to my lawyer. That's all I ask of you, to set me free."

He stood up and looked down at her, ashamed and trying to hold back tears. He then turned and strolled out the room the same way he had come in.

When Jeanine tried to stand, her legs felt as weak as a newborn colt. She slid back down into the seat, expelling a huge sigh of relief because the worse was over. The family, seeing her struggle, rushed to her side.

"Baby, are you okay?" Rose asked, worried.

Jeanine stood up, smiling ruefully at her family and said, "I feel great, I have my life back and I'm ready to leave this place. I got what I came here for ... closure. Come on family, let's stop by the hospital and see Jamal and then go home!"

LETTING
GO

One

Desiree Cooper whirled and shimmied around her tastefully decorated, tan and burnt orange paisley wallpapered bedroom, the boudoir she and her fiancé, Andre Johnson, shared. She executed a fancy spin, one that would put any figure skater to shame. The turquoise caftan she wore billowed gently around her slender ankles. She snapped her fingers to a beat only she could hear.

"I'm getting married, I'm going to be Mrs. Andre Jackson, hey, hey, hey." She hummed and chanted, while peeping at the two-carat, marquise-cut ring that glittered on the second finger of her left hand. Desiree's melodious voice articulated pure joy with the awareness that her wedding day was right around the corner. At that moment in time, absolutely nothing could spoil the happiness she was feeling. The biggest moment of her life was just days away. Desiree would be the star in the upcoming *'Cooper and Jackson'* nuptial video. So much time, energy, love, and most of all money, had been expended in guaranteeing a picture perfect wedding.

Her mother and aunts were all recipients of lavish weddings and Desiree planned to continue that tradition. Truth be known, she hoped hers would top them all. The culmination of nearly a ten-year tumultuous, but passionate, relationship would become legal and binding Saturday evening on June 28 at six o'clock during a beautiful candlelight ceremony.

The cream-colored invitations, embossed with red script, had long since been mailed to over two hundred relatives and friends. The responses were duly addressed to her coordinator Jade, who in turn, passed the final tally to the South Shore Country Club. The newly renovated building is located on the shores of beautiful Lake Michigan. Nothing less than the Grand Ballroom was acceptable for their reception.

Desiree got excited all over again thinking about the ten-day Hawaiian honeymoon cruise they'd planned. She'd just placed her requisite sexy, sequined slit in the back, after-five black dress that was hanging on the bedroom door in the garment bag. Packing for herself and Andre the past couple of weeks became her self-assigned chore. She snapped her fingers, remembering his tuxedo needed cleaning since he'd worn it to a Lion's club function earlier that year.

For their honeymoon, they were sailing aboard a Carnival cruise ship from Los Angeles. Desiree was looking forward to the pampering and indulgences one expected on a cruise. She'd been told the food was excellent, equaling any five-star restaurant. There would be non-stop dining upon the ship and Desiree didn't play when it came to food, she could throw down with the best of them. This would be her first cruise, not unless dining or sailing aboard the restaurant/ships or tourist boats along Lake Michigan and Chicago's Navy Pier counted. Working for an airline, Desiree had visited nearly every continent. The walls and tables of her home displayed the many souvenirs, art and paintings she acquired from flying the friendly skies.

Desiree is a classy, beautiful cinnamon colored woman, who stands six feet tall. Her heart-shaped face is flawless, her eyes dark brown and almond shaped. A mane of thick black hair that rests midway down her back is her crowning glory. *This is the real deal,* she'd say to her friends, fluffing it from time to time, *not that fake synthetic stuff a lot of women sport today.* Her long, slim, shapely legs seem to go on forever. Her body overall is thin, but in her opinion, a tiny waist and curvaceous butt are her best assets. Those physical attributes are what Andre loves most about her.

She's twenty-eight years old and he's thirty-seven. The tick tock of her biological clock had been pealing loudly for some time, prompting her to begin her relentless campaign for a ring from Andre, especially around her last birthday. She felt they needed to take advantage of her fertile years and start producing rug rats soon.

Desiree impatiently pushed Andre's clothing back and forth along the rack, finally spotting the black tuxedo crushed near the rear of the closet. Pulling it off the hanger, she quickly riffled through the pockets. *Better make sure he didn't leave any money or something in here,* she thought.

When she put her hand in the first pocket, it closed in on a crushed slip of paper. She rummaged through the other pocket and felt a package. With a flip of her wrist, she pulled it out and stared at it in disbelief. Desiree's face morphed into dismay, not quite believing there was an open package of condoms in her hand. She glanced at her other hand that was tightly clenching the slip of paper. Her eyes scanned quickly at the name and number of another woman. In a state of shock, she did a double take looking from one hand to the other. Her brain processed the information and she dropped both items on the bed like hot potatoes.

Desiree sucked her breath in, and her stomach contracted uncontrollably as if she'd been punched in the stomach. Bile rose in her throat and her breathing became shallow. Her legs felt as weak as overcooked noodles. Like a newborn baby out of the womb, she tumbled onto the bed.

Earlier in the relationship, and on more than one occasion, she'd caught Andre with other women. Telephone numbers were often found stuffed carelessly in his pockets and wallet. Desiree thought they had gotten past all of that. *What lousy timing*, floated through her mind, her face contorting tearfully.

"Hell naw! Oh no, he didn't go there!" she roared. "What should I do, just tear it up and pretend like I never saw it?"

Her throat choked up, eyes glistened with tears. She sat up mechanically like a robot. Her sadness quickly changed to anger, and a white fire raged through her body.

"NO!" she shrieked, aloud. "Lord, no he didn't go there."

Then the fire turned to fury. Obscenities fell from her mouth, calling Andre everything but a child of God. She stood up, stomped to the dresser drawer and irately began tossing objects about the room. A porcelain vase she'd brought while visiting Japan lay shattered in tiny pieces, books stacked neatly on a bookshelf flew across the room like moths. She rushed to the closet and began tearing and tossing Andre's clothing. How she wished he were there right at that moment so she could beat his face to a pulp. She yearned for him to feel the hurt and pain she felt right now. Finally her body crumbled on the floor in exhaustion, her anger spent for the moment. Random thoughts continued to tiptoe across her mind.

"What the hell is up with this shit?" she muttered. "I don't believe this is happening to me?" Sadly shaking her head from side to side, she thought, *Now what the hell am I going to do?*

Her body sagged forward and she began sobbing. The once neat room looked as though it had been ransacked.

Exhausted and emotionally spent, Desiree lifted herself from the floor. Dodging debris, she searched for the cordless phone, found it and dialed her best friend, Taneisha's, telephone number. She clicked it off before entering the final digit.

"No, I can't talk to Tanny, not yet. I need time to think things through." She said, sinking onto the bed. Tears seeped from her eyes periodically.

Finally, she got up and walked into the bathroom. Dampening a towel, she wiped her face while looking at herself in the mirror and thought, *"Damn, I look like death warmed over."* The pretty, vivacious woman singing and dancing a short time ago had vanished. Her blazing eyes were the only clue to the turmoil raging within her heart. She went back into the bedroom and dressed in jeans, a tee shirt and gym shoes.

As she walked heavily from the room, she made a detour to the kitchen, grabbed her purse and car keys, and stomped out of the house, slamming the door shut behind her. Quickly entering her gray Ford Expedition, she started it up, slammed it into gear and sped off. Her cell phone chimed, shattering the quietness. She glanced at the caller id unit, noting it was Andre. Taking a deep breath, she clicked the phone on.

"Hey baby, what's up?" he asked, cheerfully.

"Nothing much," she replied calmly, masking her warring emotions. What was really up was the need to curse his ass out.

"Where are you headed? Do you want company?"

It took everything she had in her to hold her tongue. "I'm just going out to pick up a few things, I'll catch up with you later."

"Are you straight? Do you need any money?"

"No, it's all good. Dre, let me call you back, I have another call coming in."

"Okay, I'll holler at you later."

She clicked the phone off, dropping it disgustedly into the seat. "That son-of-a-....!" she mumbled. Anger caused her to tremble so bad she was barely able to hold the steering wheel.

She drove a couple of more blocks, tires screeching, then quickly made a u-turn, deciding to go to Taneisha's house. She drove by rote, her emotions tightly wound. Road rage was simmering in her blood. The blaring horns of other drivers were a testament to her erratic driving. A couple of motorist gave her the middle finger as they sped past.

Having broken all kinds of speeding laws, Desiree arrived safely at Taneisha's in one piece. She jumped out the truck, set the alarm and strode purposely to the front door. She pressed the doorbell. Tanny peeped through the curtains, a smile on her chubby face. They'd been best friends since the third grade and roommates in college. In spite of arguments over the years, the friendship remained solid. Tanny pulled the door open, her smile changing to a frown when she saw the look on Desiree's face.

"Come in," she said. "Is there something wrong with your wedding gown?" She probed, as they walked silently into the kitchen and sat at the table. "What's up, girl?"

Tanny asked uneasily, after not receiving a response from Desiree.

She didn't like what she saw one bit. Her girl didn't look good, her clothes were wrinkled, shoes untied and hair pulled back into an untidy ponytail. No, this was definitely not the immaculate, well-groomed Desiree Cooper she knew and loved.

"I decided to take Dre's tux to the cleaners," Desiree explained, perfunctorily." I, being the anal person I am, went through his pockets. What do you think I found?"

"You'll have to tell me," she replied, staring at her alarmed. "I'm not up for twenty questions. I can tell from your expression that whatever it was, it wasn't good."

"Damn straight, it was nothing good. How about an opened package of condoms and a piece of paper with some woman's telephone number on it, that's what I found!" she wailed, punctuating each word by pounding on the table with a tightly clenched fist.

Tanny's eyes bucked open in shock. "No girl, git out of here!" she said, not believing what she'd just heard. "Tell me you're lying and this is a crazy prank you're pulling before the wedding. Right?"

Desiree shook her head no and began crying.

"I'm so sorry, Dessy. What are you going to do?" Tanny asked, getting up and walking around the table to gather Desiree in her arms.

"I really don't know," she replied, shakily.

"Are you alright?" Tanny asked. She passed Dessy a tissue to wipe her eyes.

"I feel numb and so fucking mad, I can't believe what happened. I really thought we'd gotten beyond this type of thing," she sniffed, blowing her nose.

"Hmm, you really don't have any way of knowing how long that stuff had been there, right?" Tanny commented, tactfully.

"No, not for sure," Desiree conceded. "The telephone number I can deal with, it's the condoms that bother me."

"When was the last time he wore the tux?"

"Let me think, around six months ago. When we went to Atlanta, he and David attended that Lion function."

"Damn girl, not when we were out of town!"

"Tell me about it," Desiree shrugged.

"So, what are you going to do?"

"I haven't figured it out yet," Desiree answered, in a low voice, almost a whisper.

"Don't you think you should talk to him?" Tanny asked.

"No, not right now. You know me, I'd just snap."

"Dessy, promise me that you're going to talk to him?" Tanny requested.

She could feel the beginning of a migraine headache coming on and began massaging her temples.

"I can't promise that, I just needed to talk to *someone*, so I came here."

The two sat in silence for a few minutes. Then Desiree stood up and said, "I'm out of here."

"Where are you going? Why don't you just stay here for a while until you calm down?" Tanny asked, troubled.

"Just out, nowhere in particular," Desiree murmured. "I need more time to think about this. And no, I don't want or need you to come with me, I just need to be alone right now."

"What are you going to say to Dre? He'll know something is wrong," Tanny asked.

"I don't know, I'll cross that bridge when I get to it."

"The timing couldn't be worse. This is just fucked up, Dessy," Tanny grumbled. "The wedding is only three days away. You're going to have to do some quick thinking."

"I know that," she nodded, solemnly. "I'm outta here, girl. I'll holler at you later."

"Okay, you know I got your back and I'm here if you need me," Tanny said, wiping a lone tear from her eye.

"That's what I'm talking about," Desiree said, smiling weakly.

Tanny stood up and hugged her tightly before she left.

two

At the Cooper/Jackson residence, Andre walked into the tan brick townhouse after deciding to leave work early. He intended to surprise Desiree, maybe take her out to lunch or dinner. They'd been so busy with the wedding plans lately that he felt now was a good time for a little rest and relaxation before things got even crazier.

"Bills and more bills," he muttered, as he quickly riffled through the mail stacked neatly on the glass table in the foyer.

He walked into the kitchen, poured a glass of orange juice and walked down the hall to the bedroom. His head seemed to pivot as he did a double take, surveying the destruction raged upon the room. Books, his cologne and clothing were strewn about the room.

"What the hell!" he said aloud, as the orange juice crashed to the floor.

His eyes alit on the tuxedo, rippled and lay heaped on the floor. As he walked over to it, remembrance dawned upon him and he frantically checked the pockets. His eyes traveled to the nightstand, tilted crookedly and then focused on the damning evidence lying in the middle of the bed.

Shit, he thought, *Des must have found that stuff.*

He picked the telephone up and dialed her cell phone number, punching the numbers with a vengeance. The telephone just rang until he was switched to voice mail.

"Desiree, it's me, I'm at the crib. Call me," Andre said, frantically.

He clicked the phone off, walked back into the kitchen and waited for her to call him back. He dropped into a kitchen chair, almost knocking it over. He sat there hunched over the table, his head in his hands.

"Hell, she's never going to understand this," he said, aloud.

Knowing Desiree as well as he did, he knew she'd assume the worst. She'd have him tried, convicted and sentenced. *I'm no saint,* he thought, angrily, *I've certainly done my share of dirt but I haven't done anything wrong, not this time. I know it looks bad, and Desiree being the stubborn Taurus she is, will never believe me.*

He thought back to when he and David, his business partner, attended the recognition dinner. Both men are members of the program committee. The club's events are usually held in a dreary VWF hall, however, when the fundraising committee exceeded in their projected goals, they decided to spare no expense and hosted a black tie gala.

Desiree and her posse, which consisted of Taneisha, Tashawn, Ranita and Kristin, planned a trip to Atlanta at the same time earlier that year. He remembered the last thing she told him, half seriously and teasingly, about not getting into trouble, admonishing him to be a good boy while she was gone. Those were her exact words when he dropped them off at the airport. *And damn it, I was,* he thought, indignantly.

The hard part would be convincing Desiree. He'd never known a more headstrong, passionate and emotional woman his entire life. She's always been somewhat of a drama queen, especially earlier in the relationship. Granted, she was young then, but she's matured greatly over the years. Still, she possessed those tendencies when riled. That was one of the reasons he'd caved in as gracefully as he did when she began pressing him into doing *"THE WEDDING"* thing.

He and David co-owned a lucrative real estate firm, which has been operational for ten years. David had come into an inheritance three years ago and decided to reinvest the money in the business, expanding into rehabbing abandoned properties in and around the Chicago area. The firm had been out of the red for five years and holding its own.

Desiree and Lenore, David's wife, who happened to be out of town with their children when the recognition dinner was held, stood by their men, knowing that at some point the company would start to pay dividends. At that time, they could all enjoy the fruits of the men's labor.

Desiree, employed by a major airline, started her career as a flight attendant and later became bored with flying. She applied for and was chosen to participate in a management training program. Her forte is organization, careful attention to details and excellent communications skills. The career move has been an excellent choice. Lately though, she's expressed an interest in joining the real estate firm. Andre has been giving it serious consideration and plans on eventually bringing her onboard.

David is cautious about the idea, saying, "It's enough you live with her, I don't know if it's a good idea for the two of you to work together. Remember your knock down, drag out fights? We can't have that spilling over into the workplace." He promised to think about it though.

Desiree owns the townhouse that she and Andre live in. The down payment was a graduation present from him when she'd graduated from Clark Atlanta University with her best friend, Tanny. Desiree majored in business administration. Ranita and Kristin, having more disposable income from their parents than Desiree and Tanny, did their college stint at nearby Spelman University. During spring break of their senior year of high school, the posse attended freaknik, which caused the onset of their ongoing love affair with Hotlanta. The weekend greatly influenced their college choice, and the fact that they'd all been raised in a nearly all-white suburb of Chicago, made them eager to partake in the "black college" experience.

Serious consideration was given to staying in Atlanta after graduation, but both Ranita and Tanny's mothers suffered serious medical problems, so back to Naperville, Illinois they returned.

Andre wasn't as fortunate as Desiree was in the financial department to be able to attend college. Simply put, his father couldn't afford to send him. His Uncle Walter, his deceased mother's brother, owned a construction firm, and Andre spent his teen years working with Uncle Walter, learning the business. When his uncle passed away, he left the business to Andre, who promptly sold it. Proceeds from the sale were used to form Jackson & Miller Real Estate Incorporated. The men did their homework as an influx of African-Americans began pouring out of Chicago and into the southern suburbs of the Joliet, Lockport area. A vast majority didn't feel comfortable dealing with white realty firms, or felt their needs weren't being met. So through hard work, the men became one of the premier real estate firms in the southern suburbs, having branched out to other surrounding communities.

Andre is a shade darker in complexion than Desiree, and stands about an inch or so shorter than her. He's chunky in build and wears his dark hair cropped short in a fade. Dre possesses a warm engaging smile, pearly white teeth, and a comical sense of humor. He's an only child, whose mother passed away when he was five years old. He and his father share a good relationship. Mr. Jackson has gone out of his way to make Desiree feel like a part of the family.

Andre tried calling Desiree one more time, unsuccessfully. As the hours continued to elapse, he began making calls to the posse and then Deja, Desiree's younger sister, and he still had no luck. At his wits end, he tried Taneisha again.

"Hello?"

"What's up, Tan Tan? Is my girl there?" he asked, trying to mask his anxiety.

"Uh no," she stammered.

"Have you seen Desiree today?"

"Yes, she came through earlier."

"Did she say where she was going?"

"I know she was supposed to pick up her wedding gown or something from the bridal shop this afternoon," Tanny answered.

"That was the last I heard from her too," he admitted. "I haven't been able to catch up with her all afternoon."

"I don't know where she is. If I hear from her, I'll tell her you're looking for her," she replied, trying to make a swift exit off the phone.

"One more question," he quickly interjected, "then I'm out. How did she seem when she was over there? I mean, did it seem like anything was bothering her?"

"Hmm, I bet he knows," she thought silently to herself. "No Dre, nothing seemed to be wrong with her," she lied.

"Okay, later then. If she calls you, tell her to give me a call."

"I will," she promised, grimly.

Taneisha quickly disconnected the phone and dialed Desiree's cell phone number. She got her voice mail. "Hey Dessy, call me back please. Dre is looking for you. He seemed to be feeling me out, as if he knew something was up. I just wanted to give you a heads up."

At that moment, Desiree was sitting at the forest preserve, her secret hideaway. It's a spot she's never even shared with Andre. There was no chance of him finding her, not until she was good and ready to be found. Usually the place brings her peace, a tranquil spot surrounded by a small lake. She often goes there when troubled about a problem, or to just chill. The waters usually calmed her, but today, the blue water wasn't working its usual magic. She sat slumped over in the seat, her head in her hands, a dejected expression on her face. She stared out of the window from time to time, but really didn't see anything except those damning objects she'd found in Andre's pocket.

I should just kick his ass and then break off the engagement, Desiree thought, breathing heavily and getting worked up. *Lord knows I've gone through a lot with this man, although it would be fair to say he's had his share of drama with me.*

She'd met Andre at a club shortly after breaking up with her high school honey, Khamal Reynolds. Theirs had been a tumultuous relationship, the break-up occurring after their senior prom. Attempting to lift Desiree's spirits, her girls urged her to go partying. They'd talked among themselves and agreed that a new man would be the best cure to help her get over Khamal. They dragged her, nearly kicking and screaming, from her bedroom to the mall. Although shopping is her favorite pastime, her heart wasn't in it. Still, she purchased a new outfit, consisting of form-fitting red Capri pants, a red and black spaghetti strapped tank top and red high-heeled sandals.

Later that evening, they piled into Kristin's Toyota Tercel and headed to Chi-town, hitting one of the local clubs with fake IDs they'd procured illegally during their junior year of high school.

Andre was instantly smitten with the tall, model looking, beautiful young lady. He bought her drinks and they spent the rest of the night conversing. Before leaving, he made sure he got her telephone number. At that time, her heart still belonged to Khamal. He'd graduated a couple of years before her and attended Kansas University on a basketball scholarship. Being an older man, Andre understood it was going to take time to win his Lady Love, and time was on his side. He was patient, giving her the space needed to get over her first love and mature into a woman. He'd traveled to Atlanta frequently while she attended school. She received care packages, greeting cards, jewelry and money from him. Flowers were delivered on a monthly basis. He even bought her a cell phone so she could call him whenever she wanted. After two years of loving, he wooed her.

Khamal became a bittersweet memory, no longer a threat for Andre. However, Andre was old and wise enough to know her former beau and first love would always hold a special place in her heart.

Dre was definitely a flirt, the most charming man she'd ever known. Right before her eyes, quite a few women had thrown themselves boldly at him. A few times, she'd happened upon him dining with other women, and telephone numbers, like speeding tickets, accumulated in the glove compartment of his ride. At that time, he still maintained his own separate residence and she'd walk in on him with other women lounging about, like they lived there. Needless to say, that resulted in some very ugly scenes.

The opened package of condoms haunted her. She was ready to settle down, the whole nine yards. One of her strong beliefs and vows was that she'd never have a baby out of wedlock. That was one of her most strict rules since both her mother and grandmother produced children before marriage. Desiree made a solemn oath never to fall into that same trap, feeling someone in the family had to break the cycle. She'd always craved the fairy tale: the man, the wedding and the babies. *All things in its time,* is her motto. Now, all of that was in jeopardy because Dre had been foolish enough to leave a telephone number and condoms in his pocket. *Either he's that sure of me, or he doesn't care,* flitted through her mind.

Her cell phone rang again, breaking her reverie. She picked it up slowly, glancing at the caller id unit. It was Andre calling for the umpteenth time. *I know I'm going to have to answer it eventually, just not right now.*

A cool breeze wafted through the car window. She rubbed her arms forlornly, started up the car and put it into gear.

three

Desiree had a primordial urge to talk to her mother, the black sheep of the family. The ambiguous emotions she felt when she thought of her mother, Mia, set in and her face hardened in a resolve not to even go there. Their estranged situation was the bane of her existence. Desiree had little respect for the woman who gave her life. To her horror, Mia is married to husband number four. Desiree and Deja are both out-of-wedlock children, unplanned pregnancies. Mia was literally ready to drop when she married their father, Martin. To Desiree's way of thinking, Mia just can't get it right, not where matters of the heart are concerned.

No way, Mia is not the one, Desiree thought, shaking her head. *She's a fool, whose judgment on the male species has only gotten worse with age.* Still, she felt a tugging in her heart to talk to her mother.

Mia's longest relationship had been with their stepfather, Rick. They divorced when Desiree was sixteen. Although he didn't sire the girls, he was the closest thing they had to a father. He later adopted them. Mia and Rick exchanged vows when Desiree was nearly six years old, not long after Mia divorced Martin because of his infidelities.

Desiree could always depend on her mother during pre-Phil days, as she called them. They were close, mother-daughter, sister-friend, until Mia began dating, and subsequently married, Phillip Jennings. Neither Desiree nor Deja could stand the sight of Phil. The sisters hated him from day one, labeling him Mr. User Loser.

He didn't make nearly the money Martin or Rick earned. They couldn't imagine what Mia could possibly see in Phil, unless it was a sexual attraction. She's an attractive, educated woman, employed by IBM as a systems engineer. The sisters would try to guess what those two could have in common. There had been plenty of speculation on that subject by other family members as well.

Desiree and Deja preferred Mia's boyfriend before Phil, Charles, but later found out he was married. It amazed Desiree that Mia was actually stupid enough to think he was going to leave his wife and marry her. The consensus between the sisters was that the woman was just hopeless when it came to men.

When Mia announced her wedding plans to her daughters, both cut her off, severing all contact. They talk infrequently on the telephone, but always at their mother's instigation. There is only polite conversation between the three. After the rift, both sisters started calling Mia by her given name, stating she didn't deserve the title Mother. In happier times, they lovingly called her *"Mama Mia"*. Now, the sisters refuse to call Mia on holidays or acknowledge her birthday. Mother's Day is just another Sunday in the month of May as far as they're concerned. However, they adore Rick's wife, Tina, so much that she has *Mother of the Bride* honors on Saturday.

The mother-daughter estrangement has even caused family conflicts while planning Desiree's wedding. Her grandmother and aunts on Mia's side of the family drove from the city to Naperville before the invitations were sent out. Big Mama sat Desiree down and told her that she was wrong in the handling of her mother as far as the wedding is concerned. In her opinion, she shouldn't be left out of the wedding plans entirely.

"It's one thing," Big Mama advised her, "to cut all ties, but another thing to air one's dirty laundry in public."

Desiree finally acquiesced to her grandmother's request and invited Mia. She had scribbled a note enclosed with the invitation requesting Mia not to bring Phil along with her.

Mia had yet to respond to the invitation. However, Desiree was certain that she'd attend the ceremony anyway. Desiree knew people, including members of her posse, thought she was being too tough on Mia, but the sisters honestly felt their mother forfeited her maternal rights when she married her fourth husband. The good relationship they once shared seeped down the drain after that union.

Desiree picked up her cellular phone and stared at it thoughtfully, then quickly dialed a number. There was no answer.

Heading towards the entrance ramp for the Stevenson expressway, she dialed Midway Airport, checking the flight availability to Arkansas.

The representative confirmed, "There's a flight scheduled to leave in ninety minutes. If you think you can be here in time, a ticket will be waiting for you at the desk."

Digesting that information, Desiree found herself at Midway Airport, impulsively deciding to go to Arkansas. It's time to pay a visit to Mia. She parked in the short-term parking lot and rode the shuttle bus to the Southwestern Airline terminal.

After checking in, she plopped down in an uncomfortable plastic seat, pulled out her cell phone and dialed her Aunt Danita's telephone number. Aunt Danita (Danny) is Mia's youngest sister and the only relative who maintains a relationship with her renegade sibling. Therefore, Desiree knew Aunt Danny would have Mia's address.

"Hello?"

"Hi, Auntie Danny," Desiree replied.

"Hi, Miss Dessy. What's up with you, girl?"

"Do you have Mia's address?"

"Sure, I have it," Danita answered. "Is something wrong?"

"You could say that," Desiree said, "but I don't want to get into that, not right now."

"Where are you, Desiree?" Danita asked. "It sounds noisy."

"I'm at the airport."

"What do you mean you're at the airport?" Danita asked. "Where are you going?"

"I'm going to see Mia," Desiree stated, firmly.

"Tonight, right now?" Danita asked, disbelievingly.

"Yes, I am."

"What's so urgent that you're leaving town tonight? Your wedding is only a few days away," Danita asked, alarmed.

"Without going into too much detail, I have something to discuss with Mia."

"Okay, but I don't get it," Danita said, wondering. "Do you have a pen and paper?"

"Yes, I do," Desiree answered. She wrote and recited the information back to her aunt. "Okay, I've got it. I'll talk to you later."

"Is Andre going with you?"

"No, this is one trip I'm taking alone," Desiree answered.

"Is the wedding still on?" Danita asked, apprehensively.

"I plead the fifth," Desiree answered, evasively.

"Well, be careful. I hope you have a safe trip. I'll talk to you when you get back," Danita replied.

Desiree sighed as she disconnected the call. She knew she should call Taneisha, knowing she was probably going out of her mind with worry right about now. She did just that and relayed the information she'd told her aunt about her booking a flight to Arkansas.

After locating her seat, she leaned her tired body against the headrest. When the plane was aloft, Desiree searched her purse and found an aspirin. She asked the stewardess for a cup of water and ingested the pill. She lay her head against the headrest, closed her eyes and let sleep claim her.

Four hours later, it was midnight and Desiree stood at the Avis Car Rental counter, completing paperwork and obtaining directions to Mia's house in Hot Springs Village, Arkansas.

Mia and Phil left Naperville a year after they married. The timing coincided with the family taking sides against her regarding the split with her daughters. Because of that, she agonized whether to attend the wedding or not. She knew that she hadn't been invited because Desiree wanted her there, but most likely because Big Mama intervened on her behalf. Phil had tried talking her into going to the ceremony. His rationale being Desiree is her oldest child, and even if she didn't participate in the festivities, it would be good if she were present for the ceremony at least. Unbeknownst to her, he'd purchased a round trip ticket to Chicago. The departure date was set for the morning of the wedding, with the return date left open.

Phil was out bowling with his buddies, while Mia snuggled in the bed, content with a book in hand and the television set muted. Her head tilted slightly to the left, not sure if she'd heard the doorbell or not. People seldom came out their way this late after dark, especially not without calling first. Again the doorbell sounded, she sprang from the bed, quickly threw on her robe and hurried down the hall to the front door. She peered out of the peephole and her mouth dropped open. Her eyes widened at seeing Desiree on the other side of the door. Her hands shook slightly as she fumbled with the lock. The look of joy on her face quickly turned to dismay when she saw the furious expression on Desiree's face. Mia wasn't sure what to do with her arms, so they dangled loosely at her sides. The two stared at each other.

Should I hug her? What if she rejects me? Mia thought.

"Desiree," she said, hesitantly, "what in heavens name are you doing here?"

Desiree walked into the house and turned to Mia, an angry expression on her face. Next, she walked up to her, hand raised as if to strike Mia, then she threw her arms around Mia's neck and began sobbing

Mia felt helpless, it had been a long time since either of her daughters required comfort from her. She felt rusty, out of practice and stood motionless for a second. Then she gathered Desiree into her arms and held her tightly. The two stood that way for a while and then Mia led Desiree into the living room. Finally, after the spate of tears dried, Desiree sat on the couch and Mia in a chair.

Desiree gazed around the room, taking in the decor. The room was tastefully decorated with a butter colored leather couch, matching love seat and chair, and several glass-topped tables. Abstract paintings decorated the walls and fresh cut flowers bloomed attractively in glass vases. Reclining on the couch, Desiree took note of the fact that Mia still looked good for her age, disappointed that her unlined face didn't show the ravages of the family feud. Instead, there was a look of serenity about her.

The long brown curly hair that formerly adorned her head was now close cropped and streaked with strands of silver. Glasses, suspended by a chain around her neck, lay perched on her nose. She was clad in peach colored silk pajamas. Somehow, she'd managed to defy father time, retaining a slim youthful figure.

Mia scrutinized her daughter, noting the misery lining her face and her hunched shoulders. She rose from the chair and stood next to her, asking, "Are you hungry, can I get you something to eat?"

Desiree shook her head from side to side dejectedly.

"I know something terrible must be going on, otherwise, you wouldn't be at my house, not this close to your wedding day. Is there something I can do?" she asked, wringing her hands together. Visibly shaken, she ran her hands nervously through her hair.

"Mia, I don't think anyone can do anything for me right about now. My life is in shambles," Desiree whispered, morosely.

"What could possibly be wrong with your life? As far as I know, Saturday is supposed to be the happiest day of your life."

"Mama, who is that?" A small boy asked, as he walked into the room and pointed at Desiree.

He was clearly sleepy, rubbing his eyes with little chubby fists. His hair was braided neatly in cornrows, with a single braid coiled at the base of his neck. Desiree's breath caught in her throat as she stared at him. He looked exactly like his sisters, the spitting of Mia, and bronze complexioned like his father.

He walked up to Desiree, smiling and patting her leg, and said, "Hey, you look like my mommy."

The lock turning at the front door signaled Phil's arrival. He walked briskly into the room, surveying the scene.

"Oh hello, Desiree," he said, tentatively.

Desiree looked seemingly through him and didn't part her lips.

Feeling abashed, Phil said, "Alex, come with me, let's get you back to bed."

"No, Dada," he whined, "I wanna stay with Mommy and the lady. She's pretty, isn't she? Don't you think she looks like Mommy?"

Against the boy's protest, Phil carried him into the bedroom.

"Humph," Desiree said, her dark eyes narrowing, "so that's your son."

"Yes, that's Alex," Mia replied, solemnly.

"No one told me he looked that much like me and Deja," Desiree remarked. "I would not have believed it if I hadn't seen it with my own eyes."

"Yes," Mia sighed, "you three definitely resemble each other."

"Well, you finally got your son, Mia. Happy?" Desiree asked, snidely.

"I guess I did," she answered. "Did something happen to Andre?" she asked, attempting to change the subject.

"No, if only it were that simple," Desiree moaned, tears springing into her eyes. "No, nothing's happened to Andre, except his ass got busted."

"Busted how?" Mia asked, bewildered.

"I don't want to talk about him now," Desiree replied.

"Okay," Mia said, raising a hand defensively. "Does anyone know you're here?"

"Tanny and Aunt Danny."

"Why don't you freshen up and I'll fix you a sandwich and tea. Then maybe we can sit down and talk."

"Whatever," Desiree said, sullenly.

"Follow me," Mia instructed, leading her to the guest bedroom.

\

f o u r

Tanny sat in her dimly lit living room, listening to Kenny G blow the blues and sipping on Martells. She picked up the telephone and dialed Desiree and Andre's number, then slammed the phone back into the receiver. She'd done that multiple times. She would call, only to disconnect before it went through. Tanny knew Andre was home. He'd only called her fifty million times in the last couple of hours. Being in coward mode, Tanny let the calls go to voice mail. She wanted to make sure Desiree had arrived in Arkansas safely before she talked to him.

She felt torn. Dessy is her girl, yet she has a strong affection for Andre too. Tanny wanted to do whatever she could to help them patch things up, but on the other hand, maybe she needed to mind her own business and let them work it out.

Tanny and Ranita have a more cavalier attitude towards cheating in relationships, and that being, *"boys will be boys"*. Maybe Andre was simply sowing the last of his wild oats. Dessy couldn't take it that seriously. Hell, he's good looking, has bank and loves her ass. What more could she ask for? Plus, they knew Dessy had cheated on Andre in the past, so she could be a little bit more understanding.

The piercing ring of the telephone cut into her thoughts. She glanced down at the caller id. It was Desiree. She snatched the telephone up.

"What's up, girl? Did you make it there okay?"

"Yes, I made it here. The flight was fine."

"I bet Mia was surprised when she opened the door and saw you on the other side?" Tanny asked.

"Yes, you could say that," Desiree replied.

"So, how long are you staying there?"

"I'll be back sometime tomorrow, I'm just not sure exactly when yet."

"You're cutting it close. You're not going to postpone the wedding, are you?"

"I don't know what I'm going to do yet," Desiree answered candidly, yawning.

"Do you honestly think Mia can help you?" Tanny asked, curiously. "It's not like you two communicate even in the best of times."

"I'll tell you this once more," Desiree said, impatiently. "I felt an urge to see her and get some things off my chest."

"Okay girl, I'm sorry. It's just that I don't get it."

"I hear you," Desiree yawned. "I'll call you tomorrow with my flight information."

"Okay. Talk to you then. Call me if you need anything," Tanny said.

"Okay," Desiree promised. "I'll be fine."

Desiree lay across the bed and fell fast asleep.

A few minutes later, Mia peeped into the room. Seeing Desiree asleep, she pulled a quilt over her body and kissed her forehead. She walked into the kitchen, wrapped the sandwich in foil paper and placed it in the refrigerator. Next, Mia turned the light off and walked into her bedroom. Phil was propped up on a pillow watching the news.

"So, what brings your prodigal daughter here?" he asked, peering at her.

"I'm not sure," Mia answered, troubled. "She said something about her and Andre having problems."

"Funny she would come here," he remarked.

Mia just nodded her head in agreement and pretended to direct her attention to the news broadcasting on the television.

Tanny sighed deeply, took a sip of cognac, and dialed Desiree's home telephone number. Andre picked up the phone.

"Desiree?" he asked, anxiously.

"You must have picked up the phone without looking at the caller id," Tanny remarked.

"Oh, it's you. I thought it might be Desiree," he said, glumly.

"Let me put you out of your misery," she said. "I just talked to Desiree."

"Where is she?" Andre asked, tiredly. "I've been calling everyone."

"Are you sitting down?" Tanny asked. "She's in Arkansas."

"Say what?" Andre snorted.

"Yep, Dessy's in Arkansas, gone to visit Mama Mia."

"I don't believe it," he said, incredulously.

"I couldn't either, but that's where she is. I also know you hurt my girl badly," she snapped.

"Tanny, you know I'd never do anything to deliberately hurt Des, I love her."

"So you say. You were an idiot not to get rid of that stuff."

"But I didn't do anything," he protested. "I swear I'm innocent this time."

"That's what they all say," Tanny said, boiling with anger. "If you're going to play, don't bring the shit home."

"I wasn't playing with anyone!" Andre shouted.

"Let me guess," Tanny said, sarcastically, "the telephone number magically appeared in your pocket. Then presto, the package of condoms jumped in to keep the telephone number company."

"Of course not!" he roared. "I know it looks bad, but there's a logical explanation for all of this."

"And what might that be?" Tanny asked, huffily.

"I, uh, don't want to get into it now. I'd rather talk to Dessy first," Andre stammered. "Give me Mia's telephone number," he said, adroitly changing the subject.

"I think it'd be better if you waited on her to call you."

"What do you mean wait on her to call me!" he yelled. "Don't you realize we're supposed to be married in seventy-two hours?"

"That remains to be seen. I think you'd better play it by ear, brotha man, and not assume anything, at least until you talk to Dessy."

"I think you're tripping!" Andre shouted. "Until I hear otherwise, I'm going to assume everything is still on."

"Okay, Dre," Tanny said, equally loud, "you keep assuming that. I just called to tell you she's alright and that she said she'd be back tomorrow."

"Fine then," he said. "Thanks for the message."

They both slammed their telephones down simultaneously, shaking their heads, irritated with the other.

"That stupid son of a ….," Tanny grumbled.
"That nosey ….," Andre complained.

five

Desiree stirred the next morning. Disoriented, she opened one eye and then the other. Suddenly, her memory returned and she realized that she was at Mia's house. A teardrop trickled down the side of her face as she glanced at the clock. It was almost 6:00 am. Desiree knew from memory that Mia was up and about. That woman had always been an early riser. Her eyes traveled to the wooden rocking chair on the other side of the room. Mia had left a change of clothing on it, along with an extra toothbrush. She sat up in the bed, hearing voices down the hall. Assuming it was her mother and Phil talking in the kitchen, she walked to the door and stood motionlessly listening.

"I guess you're not going to work today?" Phil asked.

"No, I had scheduled time off anyway in case I decided to go to the wedding, so I'll be here."

"Do you need me to stay here with you?" he asked, gently. "I know this has to be difficult for you."

"I don't know that difficult would be the word to describe this predicament," she replied wryly, nose crinkling. "Although, I'm glad she chose to come here for whatever reason."

He kissed her cheek and pulled her into his arms. "I called Sylvia, she'll keep Alex today. I've got him dressed, and he's in his room looking for toys to take along with him. I'll drop him off at her house on my way to work and I'll call you later."

Guiltily, Desiree stepped back from the door. She ran her fingers through her hair, which was a mess, and then sniffed her underarms.

"Phew, I need to take a shower," she said.

Mia sat in a lounging chair on the large wooden deck. Kirk Franklin's *"Rebirth"* CD played softly in the background. Neither Desiree nor Deja had come to her for anything in years. They never called her, although she called both of them on their birthdays and holidays. Most of the time, they didn't even take her calls. She'd end up leaving unreturned voice mail messages. Everyday she prayed her daughters would have a change of heart and allow her to become a part of their lives again.

She'd seriously contemplated suicide a few years ago, then decided to try counseling after bouts of alcoholism and depression. With the help of Dr. Lee, Phil, and the birth of Alex, she was finally able to put her life back in order. These past few years had been tough, her once brown hair turned gray overnight it seemed.

She'd left Naperville after Deja graduated from high school. Her baby girl had requested she not attend the graduation ceremony. Mia called the school almost in tears and explained the circumstances to the principal. He was sympathetic to her plight, giving her a ticket to the ceremony. Mia cried silently as she watched from afar.

Life can get so complicated sometimes, she thought, walking into the kitchen. She could hear the water from the shower, indicating Desiree was out of bed.

Mia's day of reckoning had arrived, and her stomach rumbled with tension. *I'll just have to be patient and see what she wants,* she thought, taking a sip of Pepsi-cola. Her hands shook slightly as she pulled a cigarette out of the pack and lit it.

Upon hearing sounds of Desiree moving about the room, Mia walked over to the refrigerator and removed food for breakfast. Soon, the coffeemaker bubbled and the scent of mocha filled the kitchen. Mia walked over to the patio door and stood there, engrossed in thought.

Desiree faced the bathroom mirror, pulled her long hair into a ponytail and looked at her cell phone, which was still powered off and lying on the nightstand. Taking a deep breath to soothe her quivering nerves, she dialed her home telephone number.

"Desiree?" Dre asked, impatiently. "Where are you? Are you alright?"

"Physically, I'm fine. Mentally, I don't know where I am," she answered, discouraged.

"Where are you?" Dre repeated.

"At Mia's house."

"Why Mia's of all places?"

"I guess finding condoms in your fiancé's pocket three days before your wedding might send one running to their mother," she answered, dryly.

"Anyone but you," he retorted. "You and Mia don't have it like that."

"I guess it was just one of those times, Andre. You can't imagine how I felt when I saw that garbage. I was devastated."

"I can understand that, but why didn't you talk to me first?" he asked, his voice rising with aggravation.

"That could've been an option," she said, harshly. "Excuse me, but I wasn't thinking quite clearly."

"So, I've been tried, convicted and sentenced without my input?"

"At this point, the jury is still out on that one," she replied, dryly.

"Then you need to get back here and listen to my side of things."

"Your side?" Desiree snorted. "Let's hear it."

"A woman did give me her number," he replied, "but I balled it up and stuck it in my pocket. As for the condoms, they belong to David."

"I knew you were going to say that," Desiree remarked, coldly. "Why would you have David's condoms? It doesn't add up, and how convenient for you, they belong to your best friend."

"Maybe I was wrong for not disposing of the telephone number, but did you ever stop to think, if it's crumpled in my pocket, then there's a possibility that I didn't use it?" Andre asked, heatedly.

"Sure, that's a possibility, but a little far-fetched."

"I've admitted to wrongdoings in the past. I'd do the same now, except this isn't one of those times," Andre said, quietly. "We've always been honest with each other, so give me a little credit."

"It's not like you don't have a history of doing that kind of shit!" Desiree yelled. "Maybe you aren't admitting it because it's days before the wedding."

"The same can be said of you. What about your history?" Dre remarked, chillingly.

"Anyway, all of that is in the past, and that's where we need to leave it."

"I know you don't think I'm about to just pretend it didn't happen and marry you after finding that shit!" Desiree shouted.

"What I didn't expect was for you to run to Mia of all people about this. It's personal, between the two of us. You should've been woman enough to stay here, deal with it and not run all the way to Arkansas."

"Andre, you've lost your damn mind! I don't need a lecture from you about what I should or shouldn't do. In case you didn't notice, you're the one who fucked up, not me!" she exploded. "Don't you even come at me like that. If you had handled your business like a man and disposed of it, we wouldn't be in this predicament. We have a problem here and I will deal with it as best I can. I'll be back sometime today and will see you then."

She clicked the telephone off abruptly and then threw it on the bed. As she sat on the side of the bed with her head in her hands, she began to weep.

"Desiree, are you alright?" Mia whispered, tapping at the door. "Is it okay if I come in?"

"I guess so," Desiree sighed.

Mia pushed the door open, came into the room and watched as Desiree wiped tears from her eyes. She couldn't miss the desolation on her daughter's face. The sight of it made Mia's heart drop. She walked over to the bed and sat down next to her daughter. Shaking hands betrayed her nervousness as she pulled a couple of loose threads from the comforter.

"Do you feel like talking?" she asked, glancing at Desiree warily.

"I guess so," Desiree said, nodding her head.

"What are you doing in Arkansas when you're getting married in a few days?"

"Truthfully, I really don't know why I'm here. This is the last place I should be," Desiree said. "I have a feeling that being here will only complicate matters. I found something yesterday and it threw me for a loop."

"Would I be out of line in asking what that something was?" Mia asked.

Desiree gulped. "I don't know…" She glared at her, her lips set in a thin line.

"I know this is the last place you want to be," Mia said, softly. "Usually when we're around each other sparks fly, but please let me try to help you if I can."

The angry expression on Desiree's face softened, giving her an air of vulnerability. Her mouth opened and closed a couple of times as she struggled to find the words to say.

"I found…," she stammered, "uh, a package of opened condoms and a woman's number in Dre's pocket."

Mia's eyes dropped. "I see," she said, slowly.

Desiree sagged against her, and the tears began to flow again. Mia drew her into her arms and held her. Gradually, Desiree broke down, releasing all of her frustration and anger. Finally, the tears seeped slowly, then dried. Desiree pulled away from Mia, her eyes red and puffy.

"Would you like a cup of tea or breakfast?" Mia asked, stroking Desiree's hand.

"I'm not really hungry."

"Have you talked to Andre about this?"

"We talked briefly this morning," Desiree said, ruefully. "I'm sure you heard me yelling while you were in the kitchen."

"What does he have to say about the items you found?"

"He thinks I'm being irrational and overreacting," she said, shrugging her shoulders.

"Do you believe him?" Mia asked.

"I don't know, he sounded convincing. Then again, we have a lot riding on this, the marriage, the whole shebang. The invitations have gone out and everyone have marked their calendars or palm pilots for the big event," she said, matter-of-factly.

"What do you want?"

"I want things to go back to the way they were before, that's what I really want," she wailed.

"Desiree, you're old enough to know that life isn't that simple," Mia said, stroking her hair.

"I know how old I am," Desiree snapped.

"Sorry, I just don't know what you want from me, or what to say to you," Mia mumbled, as her hand fell away from the flattened ponytail.

"I don't know the answer to that either," Desiree murmured, sadly.

"How is your sister doing?" Mia asked, trying to change the subject to a safer topic. "I talk to her every now and then."

"She's doing okay, probably going crazy with the rest of the people in my world right about now."

"Hmm, you're probably right."

"Mia, I'd like to know," Desiree asked, "how come you couldn't stay with Dad? Why did you breakup our family?"

"I, uh," Mia stuttered, at a lost for word.

"Yeah, considering you're the root of all my problems, you should be the last person in the world I come to," Desiree said, meanly. "You knew I couldn't stand Phil from the minute you introduced him to Deja and me. To make matters worse, you kept telling us to give him time. I don't really understand you. How could you put a man before your children's wishes? If there were an award for Worst Mother of the Year, you would certainly qualify for it, several years in the running."

As Desiree spoke, Mia's spirit seemed to droop. Again, forgiveness wasn't in the cards for her.

"You know what, Desiree?" she said. "I didn't ask you to come here, you made that decision by yourself. I, like most adults, have the option of making decisions for myself. I understand you're going through a bad time. I've had enough hard times to last a lifetime, but I try really hard not to complain and live my life as I see fit," Mia said heatedly, nostrils flaring. "Regardless of how you think things should have been, I tried and did the best I could under the circumstances."

"Okay, Mia," said Desiree, holding her hand up. "I need closure as to what happened to our family. Sure, I'll grant that you were a great provider, but when it came to heeding our requests, you were plain selfish and did as you wanted. That Mommie Dearest attitude is what hurt us so. You let that man, who was just your boyfriend at the time, move into our house. And Mia, you know what was really messed up, is that he didn't treat you right. But Rick, our Dad, a good man who treated you like a queen, you couldn't stay with him. Why was that, Mia?" Desiree eyes rolled, flashing a steely glint that cut Mia to the core.

"I'll try to answer your questions as best I can," Mia said slowly, taking a deep breath. "I'm sorry things didn't work out with Rick and me. You were both old enough to realize, we were two adults sharing the same space for our daughters instead of as a married couple. I've apologized for any harm that I may have caused you and Deja. As far as the divorce was concerned, I could argue your dad didn't treat me fairly at times, but that's not the issue here. I wish I could tell you life is fair and that only good things occur in life, but that's not the case, you know better than that.

Life is a series of ups and downs. It's how we deal with the down times that define us as a person. I've made mistakes in life, and if I keep living, I'm pretty sure I'll make more, just not as colossal as the one between us, I hope. Gosh, I don't know anyone who's done things exactly the way another person would want them to."

Mia continued, "I was dealing with so many unresolved issues myself, starting with my family, which shut me down and affected my decision making in a negative way. It took me a while to see that. When I married the first time, it was because I was ready to experience sex. To do that, I had to marry and get out of Big Mama's house. I know it sounds odd in this day and age, but that's how it was for us so-called good girls back in the day. Then I married your biological father, Martin, who didn't believe that being monogamous was a big part of a marriage. I had high hopes for Rick, but he couldn't be there for me emotionally, much like my family. I felt suffocated during the marriage, as if I was stuck in a box, and most of the time, the sides would close in on me, and I couldn't breathe or live. It was a sad way of life, but I tried to endure it for as long as I could because I thought I was doing what was best for you and Deja.

Phil and I have had our share of problems, just like any other married couple, and the adjustment took a while. I knew eventually that we'd get to the place I wanted to be in a marriage. My greatest regret in life is that our relationship has deteriorated to the degree it has. But you know what, Desiree? I can't live my life based one what someone thinks, or their feelings about what I should or shouldn't do with my life. In the end, I'll have to account to one person for my actions, the Lord above. Even then, I won't have to because he knows what's in my heart."

The mood in the room was somber. Both women wore the same stubborn expression on their faces.

"It all sounds good in theory, Mia," Desiree said, shaking her head. "But it still doesn't excuse what you did. You brought a man into our house knowing we couldn't stand him, and the sad thing is you never, at any time, put your children first. Our feelings weren't even a consideration."

Mia stared directly at her oldest child, recoiling from the anger that seemed to seep from her pores, and she felt such sadness for the estrangement. She prayed everyday that the time would come when her daughters would be willing to listen to her side of the story. Well, the time was now.

"We told you many times we didn't like him, but for some reason unknown to either of us, our feelings didn't matter," Desiree complained. "You did exactly what you wanted."

"I was aware that you girls didn't like him," Mia responded, "but he was and still is my choice. I had my reasons for the way I did things, and to put it simply, I love him. He touches something deep within my soul. The money wasn't a factor as far as I was concerned. When he did leave the house, at your request I might add, I realized that was a mistake. I was lonely and felt like a part of me was missing. Phil and I knew at some point we were going to marry, it was just a matter of time. We held off those plans until your sister was eighteen and set for college. Silly me, I thought I was old enough to lead my life as I wanted, not as the two of you wanted."

"Mia, you need to wake up," Desiree replied. "He's just using you, and he always will."

"How do you figure that?" she asked, confused.

"He doesn't make nearly the money Dad does. You make more than him, and I'm sure if you were honest about it, he can't even support you now."

"I didn't marry your Dad or Phil as a means of support. I'm more than capable of supporting myself," Mia said testily, clenching and unclenching her hands. "We brought different things to the table. I just happen to make more money than he does, but that was also the case with Rick and Martin. I can say that he respects my feelings, and always has. I feel loved with him."

"It makes no sense to me that you would prefer him to my Dad," Desiree said, unmoved by her words. "I guess I just don't get it."

"You may never get it, my dear. There were many times Rick was out of a job and I stuck by him. I would caution you though, until you walk in my shoes, you can't say what I should or shouldn't do. I strongly believe everyone, especially adults, have the right to live their life as they see fit."

"You're right, they do," Desiree said, her voice rising with frustration, "but not to the exclusion of family, and especially not children." She looked at Mia as if she was an idiot.

"It never occurred to me that you and Deja would cut me off. I thought our love for each other was unconditional, but I was wrong. I can't think of anything either of you could do that would cause me not to talk to you. Both of you were over eighteen and I thought I could live my life as I saw fit. You know what this has done to me?" Mia said, morosely. "Some days I feel so bad that I think I'm going to lose my mind. Can't you understand that I have feelings too? But at the same time, I can't live my life based on what you or your sister considers best for me, that's my call. I have to live it the way I see fit, do what's best for me and accept the consequences of those actions, whether it's good or bad."

"You're a piece of work, a real selfish b…!" Desiree cried in outrage, jumping up from the bed, arms folded across her chest. She managed to catch herself in time before the word escaped from her mouth. "Parents are obligated to always put their children's feelings before their own, no matter what age the child is."

"That's your philosophy, Desiree. That's what works for you. I'm not you, your sister, your aunts, or Big Mama, I'm simply myself," said Mia, earnestly. "I'm not perfect," she said, pointing to her chest, "and I don't know everything, but I do know I have to be true to me. That's been my whole problem my entire life, never fulfilling my own needs and desires to the point of suppressing my true self."

Desiree snorted with disdain, "Big Mama *always* put her children first."

"That may be the case," Mia retorted, *"but that was her choice*. I'm your mother, imperfect Mia Rosalind Jennings. In retrospect, I can see staying in the relationship with Rick as long as I did wasn't the best decision for any of us. Once again, I thought I was doing the right thing. Deja had always been closer to Rick than me when she was growing up, and I stayed with him as long as I could, knowing he couldn't be there for me emotionally.

I got tired, not selfish, but plain dog-tired. I decided at forty, it was time for me to get out of that situation. I felt like I was drowning in the middle of the ocean without a raft. I was lonely, sad and struggling with my feelings of self-worth. Getting involved with Charles didn't help me one bit. None of this is new to you, Desiree," said Mia, begging for understanding. "I've been in therapy and I've learned I was a time bomb just waiting to explode. I didn't expect anything from life except let downs, and that's because that was all I'd ever known. The same people that I thought and trusted to have my back let me down time and time again. I had to learn to love myself," she said loudly, tears filling her eyes. "Phil was the first person in my life to show me unconditional love. His methods may have been unorthodox, but I could and still feel love from him. I always have and always will."

Desiree paced impatiently, then stopped and listened to Mia's words. She knew some of what she told her was true, but she just couldn't find it in her heart to forgive her, not yet. A mother is suppose to be strong, a role model for her daughters especially, and always put her children's feelings first. That was her philosophy and she wasn't deviating from it not one bit. Mia hadn't followed the rules, thus making her a bad mother.

Mia could sense Desiree wasn't hearing her. It was as if she was talking to a deaf person. Seeing that filled her with a sense of helplessness, and tears trickled from her eyes. She didn't know a better way to explain how she felt. Her heart felt heavy with despair and rejection. Her child wasn't ready to forgive and let the healing process begin.

"I still think you're selfish, always have been and always will be."

"Then why are you here?"

"I told you I don't know," said Desiree, choking back a sob. "I'm in trouble. The wedding is almost here. I'm messed up and it's your fault."

"I know what you're saying and I could say the same of Big Mama," Mia said.
"Don't you think most parents have made mistakes one way or another in raising their children? Forgiveness is a part of life too. I did the best I could with you and your sister. I'm sorry if I fell short of your expectations. Parents don't get a handbook on perfect parenting when they leave the hospital. We make decisions we think are correct at the time, and not all of them are because no one is perfect. Yes,

our childhood affects our decisions as adults. I'll say this one more time, no one is perfect, not you, not even Big Mama. I hope one day you'll find it in your heart to forgive me."

Desiree sat on the bed next to Mia. The room was hushed for a time. Both mother and daughter faces, mirrored sadness and pain.

"I think I needed to hear what you had to say before I take that walk down the aisle," Desiree whispered, unable to look Mia. "Maybe somewhere deep inside of me there's a part of me that wants the mess to end. I'm really not sure," she said, shaking her head from side to side. "Then sometimes, I'm just afraid I'll end up a failure at marriage, like you," she confessed.

SIX

Mia rose from the bed, walked to the window and stared out at the lush rolling hills and mountains of Arkansas. She and Phil own a two-story home on a lake. Like her daughter, she finds solace in the water. Her hand nervously twisted the cord of the mini-blinds on the window frame.

"Do you love Andre?" she asked Desiree, turning to face her.

"Of course I do," she replied, irritably. "I wouldn't be marrying him otherwise."

"Come on, Desiree, I think neither one of us is naïve enough to believe that women marry only for love. If you love him, then Des, you know what to do. No one but you and Andre know how strong your love is. Can it withstand the tests of time, be it illness, financial difficulties, infidelity, even death? That's what love and life is about, my dear. Coping as best you can through good and bad times."

"Hmm, I hear you," said Desiree. "I'm just scared. What if I make a mistake? What do I do then?"

"Sometimes you have to take chances in life. Granted, marriage is a big one, but if things don't work out, you'll know what to do. What's that saying, love conquers all," she added, smiling.

Desiree smiled, the first genuine one they shared since she arrived.

"You know me," said Mia, jokingly, "I'm the master of getting out of bad relationships. I haven't been around Andre for a while, but I sense he cares for you. However, I can't advise you as to whether or not to marry him." Mia laughed. "Remember, my track record is not that good anyway."

"You ain't never lied," Desiree smiled.

"Don't base your life or decisions on the choices and the mistakes I've made. We're different individuals, alike in some respects, but different in others. What is your gut telling you?"

"Honestly, I know if Andre was fucking around, he'd just admit it. Maybe he was just sowing those wild oats."

"Andre is older than you, so I'm sure his oats are sowed by now. Therefore, maybe he's telling the truth," Mia remarked.

"It kind of makes me uneasy finding that stuff before the wedding. You know, like a bad omen or something."

"I hear you," Mia said. "All things happen for a reason, and sometimes we don't understand why. Perhaps it was the push you needed to finally make a decision about your life."

"You know what, Mia?" Desiree said, shaking her head from side to side. "You're too much!"

"Yeah, I know," she agreed, smiling. "Looking back, I see I should've done some things differently. Hindsight is

20/20, and I just didn't see the big picture back then. I often wish I was a perfect person who knows instinctively how to do things correctly all of the time, but unfortunately, I wasn't blessed with that talent," Mia sighed.

"I love Andre," Desiree admitted. "He's been there for me, emotionally, financially and physically, since we hooked up. He can be arrogant, controlling and overbearing at times, which doesn't bother me, most of the time. He's smart and he's going places, and I like that in a man."

"Well, you go girl," Mia said, clapping her hands. "If that's what turns you on, then go for it, I ain't mad at ya! But keep in mind, anything accumulated from a material standpoint can be taken away at any time. It's the love between a man and woman that sustains a relationship. Remember the vows, for richer or poorer, in sickness and in health. Life has a funny way of lulling us into a false sense of security, and then shit happens, as they say. One must be prepared for those down times."

"I hear you," Desiree replied.

"Let's say we move this discussion to the kitchen. I don't know about you, but I'm hungry."

"Fine with me," Desiree replied, "I'm starving."

The two women walked from the bedroom into the kitchen.

"It's nice outdoors," Mia remarked, "would you like to eat breakfast on the deck?"

"That's fine with me," Desiree answered, pulling the patio door open.

"I'll have breakfast fixed in a moment."

Desiree stepped out onto the deck. The clicking of crickets and cicadas serenaded her with a private song as she sat under the umbrella table. Her eyes, drawn to the lake, took in the surroundings while Mia prepared breakfast.

Desiree's cell phone went off. She removed it from her pocket and glanced at the caller id, it was Andre. She let the call go to voice mail. Next, she went through her call log and noted that both Tanny and Deja had called her earlier. She played and erased the messages.

Mia walked out onto the deck and set a plate in front of Desiree. She returned to the kitchen to get the juice and a can of Pepsi for herself. Then she sat down opposite her daughter.

"It's very peaceful here, isn't it?" Desiree remarked.

"Yes, it is. That's one of the things I like about this place. We came here for a visit and fell in love."

"It's very nice," Desiree said, looking around.

"What time are you leaving?" Mia asked.

"I called the airport and there's a 2 o'clock flight out of here. I'll be leaving in a few hours."

"Well, have you decided what you're going to do once you get back home?"

"Confront Andre, and as you suggested, I'll listen to what my gut feeling is telling me."

"Sounds like the wedding is still on then," Mia remarked.

"I guess so," Desiree said. "It would be a shame to waste all the money we've already spent."

"Just so you're comfortable with that decision," Mia warned her.

"I am," Desiree said, yawning. "Thanks for washing my clothes. I'm going to make a few more calls, change and head back to Little Rock."

"Not a problem," Mia said. "I know there are a million things you have to do."

"Did you plan on coming to the wedding?" Desiree asked, almost shyly.

"You know what? I hadn't decided, but I have a ticket just in case." Mia looked at Desiree like she wanted to hug her. "Honey, thanks for coming to see me, you don't know how good that makes me feel." She leaned over and caressed Desiree's face.

Then she stood and walked back into the house, singing and tidying the kitchen.

A few hours later, Desiree was dressed in her freshly laundered clothes and headed out the door. Mia walked her to the car.

"Hopefully, I'll see you at the wedding."

"Okay," Mia said, hugging her quickly. "I hope everything works out for you."

Later that afternoon, Desiree sat in the passenger area. She had about another half an hour before it was time to board the plane. Pulling her cell phone out of her purse, she dialed Andre's cell phone number.

"Hello," he answered.

"Hi yourself," Desiree said.

"So, where are you now?" he asked. "Headed home, I hope."

"Yes, I am."

"So, are we still on?" he asked, cautiously.

"I guess you'll find out when I get back there, now won't you?" she answered coolly, determined to let him sweat a little while longer.

"Do you need me to pick you up from the airport?" he asked.

"No, I parked in the short-term lot."

"What time does your flight arrive?"

"I'll call you when I arrive in Chicago." She powered the cell phone off, stood and walked over to a newsstand, and purchased a couple of magazines for the flight home.

The flight home was uneventful. Desiree stepped off the plane and walked slowly through the ramp to the passenger area. As she exited, she caught sight of Andre standing nervously near the gate. His face was covered with prickly hairs, and his hair looked mused, as though it hadn't been brushed. She suspected he would be there.

"Hey baby," he said, solemnly.

"What are you doing here?" she asked.

"I just couldn't sit in the house another minute," he confessed.

"I told you I'd see you at home, and I will in about thirty minutes."

"Okay," he said, holding up his hands. He made a move as if to touch her, but she drew away.

Shortly after leaving the airport, she drove along I-88 expressway, cruising towards home. Her cell phone rang and she quickly scanned the caller id.

Clicking the telephone on, she said, "Hello?"

"What's up, girl?" Tanny asked.

"I'm on my way home."

"So, are we still on for Saturday?" she asked. "I picked up my dress from the shop today and it's a perfect fit."

"Tanny, Tanny, Tanny," Desiree said, "I'll let you know soon enough."

"Which way are you leaning?" she asked, nosily.

"This is not a movie, there's no sneak previews here," Desiree laughed.

"How was your visit with Mia?"

"It went okay. Her house is nice, paid for with her money, I'm sure. I suspect Phil is mooching as usual."

"Is she coming to the wedding, assuming it's still on?"

"She said she may. I reminded her that Phil is still not welcome though."

"Damn, I hope I never get on your bad side," Tanny laughed.

"Humph," Desiree snorted, "I don't know what you're talking about, you've been there a time or two."

"Let me change that, I hope I never really piss you off. Girlfriend, you can definitely carry a grudge. So, you'll call me later?"

"Hmm, I think I can do that. I'll talk to you."

"Later girl," said Tanny.

Desiree clicked off and dialed Deja's cell phone.

"I don't believe you!" Deja snapped, crossly. "You just up and leave town and can't even call a sista."

"What can I say? I just wasn't thinking straight," Desiree replied.

"Tanny called and told me you went to see Mia. What possessed you to do that?" Deja asked.

"Um, I don't know, maybe the whole marriage thing."

"Girl, please," Deja said. "How is *she* doing anyway?"

"She's fine, living in a big house on a lake. I thought I saw a boat on their dock."

"Wow, I guess they must be doing okay then."

"Oh, I almost forgot to tell you. I saw their son, little Alex, too," Desiree added.

"Did you really?" Neither sister had ever expressed any interest in their half brother.

"Yeah really, and let's keep it real," Desiree remarked, "you and I both know that it's Mia's money keeping them in that lifestyle."

"Desiree, she told Big Mama that he's been working since they moved there, so maybe he is contributing," Deja replied, cautiously. "Is she coming, and does that mean the wedding is still on?"

"She says she might, but I bet she won't leave Phil behind."

"Did she actually say that she'd consider coming?"

"Yes, she did. I guess we'll have to wait and see if she shows up or not."

"So, is the wedding still on?"

"I honestly don't know yet," Desiree confessed. "I'll let you know in about an hour or so."

"Okay, big sis. If you need me, just hit me on my cell."

"Will do. I'm coming up to my exit off the expressway, so I'll talk to you later."

"Okay, peace out."

seven

Desiree pulled her truck in the driveway, noting Andre had beaten her home. She hopped out of the truck and started walking up the walkway. Andre opened the door as soon as she reached the top stair. She strolled into the kitchen, pulled open the refrigerator door and took out a bottle of mineral water. Twisting it open, she greedily gulped it down.

Andre went into the den and sat in the reclining chair, looking dejected. Desiree took her sweet time before entering the room. She dropped ungracefully on the couch, attitude written all over her face.

"So, I guess we need to figure out what we're going to do," she said.

"Yeah, you're right," he sighed. "First, I'll say this again. I apologize for putting us in this situation. If I had known the confusion leaving that stuff in my pocket would cause, I would've thrown it away immediately."

"A little late for that now, isn't it?" Desiree said, coolly.

"I'm sure from your standpoint it is," Andre replied. "What do you want to do, Dessy?"

"I want you to explain to me how we got like this, beginning with the dinner."

As Andre had feared, she was definitely in lawyer mode. "David and I went to the Lions' dinner. It was the same time you went to Atlanta."

"I know that part," Desiree snapped.

"Okay," Andre said. "David and I went to the dinner. It was a lively set, there were tons of women there, and a couple of them hollered at me. I was merely mingling as any good businessman would. Then David and I ended up at the bar, and one sister in particular came onto me. You know how that goes."

"And you didn't know how to just say no?" Desiree interrupted, an angry scowl on her face.

"Now, you know I wasn't about to come off as whipped in front of the fellas. I'm not going out like that. Anyway, she wouldn't take no for an answer, so I just took the number. I meant to throw it away and forgot. You have no reason to assume things went any further."

"I'd say due to those condoms in your pocket, I have a very good reason to suspect things went further."

"I see your point, but that wasn't the case."

"So you say," Desiree said stubbornly, her arms folded tightly across her chest.

"It's merely incriminating, that's all."

"So, whom do the condoms belong to?" Desiree asked.

"Like I told you before, they're David's."

"Last time I checked," Desiree said, loudly, "David was a grown man. So why the hell would his condoms end up in your pocket?"

"We rode to Joliet together. I drove. David asked me to stop at a drug store and that's when he purchased them."

"I know how men stick together. You and I both know he'd lie for you anyway."

"Somehow, I knew you'd think that," Dre said, frustrated.

"Your best bet is to just come clean with me. It wouldn't be in our best interest to start a marriage with this issue hanging over our heads. So, give it your best shot, convince me," Desiree said.

She tapped her foot, her body taunt and eyes glowing with pain. Black circles smudged her eyes, like she hadn't slept for a couple of days. Tracks of tears disfigured her face like scars.

Andre's stomach danced with tension as he watched the emotions play across her face, disgust being the most apparent. It was an expression he hadn't seen for a long time. The last time he saw it was nearly six years ago, and he vowed no one would ever hurt her like that again. Now, here it was back to haunt him, a couple days before their wedding. This should've been a joyous time for both of them, attending bachelor and bachelorette parties. They'd plan to thumb their noses at traditionalists and spend their last single night together. Instead, Andre was in for the fight of his life. One misstep and he knew it'd be over.

"If I could go back and relieve that night over, Des, I would in a New York minute. After David bought the condoms, he took one out of the package and put it in his wallet, just in case he got lucky. He then gave me the package, which I put in my pocket."

"But he's married!" Desiree cried.

"Yeah, that's true. I never told you this, but he cheats on Lenore. I don't agree with it, but it's his marriage and his choice. That's all I'm going to say on the matter. I know what you're thinking, and no, our marriage won't be the same way. All I'm open to is a one-on-one relationship."

"You damn well better be," Desiree said, hot by now. "Otherwise, you can get your black ass out of here now! Why didn't David just keep the package himself?"

"Truthfully," Dre said, looking sheepish, "he told me to keep them in case I got lucky. He knew the wedding was coming up, and mentioned something about me getting some booty before you put me on permanent lockdown."

"And this from your best man," said Desiree, shaking her head and cutting her eyes sharply at Dre.

"Baby, you've got to remember his philosophy isn't the same as ours regarding marriage He really doesn't look at it as cheating. He's just greedy like that, always has been, and always will be. So what do you want to do, Des?" Andre asked, tiredly. "I can only tell you what happened, whether you believe it is up to you. I love you and have for many years. From the moment I saw your beautiful face at Chic Rick's, I knew that you were the one for me, despite the difference in our ages. I knew that I had to give you the space you needed to grow and come into your own. You've blossomed into a beautiful woman. I'd never knowingly do anything to hurt you, baby. I apologize for my stupidity and hope you can find love and trust in your heart for your man. I love you, Desiree, and that's all I can say. It's up you now."

As Andre declared his intentions, Desiree just stared at him wordlessly. *This must be how Mia felt when Deja and I came to her complaining about Phil. She had a make a call, it was a tough one, and she followed her heart. Unfortunately, in doing so, she messed up our family bad. What consequences will my choice bring if I choose incorrectly?*

"If you want to call it off, Des, now is the time," Andre continued talking. "I don't want you to. What I do want is for you to be sure of your decision, as sure as you can be under the circumstances."

The doorbell sounded loudly and long. Andre sprang from the chair and went to the foyer. Peeping through the curtains, he saw David standing there and opened the door. Their low murmuring could be heard as they walked back into the den. David sat down on the couch next to Desiree.

"What's up, Des?" David turned to kiss her cheek. She pulled away slightly as his lips drew near. "Dre told me about you finding the condoms I bought and had him put in his pocket," he admitted. "I guess I really didn't think about you finding them when I put them there."

"You're damn right about that," Desiree said, heatedly. "It's obvious you were thinking with the little head, instead of the big one. I don't know what you thought would be accomplished by having David come over," Desiree said, glaring at Andre.

"By any means necessary, if my best friend has to come clean in his part in all this, then that's what he has to do," Dre said.

"Hell," Desiree exclaimed, "he'd lie for you anyway. All three of us know that."

"True, I'd lie for my boy," David said, seriously, "but not if your future is on the line. I may be a bad boy, but even I have some principals."

"Sorry, David, you have zero credibility as far as I'm concerned."

"Okay," said David, eyes narrowing, "you can't say I didn't try. One thing I never admit to anyone is that I cheat. Some men are like that, and I'm one of them. My daddy and granddaddy were like that, three generations of players," he mused. "I know it's not right, but I can't help myself. I love Lenore and always will, it's just something about the challenge of pulling in women. That's my biggest shortcoming and I'm man enough to admit it. You and Dre, on the other hand, have something different that Lenore and I have. Once again, I'll say I have no reason to lie. My man doesn't either, especially about something as important as this. The condoms belong to me, so you can choose to believe me or not. I'm out of here." He looked at Desiree one more time. "Maybe you need to check yourself, Desiree. Maybe the problem is you aren't ready for marriage."

He went on, turning to Dre, "I'm sorry, man. You know where to find me if you need me." With that said, he departed.

Andre walked over to the couch and sat down next to Desiree. "Is all this really about Mia?" he asked, grabbing her hand.

"Could be," Desiree replied, tugging her ponytail. "She offered excuse after excuse to try to justify her actions. Still, the bottom line is that she's selfish."

"If that's not it, Desiree, then is it your Dad and Mia's not making it? Do you feel our marriage will fail because of what happened with them, or because of Mia's many marriages?"

"Probably all of the above."

"It doesn't matter now anyway. They've been divorced for a long time and have moved on with their lives."

She leaned against him and just lay there for a few minutes, then she pushed away.

"Deja and I both felt we'd never be lucky in love. I still feel such animosity against my mother."

"You know what I think?" he said. "Mia is leading her life and we should all do the same. Maybe something happened to her when she was younger that made her the way she is. Honey, I think you should let it go and try to make up with her, both you and Deja. Let it go, baby, so you can begin healing and become the wife I want you to be. You know if I cheated, I would admit it. Hell, haven't I done so in the past. Don't use Mia or the condoms as an excuse to get out of marrying me, no matter how scared you are."

Tears trickled down her face. She knew he was telling the truth.

"One step at a time," Andre said, rubbing her back. "Ms Desiree Nicole Cooper, would you do me the honor of marrying me on Saturday?" he asked, getting down on one knee.

She took a deep breath, and replied, "Yes, Mr. Andre Jackson, I will."

He stood up, pulled her into his arms and held her tightly. They stood that way for a while. Then Andre kissed her tenderly on the forehead.

He looked upward mouthing, "Thank You, Lord."

They sat back down on the couch.

"Let me tell you about my visit with Mia," Desiree began.

eight

Saturday evening, 6:30 p.m., South Shore Baptist Church...

Desiree stood outside the closed sanctuary door clad proudly in her wedding finery. She was the epitome of a breathtaking bride. Her gown was beautiful, beaded and lacey. The back heart-shaped opening was dotted with tiny pearls. The cathedral train billowed behind her. Rick stood next to her clad in his rented black tuxedo, every inch the proud Papa, dabbing his shiny forehead nervously with a white handkerchief. Desiree peeked in the sanctuary earlier and caught a glimpse of Mia sitting in the back row. Their eyes met and she nodded at her.

The organ strains of *"Here Comes The Bride"* floated through the door. She peeked in and spied Andre fidgeting nervously at the front of the altar, along with David and his groomsmen. The church was brilliantly decorated with red and white roses perched on the end of each aisle. The lights were turned low as candlelight gave the sanctuary an ethereal glow. Deja looked gorgeous in her off the shoulder red silk dress and matching cloth shoes. A tiny red, veiled pillbox hat sat on the side of her upswept hair. The bridesmaids looked their best, coifed, exquisitely made up and wearing red and white dresses. The ushers, Desiree's cousin, Dimitri, and Andre's cousin, Michael, unfurled the white carpeting for her to make the journey to her future husband's side.

She floated gracefully down the aisle as the guests oohed and aahed at her appearance. When she arrived at Mia's aisle, Desiree flashed a beguiling smile in her direction and continued her trip to the altar. When she stepped under the flowered arch, Andre grasped her hand. His loving smile caressed her face. Rev. Smith nodded approvingly.

"Dearly beloved, we are gathered here today to join together this couple in holy matrimony..."

FAMILY
meetings

One

It seemed only a short time ago that Marsha had laid her head on the pillow. She was so very tired and her head throbbed non-stop. It just plain ached, feeling as though someone had used it as a punching bag. The shrill ringing of the telephone startled her, causing her to jump slightly and then stare at the telephone with trepidation. She picked up the cordless telephone, looking anywhere except at the lit caller id. Marsha was well aware that if the telephone rang at one in the morning, it was never good news. She didn't really want to answer because she had a feeling that it was the hospital calling regarding Mother.

"Hello," she said, fretfully.

"May I speak to Mrs. Douglas please?"

"This is she," Marsha said, dispiritedly.

"Hello Mrs. Douglas, I'm sorry to disturb you this early in the morning. This is Ms. Finley at Mercy Hospital. Dr.

Williams has requested you come back to the hospital as soon possible."

"Is it my mother?" Marsha asked, almost timidly, her heart pounding rapidly.

"Yes Ma'am, there's been a change in her condition."

"Is she...?" Marsha couldn't seem to speak the words, her throat choking up. Tears sprang into her eyes.

"We can't give that information out over the telephone. We do need you to return as soon as you can."

"Okay, I'm on my way," Marsha said sadly, clicking off the telephone.

She turned the lamp on and tapped her husband, Howard, on his back to awaken him. He turned over heavily, rubbing his eyes and squinting as the glare of the bright light greeted his eyes.

He asked, although he knew the answer, "Who was that?"

"A nurse at the hospital," Marsha sighed. "She said there's been a change in Mother's condition. Although she didn't come right out and say it, I think she's taken a turn for the worse. They want us to come there as soon as possible."

"Seems like we just got home," He observed, as he arose from the bed.

"Yeah, we did, but you know Dr. Williams said that Mother could go at any time..." she said, her voice deserting her once again.

Howard immediately got up from the bed and began putting on his clothes.

"Come on, get up, Marsha, let's go," he said, as he spied her still sitting inertly on the side of the bed.

He had almost gotten completely dressed while Marsha still sat paralyzed with fear. Her body didn't seem to want to cooperate with the message her brain signaled for her to get up. She was simply unable to move.

"I'm so tired," she moaned.

"I know, baby," he said, sitting down beside her, "but we have to go regardless of how you feel. She's your mother. We talked about this, remember?"

"I know we did," she replied, "but I don't know if I can do this."

"You're strong. I'll be there with you." He reached over and hugged her, then gently pulled her up from the bed.

Thirty-five minutes later, they arrived at the hospital and rode the elevator to her mother, Anna's, room. Marsha began trembling uncontrollably. Howard, seeing her losing the battle with her emotions, slipped his arm around her waist. She leaned into his body, as if seeking strength for what lie ahead. They walked slowly down the hall towards her mother's room. Marsha's feet didn't want to take another step. Finally, they were standing at the door to her mother's room. Stepping across the threshold, the whooshing sounds of the respirator hailed their arrival.

"This is new," she remarked, looking around the room, anywhere but at the bed. "Mother wasn't hooked up to all of this when we left earlier."

In her mind, the machinery resembled a sci-fi monster, although she knew it was the mechanism keeping her mother alive. The drip of the IV seemed unnaturally loud to her ears. Marsha finally focused on the bed and walked over to it. Her eyes filled rapidly with tears as she looked at her mother's pale, ashen face. She lovingly stroked her brow. Her skin felt cold and clammy to the touch.

"Mother, can you hear me?" she asked.

There was no response, she just lay in the bed peacefully, as if in a deep sleep. Marsha turned away from the bed to look for Howard, but he wasn't there. She walked over to the door, peeked out and saw him talking to the nurse.

"Dr. Williams is here in the hospital and he's on his way now," he said, after re-entering the room.

"God knows I can't bear to see Mother like this," Marsha moaned.

"I don't know, Hon. Like you said, perhaps it's time. We'll just have to wait for the doctor."

She sat in the chair next to the bed and waited for Dr. Williams to appear. Fifteen minutes later, he walked into the room, fatigue and sadness imprinted upon his face.

"Hello, Marsha and Howard," he said, greeting them.

"Hello," they both said in unison.

"Is it time? Is Mother … Why is she hooked up to this, this thing?" Marsha asked, pointing at the respirator.

She was incapable of saying the words she really wanted to. Asking if one's mother was dying would be blasphemous to her way of thinking. And Marsha wasn't quite ready to face that fact, even though her eyes told otherwise. She began sobbing softly.

"Marsha," Dr. Williams said gently, kneeling down beside her, "you know we discussed this months ago. I explained this would be the next step. She'll only be on the respirator until the rest of your family arrives."

"I know you did," she cried, wounded to the core of her very heart, "but I just didn't expect it to be like this. And that noise, it sounds terrible."

"I know," he said, "but this is where we are. Anna's heart is failing, as I explained to you it would. Her condition began deteriorating shortly after you left."

"Why didn't you call me on my cell phone then?" asked Marsha, angrily. Her voice rose uncontrollably. "I left the number at the nurse's station."

"I know you did, but you'd been here all day and I personally felt you needed the rest. So, blame me and not the nurses."

"How long?" Marsha asked pitifully, her face dripping tears. She unconsciously began swaying back and forth in the chair.

"Not too long, tonight more than likely. I suggest you call your sister, brother and any other family members you feel should be here."

"Thank you, Dr. Williams," Howard replied. "We'll do that."

"I'll be here in the hospital and will stop by later."

"All right," Howard said, shaking his hand.

Marsha continued to sob, looking at Howard. "I guess it's really time. Now what do we do?" she asked.

Her mind was befuddled. She was unable to take her eyes off her mother's still form.

"The first thing we need to do is call your sister and brother as Dr. Williams suggested. They should be aware of what's going on."

"I can't make those calls, Howard," she said sadly, wiping her eyes.

"I know, Hon, I'll make them."

"Thank you, Howard," she said, weakly. "That'll give me time to get myself together before they get here."

"Now, I want you to calm down. I'll be back in a few minutes." Howard left the room and headed outside to use his cell phone.

Marsha turned back to her mother, got up and sat on the bed next to her. She laid her head gently on her shoulder.

"Mother, please don't leave me, not now. I don't think I can take it. Please, Mother, don't leave me," she pleaded over and over.

Howard stepped outside the hospital door and quickly flipped open his cell phone to call Martha. He glanced at his watch, which read two o'clock am.

Martha answered the telephone groggily. "Hello?"

"Marty, this is Howard," he said loudly, clearing his throat. "We're at the hospital. They called around one o'clock asking us to come in."

"Oh God," she moaned, "it must be time."

Howard answered sadly, "It looks that way."

"Mother, is …?" she asked, with sad resignation in her voice. Like her sister, she really didn't want to know the answer to the question.

"I don't know. It doesn't look good, but she's holding on though."

"I'll see you shortly," she said, more alertly.

Howard sighed audibly as he punched in John's number. John answered quickly on the first ring, as if anticipating the call.

"John," Howard said, "it's me, Howard. Marsha and I are at the hospital. Dr. Williams has asked that the family come in. Looks like it's time. Try to get here as soon as you can."

"Okay, brother-in-law, I'll see you in a minute."

Howard closed the cell phone thoughtfully and hurried back into the hospital. Something told him it was going to be a long night. When he arrived back at the room, Marsha was still standing next to the bed clinging to her mother. Tears continued to trickle down her face.

"Oh Howard," she wailed, as he entered the room, "I think Mother is going to leave me. I just can't take it!" she cried out, turning and collapsing into his arms. He led her over to the chair.

"You've got to hang in there, baby. Remember, we don't want her to suffer. I know it's hard on you, but we've got to put her feelings first and do what's best for her," he murmured, soothingly. "We agreed to do this her way."

"I know," she replied morosely, wiping her face as the tears flowed copiously from her eyes, as if someone had turned on a faucet. "Did you talk to Marty and John?"

"Yes, I did. They're on their way."

"Okay," she said.

two

Mother, or Mrs. Anna Mae Smith, suffered a stroke a year ago. She'd developed a mild heart condition five years ago. That factor, combined with her age of eighty years, didn't make for a good prognosis. Dr. Williams had told them back at the onset of the stroke that at best she'd live another nine months to a year.

Mother has always been a quiet, unassuming woman, who put God and her family first. She's been a widow for the past twenty years. She, Marsha and Howard reside in a converted brownstone, located on the south side of Chicago in the historical African-American community known to Chicagoans as Bronzeville. Anna and her husband John Sr. purchased the family home fifty years ago. Howard and Marsha live in the second floor apartment and Mother on the first floor.

Marsha is her oldest child, followed by Martha (Marty), and her baby boy, as Mother calls him, John Jr. Marsha is fifty-nine years old, Marty is fifty-five years and John fifty years of age.

Marsha and Howard are the parents of two children. Their son, Howard Jr., resides in Michigan along with his wife, Betty, and son, Howard III. Their daughter, Melinda, and son-in-law, Michael, have three children: two daughters, Anita and Jonita, and one son, Michael Jr.

Marty has never married.

John's wife is Cloris, and they're the parents of three sons. John III, who's married to Felicia, is the parent of twin daughters, Asia and Paris. Joshua is married to Janis, and they have one son, Clarence. James, their youngest son, is not married, just like his Aunt Marty.

Mother's stroke had changed life as they'd known it. Though a quiet, reticent person by nature, she's always been there for her family and close friends, be it advice, money or just moral support. Friends and family described her sense of humor as quirky. She's a tall, five foot ten inch, big boned woman in stature and weighs about two hundred and twenty pounds.

You can still see vestiges of the attractive woman she'd once been. Though her face is now wrinkled, jowls now sagging and crow's-feet etched around her eyes, she still possesses a warm, kind smile and believes in spreading God's word to all that pass her way. Her high cheekbones hint of Native American ancestry. Her complexion is pecan brown and her coarse hair has thinned to the point that she wears wigs whenever she leaves the house. Her hair is her one sign of vanity. She's often told Marsha and Marty that they're too old fashioned when it comes to hair. The granddaughters take her hair shopping, as she calls it, every six months. She loves the outing and trying on different colors and styles of wigs, before settling on her usual conventional style that she mostly wears to church. Every now and then, she'll buy one out of character, like braids or an afro wig. Often times, they'd make a day of it and dine out for lunch. When Mother felt up to it, although it's been a while, they'd take in a movie as well.

When she had the stroke, it literally threw the family into a tailspin. Her failing health really drove home the issue that she was getting up in age and her time on this earth was limited. What they didn't see, nor imagine, was the extent of how her illness would drastically change the status quo, life the way it had been. They relied on Mother heavily, and now, she could no longer be there for them as she had in the past. Everyone knows someone like her. That special person you can talk to and not feel judged, tried and convicted.

It was important to Mother that as family crises arose, they discuss them as a family unit, a group. *If you live as long as I do,* she'd often say, *then you know life is full of good times and bad, ups and downs.* She proclaimed that they'd always meet and discuss family problems as a group, and between all of them, they'd come up with a solution to anything. It didn't matter how big or small the issue. She felt by doing things that way, everyone would know that not one of them was perfect and that they're all God's creatures. *We all have our good points and bad,* she'd say, and then add, *no one person is better than the other.* That was the way she believed a family should conduct itself. That became the Smith family philosophy and they practiced it daily.

As Marsha sat in the chair next to the bed waiting for the family members to gather, she recalled that horrible morning just nine months ago.

Sitting at her desk at work, she'd telephoned Mother as she sorted through the mail. The telephone continued to ring and there was no answer. Marsha immediately became alarmed and called Howard, asking him to go downstairs and check on her. While waiting for Howard to call back, she sat hunched over her desk, worried sick. Second-guessing her actions, she wondered if she should've called 911 instead. She tried unsuccessfully to calm down while she continued to wait. Time seemed to slow down, creeping like a snail crossing a road. It seemed it took forever for him to call back. Finally, the telephone rang, and quickly snatching the receiver from its base, she accidentally hit herself in the head.

"Marsha," Howard said, somberly, "I'm down here in Mother's place. I found her unconscious on the kitchen floor. I've already called an ambulance. They should be here shortly, meet us at Michael Reese Hospital," he instructed.

"Okay," she replied, shakily, "I'm on my way."

Her mind went blank for a minute, like a freshly erased blackboard. It took her a few minutes to figure out how to get to the hospital. Then she couldn't remember if she had drove to work that morning or taken public transportation. She knew Marty, a high school assistant principal, was in route to work, and John was already at his factory job. However, she couldn't seem to remember their cell phone or work telephone numbers. Finally, she gave up trying. Her hands shook slightly as she looked the numbers up in her telephone book. She called their jobs and left messages for them to come to the hospital immediately. Then she locked her desk, powered off her pc and sped out the door. As she rode the elevator down to the first floor, she remembered that she had in fact drove to work that morning. Her legs were trembling so badly though, that by the time she got off the elevator, she had decided to take a cab to the hospital.

Marsha is employed as an office manager for a financial planning firm located on Financial Row in the loop, or downtown area, of Chicago. She was able to find a taxicab quickly and the ride to the hospital didn't take very long. After exiting the vehicle, she looked up at the flashing red and white emergency sign and began shivering. She quickly walked through the doors, not sure what might await her on the other side. Once inside, Marsha began walking so fast in search of the nurse's station that she almost walked right past Howard.

"How is Mother?" she asked, breathlessly.

"Honey, she had a stroke," he said, softly.

"A stroke?" she repeated, in disbelief. "Is she conscious?"

"She wasn't on the way here in the ambulance," he said, putting his arm around her shoulder. "They're still working on her. Come on, let's sit down, the nurse or doctor will come to see us when they have something to report," he said, leading her across the room.

She almost tumbled into the hard plastic orange chair.

"Mother, a stroke?" she repeated.

She sat trembling with her hands on her face, shaking her head from side to side. The wait to see the doctor seemed to last an eternity. Thirty minutes later, Marty rushed into the room with John and Cloris trailing behind her. They hurried to the nurse's station. Marsha and Howard got up and walked towards them. Cloris glanced their way as John began questioning the nurse. Once she spotted them, she tugged at John's arm and pointed to Marsha and Howard. All three turned away from the nurse and walked up to Marsha and Howard.

"Any news?" Marty asked.

"What happened?" Cloris asked at the same time as Marty.

"I called her this morning," Marsha explained, in a leaden voice, "but she didn't answer the telephone. Then I called Howard and asked him to go down and check on her. When he got there, he found her unconscious on the kitchen floor."

"My God," said Cloris, "do they know what's wrong with her?"

"Howard thinks she had a stroke, but they're still working on her now."

"So you really don't know if she's dead or alive?" asked Marty, matter-of-factly.

"I assume she's alive since they're still working on her," Marsha snapped, "and they haven't said otherwise. How could you even ask that question, Marty?"

"Obviously, I wanted to know," Marty replied, equally harshly.

"Ladies, ladies," said Howard, quickly stepping between the two sisters. "This bickering isn't doing anyone a bit of good. I suggest we sit down and wait for the doctor to talk to us. I'm sure he'll have something to report shortly."

They sat down in a row on the hard seats, concern and worry lines creased on each face. There was no further conversation after that little incident. Each was lost in their private thoughts. It seemed an eternity before Dr. Williams finally walked down the hall from the emergency room. They all stood up simultaneously.

"Is she alright?" Burst from their lips at the same time.

Marsha's face was a study of terror, John's concerned and Marty curiously detached, as if the morning events had no bearing on her at all.

"We've managed to stabilize her for now," he said, clothes rumpled, his face and body conveying tiredness.

"Is she awake?" Marsha asked, anxiously.

"No, not yet," he said. "We've sedated her and still have more tests to run."

"Was it definitely a stroke?" Cloris asked.

"Yes, it was definitely a stroke," Dr. Williams answered.

"How long will she be in emergency?" asked Howard.

"She won't be here long. We'll be moving her to the cardiac intensive care unit shortly. They're preparing her bed as we speak. She'll need round-the-clock monitoring for at least a couple more days. We should have more tests results available later today. After I study them, I'll have a better picture of what's going on with her heart, as well as what further steps to take."

"Can we see her?" Marsha asked.

"Yes, two people at a time, fifteen minutes hourly. I'll be leaving shortly, but my associate, Dr. Martin, will continue her care in the interim. I'll be back later."

"Thank you, Dr. Williams," Howard said, shaking the doctor's hand.

"If no one has any objections, I'd like to go in to see Mother first," Marty said, narrowly cutting her eyes at Marsha. "I have to get back to work."

"Marty," Marsha said, disapproval written all over her face, "I don't understand you sometimes. How can you think of going back to work at a time like this? Don't you care about Mother?"

"Of course, I do," Marty replied, disgustedly, "but there's nothing we can do right now but wait. Who knows what's going to happen next. We may need to take time off from work anyway, so I may as well go in now and come back this afternoon."

Marsha shook her head in disagreement. "I think you should stay, her condition is serious. My God, she's going to be in the intensive care. We should all be here when she wakes up."

"Marsha, I'm going back to work," Marty said, firmly. "I think we need to talk to Dr. Williams further before we start scheduling days off. As I said before, I'll be back later. If something happens in the meantime, I can always come back."

"Okay, you do that," Marsha said resigned, but her eyes were glaring daggers at Marty. "What are you going to do?" she said, looking at John. "Are you going back to work too?"

"Yes, I am. I'm with Marty on this. I can get back here pretty quickly if something comes up.

"I'll stay with you, Marsha. Today is my off day," Cloris offered, graciously.

She was trying hard to be helpful and keep the peace between the sisters and her husband. At that moment, the nurse walked up to the group. She informed them, two family members could now see Mother. Marty began walking, then stopped and looked around.

"Who's coming with me? John?"

"Honey, go ahead," Cloris said, making shooing motions with her hand. "I'll see her later."

The two walked down the hall and disappeared behind the doors. Marsha sat back down heavily into her seat, watching John and Marty go into the room.

"Marsha," said Howard hesitantly, not wanting to upset her further, "I think I'll go back to work too."

Cloris stepped away a few feet away to give them privacy.

"Howard," Marsha said, her voice wheedling, "I want you to stay with me. I don't really want to be here alone."

"Now Marsha," he said patiently, as if talking to a child, "Cloris has offered to stay with you. Marty is right, we don't know what's to come. As she said, we may need to take days off. Anyway, what's wrong with you staying here with Cloris?"

"I want my blood here, not an in-law," she said haughtily. "What if something bad happens to Mother?"

"Marsha," he said gently, "you're not thinking straight. She's at the hospital where she should be if something happens. I'll try to get off early, that's all I can promise for now. You know Mother thinks of Cloris as her daughter, so blood doesn't matter."

"I'd call Melinda to come sit with me," she remarked, "but I know this is one of the days she had to go into the office to work."

"You're going to have to be a big girl, Marsha. Now, you can stay here alone if you choose to. Personally, I think you should take Cloris up on her offer."

"Okay, okay, I'll ask her if she'll stay with me," she replied tersely, throwing her hands up defensively.

Marty and John emerged from the room. Marty dabbed her eyes with a tissue, and John looked visibly shaken. They walked over to Marsha and Howard.

"I guess I don't have to ask you how she looks," said Howard, somberly.

John replied, as his voice crackled with emotion, "She doesn't look good at all, and judging by all the equipment they have her hooked up to, the stroke must've been severe."

Marty suggested Marsha and Howard go see Mother. She'd wait until they returned before she left to go back to work. John decided to return to work then. Marsha promised him that she'd keep him updated on Mother's condition. Cloris walked with John to the hospital parking lot.

She told him, "I'll call the children and tell them what has happened."

The third generation Smiths was still children in her eyes, even though most of them were at least thirty years old.

"Don't forget to call Rev. Davis," he urged. "Mother would want him to know what's going on."

Back in the waiting room, Marty impatiently asked Howard and Marsha to go ahead and see Mother so that she could get back to work.

"Tell you what, Marty," said Marsha, spoiling for a fight. Her body seemed to pulsate with anger. "Since you're in such a hurry, go ahead and leave now. One of us will let you know if anything changes."

Howard took Marsha's arm and quickly steered her down the hall to the room. As they entered the room, a nurse stood beside the bed checking Mother's vital signs and the IV drip.

"Good Morning," she said, nodding as they walked into the room.

Marsha felt immense terror and despair as she walked toward the bed. Her body drawn tightly, she seemed to quake with fear as she stood silently staring. Mother's face was contorted on the left side, her breathing sounded thin. Odd wheezing sounds emitted from her mouth. For a large sized woman, she looked small and frail lying in the bed, her hair closely matted to her head.

"Are you sure she's all right?" Marsha asked the nurse, nervously.

"Yes, she's doing as well as can be expected," she replied. "We'll keep an eye on her, I promise. You have fifteen minutes, and we ask that you adhere to the rules," she said, glancing down at her watch. "We'll take good care of her," she said reassuringly to Marsha, squeezing her arm as she left the room.

Marsha continued to stare at Mother intently, as if to verify with her own eyes that she was breathing. She watched her chest rise and fall as if mesmerized, all the while tears leaking from her eyes. She gently patted her hair back in place as best she could, her hands trembling. Then she caressed her cheek. Howard was standing at her side, looking worried and patting Mother's hand. They stood watching her until the allotted time was up and then they walked back out into the waiting area.

"I don't like this at all," Marsha said. "She doesn't look good at all."

Marty replied, "I agree with you, but gracious, Marsha, she just had a stroke. The hospital is the best place for her now. Please call me if there's any change in her condition."

"We'll keep you updated," Cloris said tactfully, as Marsha looked away.

After exchanging goodbyes, Marty and Howard departed for work.

Clearly embarrassed, Marsha turned to Cloris and said, "If you don't mind, would you stay at the hospital with me?"

"Of course," Cloris smiled, diplomatically, "she's my mother too."

The women walked to the nurse's station, informed the duty nurse they'd be in the waiting room and asked that she inform them of any changes.

"Are you hungry?" Cloris asked, as they walked back to the waiting area. "It's already ten o'clock."

"My goodness, I didn't realize it had gotten so late," Marsha remarked. "I could use a cup of coffee."

"Me too, let's go to the cafeteria."

"Sounds good to me."

Marsha went to the nurse's station and informed them of their change in plans. Soon, they were sitting in the cafeteria sipping coffee. Marsha thanked Cloris again for staying and calling the children.

"Oh, I didn't mind, not at all. I know this is a tense situation for everyone. I went through the same thing with my father a couple of years ago. It was truly a trying time for us," she murmured.

"I'm trying to be strong," Marsha replied, "but right now, I just feel so scared. What if Mother doesn't make it?"

"It's in the Lord's hands, He knows best. I'm sure she'll be okay. Keep in mind that we don't have all of the test results back yet. So, let's not make any assumptions and just wait to see what the doctor has to say."

"I know you're right," whispered Marsha. "I'm just so frightened." The agony she felt was apparent on her face. "You know, Cloris, it's ironic. As we get older, we don't seem to realize our parents are aging right along with us. I guess in my mind, I thought Mother would be here the rest of my life. Now reality has barged in and I realize she could go at any time. You think you're prepared for these things, but I guess I'm really not."

"Have faith, it'll be okay," Cloris said firmly, patting her hand. "Let's just finish our coffee and see if Dr. Williams has returned yet."

They did just that and took the elevator back up to the waiting room. Marsha and Cloris checked on Mother hourly. She still hadn't regained consciousness. The nurses informed them she was heavily sedated and didn't expect the medication to wear off until later in the afternoon. Finally, by eleven-thirty Mother was settled in CICU. When Cloris got around to calling Rev. Davis, he said he'd stop by the next morning and the entire family would be in his prayers.

three

At twelve o'clock, Dr. Williams came into the waiting room to talk with the two women. The diagnosis was she'd definitely suffered a stroke, leaving the tissues and muscles surrounding her heart damaged. He would continue to run tests to access the severity of the damage.

"Don't strokes affect the brain?" Marsha asked.

Dr. Williams replied, "Yes, they do. When was the last time you talked to your mother?" he asked.

"Um, let me think," Marsha said, rubbing her closed eyes, "around ten o'clock last night. She's a night owl and tends to stay up late at night and sleep more during the day."

"Has she complained of not feeling well lately?" he asked, inputting her answers into an IBM think pad handheld computer.

"Not that I can remember. She always seems to have little ailments of sorts. We just attributed it to old age. Why do you ask?" said Marsha, curiously.

"We're just trying to pinpoint when the stroke may have occurred."

"Let me check with my husband. Howard usually checks on her before he goes to bed, since he goes later than I do."

"If you can find out, that would be helpful," Dr. Williams said.

"How long will she stay in CICU?" Cloris asked. "And when will she be moved to a private room?"

"We'll monitor her vitals tonight, and if all goes well, tomorrow or the next day."

"Is she going to make it?" asked Marsha, frightened. Her heart rate thudded, like horses running the Kentucky Derby.

"Tonight is very critical, as well as tomorrow, so let's wait and see," Dr. Williams advised, cautiously.

"Do you think one of us should stay the night with her?" asked Cloris.

"I don't think that'll be necessary," he answered. "She's in very capable hands, however, that's entirely up to you."

"I guess we need to see what happens in the next couple of days before you can prescribe what sort of treatment will be needed?" Marsha asked.

"You're correct, let's just take it one step at a time," Dr. Williams counseled. "Do either of you have any further questions?"

They shook their heads no.

"Okay, ladies," Dr. Williams said, arising from his seat, "I'm going to continue my rounds. I'll be in the hospital for a couple more hours. Don't hesitate to have the nurses call me if anything comes up. Also remember my associate,

Dr. Martin, will be available for questions." He stood up and shook their hands.

Cloris and Martha looked at each other, and then Marsha said, "I don't know if what he said was good or bad news."

"We'll just have to play it by ear," Cloris suggested. "Why don't you call Howard?"

Howard confirmed he'd seen Mother around eleven o'clock the previous night and that she appeared fine. The two women continued their vigil in and out of her room. As the day progressed, Marsha became tired, her energy level flagging drastically. By the late afternoon, she began feeling very fatigued. She and Cloris dozed off at intervals. Marsha woke up, remembering she'd forgotten to call her son, and left the waiting room to use the telephone. When she returned, Cloris asked how he was doing.

"They're all doing fine. He was upset, of course, when I told him about Mother. They're going to try to come here this weekend to see her," Marsha said.

The nurse informed them that Mother would probably be awake by six o'clock that evening. She added that she wouldn't be able to talk and would only be awake for a few minutes. She also cautioned them not to be alarmed if she dozed off frequently. Her body had suffered a trauma and the medicine was of a strong dosage. Therefore, sleeping and dozing off was considered normal. After the nurse left, they called the family members, urging them to try to be at the hospital when she awakened.

That evening, the Smith family gathered at the hospital en masse. Since theirs was a fairly large group, the hospital provided a small conference room to talk to Dr. Martin privately, who was due to arrive any minute. Dr. Martin walked into the room and greeted everyone. He explained that Mother's vital signs had been fair thus far.

"If there are no setbacks tonight, that would be most favorable. The next few days and nights are most critical to her recovery. If she continues to do well, then we'll move her to a private room in another day or two. Great strides have been made in stroke medication. Dr. Williams and I have prescribed a blood thinner, which she's taking intravenously. We plan to run additional tests tomorrow. I assure you she'll have the best of care." With that said, he asked them if they had any questions.

"What type of permanent damage could be caused by the stroke?" Marty asked, raising her hand as if in a classroom.

"It differs by patient," Dr. Martin said. "Short-term effects include paralysis usually on the left side. The speech could possibly be impaired, and the patient may appear to be confused or disoriented. We'll just have to wait for Mrs. Smith to awaken and study the test results."

"Dr. Martin," Marty said, "it doesn't look like our mother will be able to stay home alone based on your earlier statement regarding the damage to her heart, am I correct?"

"Given her age and existing heart condition, I don't think that it would be advisable," he answered.

"Will she need physical rehabilitation of any kind?" asked Melinda.

"I'm almost sure she will," he nodded.

There were a few more questions, and after answering them all, Dr. Martin excused himself saying, "Dr. Williams or I will give an update to whoever is available tomorrow morning. Don't hesitate to call either of us if you have any further questions."

The family decided to remain a little longer, as Mother seemed to be regaining consciousness. It was decided Marsha and Marty would go in first to see her. The nurse came into the meeting room to report Mother was starting to stir and would be awake very soon. The sisters walked into the hospital room. Mother's eyes were still closed, but fluttered. They both stood on each side of the bed talking to her.

"Mother, open your eyes," Marty said. "Come on now," she urged, "we want to see your beautiful brown eyes."

Marsha crooned softy, "We love you and are we're all going to be here for you."

"You're in the hospital., Marty followed. "I promise you're going to be alright."

The sisters continued talking to her. Then Mother opened her eyes, looking quizzically around the room.

"It's okay, Mother, you're in the hospital," Marty said. "You've had a fall. Everyone is in the waiting room."

Mother moved her head from side to side, looking at both of her daughters. Then she rearranged her cheeks into something resembling a lopsided smile.

"Are you in any pain?" Marsha asked.

She wished to God that she could take the pain herself. It was hard for her to see her mother suffer so. She just lay there and continued to stare at her daughters solemnly.

"Do you want us to call the nurse?" asked Marty.

She shook her head no slowly and then nodded her eyes imploringly at them. She tried moving her left arm, gesturing as if to ask just how bad her condition was.

"They're still running tests," Marsha said, "so they don't know anything definite yet."

She nodded her head, closed her eyes and fell back to sleep suddenly, as if a light switch had been pressed. The nurse came into the room, pointing to her watch and indicating the allotted time was over. They walked back to the waiting room, telling the family Mother had awakened and seemed fairly alert.

"She couldn't talk like they said. There's a tube in her mouth, but she seemed to know who we were," said Marsha, optimistically.

The long, emotional day's events seemed to hit her at once, weariness seeping into her bones. Her equilibrium seemed to be off, leaving her weak and slightly dizzy.

Having noted her appearance, Howard said, "I think we should go home now. Marsha, you've been here all day."

"Oh no," she cried, stubbornly, "I'm not going home. I plan on spending the night with Mother."

"Mom," Melinda said, patiently, "I think you should go home with Dad. I can stay tonight, unless you're staying?" she asked, looking at Marty.

"This is a busy time at work for me," she replied. "Report card day is next week. I'll go home tonight and come back tomorrow. If I can move some things around at school, I'll try to stay tomorrow night."

"One of us should be here with her," Marsha said, clearly agitated. "She's your mother too. We're her only daughters. If I hadn't stayed all day, I'd stay myself, but I must admit I'm tired."

"I can't stay the night and go to work tomorrow," Marty said, nonchalantly. "I told you it's a critical time at work for me. I *have* to be at work."

"Nothing ever comes before your job, does it?" observed Marsha, dryly. "Not even Mother being sick."

"It's okay, I can stay," Melinda interjected, stepping between the two. "Please don't act this way. Come on, Mom," she begged, "we have our hands full coping with Grandmother's illness as it is. It's not a problem, I'll do the night shift until someone comes in tomorrow morning."

"Time out, ladies," said Howard, forcefully. "Let's sit down like adults and discuss this."

"Well, I just want to say, I agree someone should be here at all times with Mother. I just need time to move some things around at work," Marty pronounced, fuming from Marsha's comments.

"It's funny you should say that, considering you can't make the time yourself," Marsha said, contempt dripping from her voice.

"Come on now," John said, imploringly, "we want to do what's best for Mother. Let's try to stick to the subject at hand."

"You're right," said Howard, looking at Marsha and shaking his head as if to say all that was just plain unnecessary.

"I'm sorry, I'm a little tense and tired with Mother and all. Someone should be here with her at all times," Marsha said, apologizing.

"Let's not jump the gun here. Let's wait until we get a report from the doctor before we make long range plans," Cloris added. "At this point, we still don't know how severe the damage is or how long Mother will be here."

"That's true," said Melinda. "I don't mind staying, and luckily, my schedule is pretty flexible. I work from home most days anyway. I went into the office today, so that leaves me open for a few days. I can pick up some of the slack and pitch in mornings or nights, whatever is needed."

"Thank God none of us have small children," added Joshua's wife, Janis. "There's more than enough of us in this family to share in Grandmother's care."

"We should be able to cover all the bases," John said.

"Okay, Melinda, it's unanimous. You stay tonight," Howard said. "I'm taking your mother home with me."

"I can switch my days around if needed," Cloris added.

She works part-time in a department store and retired earlier in the year from her job of forty years at the same factory John is employed.

After further discussion, a consensus was reached. Melinda would stay the night, and Marsha would go home and then come back in the morning. Marty would come in the next afternoon when she got off work and stay the night, if her workload permitted. As soon as they got the results of the tests, they'd schedule another meeting with the doctors to determine the best care for her. That being said, James, being the charming, persuasive man he is, talked the nurses into letting them peep in on Mother one more time without adhering to the "two per hour, fifteen minutes" rule.

Melinda promised to call the relatives if there was any change in Mother's condition. That task accomplished, they departed for home and Melinda settled in for a long night.

four

When Marsha and Howard arrived home, he told her to sit down on the couch and rest her feet, he'd warm up dinner. Having stopped at a local Chinese take-out restaurant before going to the hospital, all he had to do was zap the meal in the microwave oven. Marsha sank into the couch, stretching her legs. They telegraphed, *"no more walking for you today, time out, old girl."* She rubbed her neck and massaged her ankles, informing Howard she was more tired than she'd thought.

Within a few minutes, he brought a hot plate of food to her. While she ate, he went into the bathroom and ran a tub full of hot water for her to soak and bathe in. As she sat in the tub, she began nodding, her head bobbling almost rhythmically. Twenty minutes later, Howard entered the bathroom to rouse her.

"Marsha," he said softly, patting her shoulder, "it's time for you to get out of the tub. Come on, honey, wake up."

"Huh?" she muttered, her eyes widening at him. "Mother's all right, isn't she?"

He encased her body in a large towel as she got out of the tub. She clung to him for a few minutes, and then sagged as the seriousness of Mother's condition began to sink in.

"What's wrong?" he asked.

She replied, "It just dawned on me that Mother could die, Howard." She bit her lip, wondering what possessed her to speak such a thought aloud. Her eyes brimmed with tears. She said sadly, "I should've stayed with her, Howard. I don't know what I was thinking, maybe I wasn't thinking at all."

"What you need to do is rest," he gently chided her. "You're overreacting, Hon. Melinda is more than capable of sitting at the hospital with Mother. If something comes up, she'll call us. We can be back at the hospital in a matter of minutes. Now, put on your gown, before you catch cold," he ordered her.

"I know what you're saying is true, but I still feel guilty. I'm her daughter, the oldest, I should be there with her," she confessed, her eyes streaming tears again.

"If you let yourself get run down," he replied, "you won't be any good to Mother or yourself. Her illness doesn't just affect you," he continued, sternly, "it affects the entire family, and it's something we're going to deal with as a family. No one person is going to take the entire burden upon themselves and that includes you, my dear."

"You're right," she yawned, "I can barely keep my eyes open. I think I'll just go to bed."

"Do that," he ordered as he kissed the top of her head. "I'll call Melinda before I come to bed. I'll wake you up if there's any change. If not, you will sleep, got it?"

"Yes, Sir," she replied, pertly. She was in the bed asleep and snoring before too long.

Meanwhile at Marty's house, she sat in the living room on her favorite reclining chair, re-hashing the day's events. *It's certainly been a long day,* she thought. *I could hardly believe it when I arrived at work and the school clerk gave me Marsha's message to come to the hospital.* She'd instantly become alarmed after Marsha's frantic message was relayed to her. The telephone rang loudly, interrupting her thoughts. Her best friend Constance was on the telephone, inquiring about Mother's condition. Marty explained the situation to her and Connie asked if there was anything she could do.

"She's certainly not out of the woods yet. We're at the point where we just have to wait and see what happens. Mother regained consciousness this evening while Marsha and I were with her. She definitely recognized us and I consider that a good sign. I don't think there's anything you can do at the time. I'll keep that in mind though and let you know if anything comes up."

"I'll be praying for you and the rest of your family," Connie told her. "I know it's been a long day and you're tired. We'll talk tomorrow."

After ending the call, Marty sighed, got up, went into the kitchen and put the teakettle on the stove. She hadn't been at the hospital all day like Marsha and Cloris, but still felt tired and mentally drained as she imagined they did. After the water boiled, she poured it into a cup and dipped a teabag into it. She walked over to the cabinet and pulled out a bottle of whiskey, pouring a hefty amount into the cup.

Her thoughts drifted to Marsha. She shook her head, realizing they'd never really gotten along, embroiled in a case of sibling rivalry that extended to adulthood. For the most part, they'd managed to keep their differences at bay. But with Mother ill, who knows how long they'd be able to cope with the crisis without one of them saying something that they'd regret or, as Mother would say, showing their behinds. *I'll always be the odd person out*, she thought bitterly. *So now, I'm going to have to kowtow to Miss Marsha Ann.* A tear escaped from her eye and she prayed, closing her eyes. "Lord, please don't let my mother die." She sipped the rest of her special brew, rinsed out the cup, turned the lights off and headed to bed.

Marty favors her father, John Sr., in looks, only inheriting Mother's brown complexion. She wears her short hair in an Afro, the same style she's worn since the seventies. Her bone structure is not large like Mother and Marsha's, but more slender. She wears tortoise shell glasses, and her manner is very intimidating and aloof. She's a serious, no-nonsense person and doesn't suffer fools lightly. She believes in speaking whatever is on her mind, she doesn't bite her tongue for anyone, except for maybe Mother. She and John resemble each other greatly, although one can tell all three siblings are related. However, John is heavier. Marsha, on the other hand, looks like Mother's people, big boned, although her complexion is the same café-au-lait complexion as their father's. John and Marty are both tall like Mother, whereas, Marsha is shorter.

Meanwhile at John and Cloris' house, the two lie in the bed discussing the day's events also.

"It breaks my heart to see Mother like that, Clo," he said.

"I know it's hard, baby," she replied, trying to console him. "I went through the same thing with my daddy. It's definitely not an easy thing to see at all."

"Did you see all the machines and tubes in her room?" he asked.

She nodded her head yes.

"For a minute there," he said sheepishly, "I thought she was dead and the equipment was the only thing keeping her alive."

"Dr. Williams explained all of that to us. He wants her as comfortable as possible because of her age."

"I don't know," he murmured. "If something happens to her, I'm not sure what would happen with those two sisters of mine. I feel a storm brewing as it is. Thank God, I'm just the son." "John Smith Jr.," Cloris scolded, "I don't want to hear you talk like that. Family crises sometimes bring out the worst traits in people. I believe your family will be the exception. Mother has always shown us a good example. Adjustments will be needed, no doubt, and unfortunately, this is only the beginning."

"What do you mean by that?" he asked.

"I'm sure Mother will remain in the hospital for a while, maybe a couple of weeks at the most. She'll more than likely need physical therapy, like my daddy. You remember he stayed at that nursing home for a couple of months."

"Damn!" he swore. "You're right, I didn't even think of that. There's no way my mother is going to stay in a nursing home. If we have to bring her here, then we'll do that. Those two sisters of mine are already going at it like cats and dogs, I don't know how we'll survive the feud long-term."

"We'll pray," Cloris said. "If it's the Lord's will, Mother will be alright. We just have to have faith in the Lord. If I have to take a leave from work, I can do that. We'll get through this," she promised.

They lay silently side-by-side, consumed with their own thoughts. Cloris drifted off to sleep and John turned the light out after kissing her softly on the cheek. His last waking thought was, *I'm so glad I have you, baby, to lean on.*

f i v e

Melinda had just come from Mother's room and back into the waiting room. She called home a couple of times, checking on her children. She's a light skinned, pleasant, helpful woman in her mid-forties and resembles her mother. Michael had left the hospital an hour ago to bring her snacks. Since she'd been at the hospital, she completed her work assignments for the week and e-mailed her manager a status report of her projects. One of the nurses brought her a blanket and pillow, informing her to let them know if she needed anything else. Melinda stretched her long legs across the two chairs trying to get comfortable, tossing and turning.

Her mind dwelt on Grandmother. Like other family members, she couldn't get past her declining physical state. It broke Melinda's heart to see her face that way. She'd awakened once when Melinda went in to see her. It seemed to Melinda, she winked at her. Seeing that made her feel much better, uplifting her spirits. *Grandmother recognized me,* she thought, happily.

Howard called later in the evening to get an update on Mother's condition. Melinda told him there hadn't been any change.

"With Grandmother on a respirator, I don't know whether it's good or bad, Daddy," she said, dejectedly.

"Don't go trying to read into things," he warned. "If the doctor has her on a respirator, then there's obviously a need for it."

"Mother seemed awfully tense this evening," Melinda remarked, carefully. "I thought she and Aunt Marty were going to go at it."

"You know your mother," Howard sighed, "she gets a little high strung at times. They'll both be okay. This is just an upsetting situation for the two of them, as well as all of us."

"I guess so," Melinda said, doubtfully. "Anyway, how is Mom?"

"She's knocked out," Howard replied. "I managed to get her to eat and soak in the tub. She's very tired, but she'll be okay in the morning."

"Tell her I'll call first thing in the morning."

With that said, they both got off the telephone.

Melinda was too wired to sleep, tossing and turning as she lay on the couch. Grandmother on a respirator really ate at her. She felt Dr. Williams just didn't want to come out and say the life support unit was the only thing keeping Grandmother alive. The explanation that it was a precaution was just double talk. However, she knew it wouldn't be wise to voice those opinions to the family. Comments like that would set off a chain reaction, and they'd all be back at the hospital, demanding answers from the doctor. Michael came back to the hospital later, bringing dinner and a few snacks.

"I thought at some point you'd get tired of the cafeteria or vending machines." He said, sitting beside her. Noticing the worried expression on her face, he asked, "What's wrong, did something happen to Grandmother?"

"No, but for some inexplicable reason, I feel like the respirator is keeping her alive and it's not a precaution like Dr. Williams said."

"Come on, Lin," he urged, wrapping his arms around her, "could it be your fears about her mortality are making you a little apprehensive? We had a scare this morning, a big one, maybe it's just starting to sink it."

"You could be right," she admitted reluctantly, her eyes filling with tears.

He pulled her into his arms and held her, embracing and rubbing her back. He murmured words of solace, trying to bolster her flagging spirits.

"I know it's tough. I just know that Grandmother will pull through. Do you want me to stay the night?" he asked.

"No, you go on home, I'll be fine. Tomorrow is a workday."

They talked a while longer and Melinda gradually felt herself calming down. He left, promising to come back in the morning to pick her up.

"If you want me to come back tonight," he said, "just call me." He advised her to hang in there and they hugged each other tightly before he left.

Her mind drifted back to more pleasant childhood memories. Grandmother was the official family babysitter. She took care of her grandchildren while the parents went off to their various places of employment. They'd all grown up and continued to live in or close to Bronzeville. Melinda and her family reside in Prairie Shores, a high-rise apartment complex. Marty lives in Lake Meadows, another high-rise nearby with a stunning view of the lakefront. John and Cloris made their home five blocks from Grandmother, Marsha and Howard's house. Their sons live within a block of each other and their parents' house.

The three brothers are employed in the construction business, each armed with their own area of expertise. They are strongly considering starting a family business within the next year. They'd shared those plans with the rest of the family, and that generated many discussions. Before Bronzeville became gentrified, the brothers found, purchased, and later restored, three-story brownstones. It took them a couple of years to complete the project. They'd asked Melinda if she was interested in purchasing a building in need of repair they'd happened to luck up on, but she and Michael declined. With Michael in the military, they didn't want the additional pressure of a mortgage at this time, since he travels frequently.

Back in the day, all of Grandmother's children dropped their offspring off at her house on their way to work. She took care of them before and after school, as well as nursing them back to health whenever they were ill with miscellaneous childhood illnesses. She'd attended school assemblies and plays, piano and dance recitals, and sporting events. Melinda mused, *She's always been there for us.* The cousins married people in the neighborhood and had all grown up together, except Joshua's wife, Janis. They shared a close bond of socializing, as well as vacationing together. The relationships were so close it seemed they were more like sister and brothers instead of first cousins. All holidays were held at Grandmother's house, even now. She prayed to herself, *God, please don't take Grandmother from us yet, I don't think we're quite ready. And Lord, please let Mom and Aunt Marty act civilly, it just wouldn't be right if they don't. Amen.*

The next morning, Mother was still holding her own, she'd had a decent night, there hadn't been any setbacks and she was still resting comfortably. Melinda freshened up as best she could, went to the cafeteria and treated herself to breakfast. When she returned to the waiting room, Dr. Williams stopped by to talk to her. He told her if all continued to go well, Mother would be removed from the respirator. He cautioned Melinda that she wasn't out of danger yet and they'd have to wait and see what the day would bring.

By nine o'clock, Marsha was back at the hospital, looking rested and relaxed. She brought along a change of clothing for Melinda with her.

"Darling, I'm so glad you stayed with Mother," she said. "Your dad was absolutely right, I needed some rest. I feel like a different person this morning."

"She's my grandmother, I didn't mind staying, not at all. Last night, I thought about how Grandmother took care of all of us when we were children. Staying here last night was no problem, none whatsoever."

"What time is Michael picking you up?" Marsha asked. "Would you like to go to the cafeteria and have breakfast?"

"He's on his way as we speak," Melinda answered. "Thanks, but I've already had breakfast. Why don't you go in to see Grandmother? I'll wait until you come back."

"Good idea, I'll do just that," Marsha replied.

Fifteen minutes later, Marsha came out of the room with a smile on her face.

"Melinda, I think Mother winked at me!"

Michael walked in as they were talking. Mother and daughter chatted a bit more and then Melinda left for home, promising to call her later.

Marsha sat in the waiting room, only leaving to check on Mother. Dr. Williams stopped to see her after making his rounds. He reported that Mother was doing fairly well, but he wanted to hold off moving her to a private room until the following day.

"Did something happen?" Marsha asked, fearfully.

"No, I just don't want to move her prematurely yet. Another night in CICU won't hurt at all."

Marsha reported the latest turn of events to the family. When she talked to Cloris, she suggested Marsha ask Dr. Williams to set up a time to sit down and discuss Mother's condition in more detail, specifically what the next step would be and the kind of care that would be needed in the long term.

"That's a good idea, Cloris," Marsha exclaimed. "I'll ask him the next time I see him."

When she got off the telephone, she asked the nurse to page either doctor. Thirty minutes later, the nurse called her to the desk, saying the doctor was on the line.

"Good Morning, Dr. Williams," she began, "I was wondering if you could schedule time to meet with my family to discuss Mother's condition."

He replied, "I have no problem with that, but let's wait until tomorrow. By that time, I should have all the test results in."

"Thank you," she replied, gratefully.

"Sure, no problem," he replied.

"I also wanted to thank you for taking such good care of Mother. There's no doubt in my mind you saved her life," gushed Marsha.

"I try to do my best when treating all my patients. I've been seeing Anna for about ten years now. We've had many conversations and I'm quite fond of her. Now, about this meeting, I assume the family would prefer to talk in the evening."

"Yes, that's correct," Marsha answered.

"Let me check my schedule and I'll touch bases with you later. What I'll do now is tentatively set up the meeting for six o'clock tomorrow evening. That should allow your family plenty of time to arrive here from work. If I have a conflict with that, I'll have my nurse contact you or any other family member at the hospital. How does that sound?"

"That sounds like a plan," smiled Marsha, as she hung up the telephone.

Rev. Davis came to the hospital to visit Mother a little after noon. Marsha explained the events from the day before to him. He'd brought a lovely bouquet of flowers from the church and didn't stay long as she was still in CICU. He and Marsha joined hands as he prayed for Mother. As he took his leave, he asked Marsha to call him for anything the family might need.

"I'll return to visit her in a couple of days," he said. "Remember, call me if anything comes up. Day or night, it doesn't matter. You all will be in my prayers."

"Rev. Davis," Marsha asked, "I was wondering if the senior citizen's center provides rehabilitation therapy? I know there are doctors and nurses on staff, I just wasn't sure about physical therapy."

"Yes, Marsha, we do," he replied.

"I'm almost one hundred percent sure that Mother is going to need rehab of some type. We haven't checked her insurance yet, but I thought I'd ask about that anyway."

"You know, Marsha, it's a sad thing the leaders of our country haven't done a good job of addressing health issues for our seniors. Medical costs have skyrocketed over the past years and most of the elderly are on a fixed income and don't have adequate health insurance. One of our goals was to offer alternatives to traditional health care insurance, and by doing so, address those issues. It isn't always profitable to do business that way and I won't go into specifics today. If there are any problems with your mother's insurance coverage, let us know. I'm pretty sure we can work something out to your satisfaction. After all, she and your father were founding members of the church."

"I'll keep that in mind," Marsha said, grinning from ear to ear. "And I promise to call you if anything else comes up."

"You do that," he replied, smiling at her and patting her on the back before he departed.

S I X

Beautiful floral arrangements continued to pour into the hospital. With Mother still in CICU, the flowers couldn't be taken into her room. Therefore, Marsha distributed most of them to the elderly patients on the hospital's private floors, feeling Mother would appreciate the gesture. At four o'clock sharp, Marty arrived at the hospital. Marsha assured her all was well. Shortly after that, Howard made his appearance, and John and Cloris a little later. Dr. Williams stopped by and reported that if Mother's condition continued to improve, she'd be moved to a private room the next morning. In addition, he had good news to report.

"The nurses are removing the respirator as we speak."

"Dr. Williams, are her facial features eventually going to return to normal?" Marty asked.

"Yes," he replied, "just give it time. We'll talk about that in more detail tomorrow." He left shortly after the conversation.

They walked quietly into Mother's room. The nurse had just removed the life support apparatus. Mother stared at them sadly, with a shaky hand rubbing her face. She intently stared at her left arm for a time.

"You'll be okay, Mother. All of that is a result of the stroke," Marty said.

Mother tried to speak, but only guttural sounds came from her mouth and she shook her head in frustration.

"That's another after effect of the stroke," said Marsha, full of fake bravado. "They're going to schedule you for physical therapy as soon as Dr. Williams gives the okay. All of that will come back, it'll just take time."

She stared at them for a time, laid her head back down on the pillow and turned her face towards the wall.

"Are you tired?" Marty asked. "Do you want us to call the nurse?"

She ignored them.

"Mother," Marsha said, gently, "we know this is difficult for you, just be patient. You've gone through a lot these past couple of days. Recovery will take time."

"Yes, Mother, Marsha is right," Marty interjected. "Please don't shut us out."

She didn't move a muscle and wouldn't look at them. They didn't want to tire her out, so the room was silent for a while. Marsha mentioned Rev. Davis had been to see her and would return tomorrow and that many people had called offering prayers.

The sisters talked until she drifted off to sleep. They left the room, shaken by what they'd just witnessed. Marty walked to the nurse's station and demanded Dr. Williams be called immediately. Hands on her hips, Marty explained to the rest of the family what had just happened. Marsha turned to Howard and began to cry. Minutes elapsed and Dr. Williams still hadn't put in an appearance.

Marty walked back to the nurse's station, irate by now, and asked the nurse angrily, "Did you call Dr. Williams as I asked?"

"We paged him, ma'am. I'm sure he'll be here any minute," the nurse said.

Marty turned away from her and returned to stand with the family. Daggers fired from her eyes as she glared at the helpless nurses. Finally, Dr. Williams stepped off the elevator and walked towards them.

"Dr. Williams," said Marty testily, "Mother wouldn't talk. We expected that, but she even refused to look at us." Marty's body language communicated how furious she felt.

He apologized, saying, "I should've mentioned that possibility. We just weren't sure how she would react. I explained to her earlier this afternoon everything that has happened and told her where we'll go from here. You have to understand her body has sustained a great trauma. Let's not forget, she's also on heavy dosages of medication. No doubt she's feeling depressed. The severity of her condition is a lot for her to absorb mentally."

"I would think it has to bother her not being able to talk clearly," said Howard.

"I'm sure it does. Anna is a proud woman," Dr. Williams nodded, "so give her a few days to settle down and come to terms with everything. If there's no improvement in her mental attitude in a couple of days, we have psychologists on staff. Someone will be available to talk to her."

The family reluctantly agreed. They left the visitor's area and headed to the meeting room, where they sat quietly for a while. Cloris was the first to break the silence.

"Really, Mother's behavior is normal, considering all that has happened. My father was the same way after his stroke. To be honest, no one in the family could do anything with him. He cooperated with the therapists though, which hurt us. They were able to bring him around after a few sessions. Dr. Williams is right, we'll just have to give it time."

"You just don't know," Marsha said, her voice rising a decibel level, "how it hurt me to see Mother that way. My God, she can't even talk."

"She's our mother too," said John, understandably. "Believe me, Marsha, we know how it feels."

"It's a sad thing, that's for sure," Howard said.

"Cloris," Marty asked, "did your father recover one hundred percent?"

"Not quite," she answered, evasively. "He was able to perform menial tasks by himself by the time therapy was concluded."

"Okay, we'll wait and see. Plus, we meet with Dr. Williams tomorrow," Marsha said. "Hopefully by then, he'll have something positive to tell us. So who's staying with Mother tonight?"

Marty indicated she'd be staying. Cloris volunteered to relieve her the next morning since she would have the day off. They all agreed to meet at the hospital the next evening at six o'clock to talk to Dr. Williams.

"Is it really necessary that your children attend the meeting?" Marty asked.

"What's wrong with that?" Marsha and Cloris asked at the same time.

"Realistically, the three of us will be the ones making decisions as to her care anyway. I don't really see a need for all of us to be here."

"Marty, Marty, Marty," Marsha snorted, "you just don't get it, do you? We're still a family and anyone interested in attending is more than welcome to do so. We still make decisions as a family, so I don't know where you get off saying something like that."

"She's right, Marty," Cloris interjected.

John added, "We've always discussed problems as a family, and just because Mother is ill, is no reason to change the program. The subject is closed."

"Well, sorry," said Marty, elongating the word, "I was just asking. Didn't Marsha talk to Rev. Davis about Mother's rehabilitation? That could be categorized as a subject that the family should discuss."

"I didn't make any decisions, Marty, only inquiries. I think that's a little different."

"Whatever," Marty said, shrugging her shoulders. "If no one has anything further to add to this conversation, I'm going to look in on Mother. Maybe I can help get her out of that funky mood," she said, walking down the hall to the room.

seven

At six o'clock the following evening, the family gathered in the same conference room as before. The mood was grave and feelings of nervous anticipation seemed to saturate the room. Soon, both Doctors Williams and Martin walked into the room and sat down. Greetings were exchanged.

"First of all, on a positive note," Dr. Williams began, "your mother is recovering fairly well. We expect she'll pull through. If everything continues to go well, I'll release her next week after physical therapy. On the other hand, I don't want to give you false hope. I believe in being honest with my patients' families. Because of the stroke, the tissue and muscle damage was severe. The damage is of such a high degree that the only means to correct it would be surgery. We could repair the muscles artificially, or put her on the list for a transplant, but your mother has refused to consent to surgery."

"I don't see that as being a problem," Marty said. "We can overrule her if necessary. As a rule, our family generally votes on major issues."

"I thought the combination of physical therapy, along with a medical regiment, produced great results for those suffering from strokes," Melinda commented.

"At this point, physical therapy along with a medication is our only options."

"What exactly are you saying?" asked Marsha, visibly flinching as ominous thoughts filtered through her mind.

Her palms became moist and she unconsciously rubbed them together. A cold feeling of dismay crept into her soul. She knew in an instant that whatever Dr Williams was about to say wasn't going to be pleasant.

"In the long run, we're only men and can't predict the future. However, we do know from experience that due to the stroke, Anna's heart muscles and tissue will continue to deteriorate over time."

"What does that mean in laymen's terms," Marty asked, emotionally. "Are you saying our mother isn't going to make it?"

"She'll pull through this time, but not in the long run, not without surgery," Dr. Williams remarked heavily, his face as stricken as those gathered with him. "We are almost certain your mother will suffer another stroke or heart attack in the future. That one will prove to be fatal. More than likely, she won't survive that one."

The family sat dumbfounded in shock, unable to believe what Dr. Williams had just told them.

"So, you're saying Mother will die?" Marsha whispered, her eyes brimming with tears. "And you won't do anything to prolong her life?"

"Marsha," he answered, sighing, "your mother and I have had many conversations in the past regarding prolonging her life. She was quite adamant that wouldn't be an option for her."

"Could she just have been philosophical? Maybe she didn't mean in reality," Melinda asked.

"I consider your mother a patient as well as a friend. Your mother and I have talked regarding your father's bout with cancer. She felt he suffered unnecessarily towards the end. Her exact words to me were that she doesn't want any extraordinary measures to prolong her life, which includes surgery, resuscitation and life support. When your father was ill, those were her feelings as well, but you overruled her. When I saw her six months ago for her physical examination, she did admit to having slowed down somewhat. I wanted her to come into the hospital at that time and let me run tests then but she refused. She bluntly told me when it's her time, just to let her go and not keep her here, especially if she were suffering. She wants to be kept comfortable and pain free..." His voice trailed off.

"I don't believe you," Marsha said angrily, shaking her head from side to side. "Mother is a Christian, there's no way she'd deliberately try to end her life. She knows that's against our beliefs."

"I assure you, Marsha, I have no reason to lie to you. Those are your mother's feelings and I hope for her sake that you respect them. She feels surgery is for young folks, only to be performed in life-threatening situations, like an accident. I think in the back of her mind she still feels that wouldn't be a good enough reason to prolong her life, not at her age. It's a moot point anyway," Dr. Williams added. "Your mother is in full command of her faculties and she's refused surgery."

The family sat in stiff, stunned silence with shock expressions on their faces. The women began sniffling. Janis and Felicia started sobbing aloud. Melinda shook her head in disbelief. This couldn't be happening, not to her family, and especially not to Grandmother. The grandsons wore stoic, but sad expressions, much like their father's.

"I know this is a lot for you to comprehend and I'm very sorry," Dr. Williams said. "I feel we needed to be truthful about what we're facing here. The physical therapy and medication will allow us to get her back on her feet. She won't be able to do as much physically as she could in the past."

"But what about the quality of her life?" Melinda whimpered. "Will she be in pain? Can she even withstand rehabilitation?"

"We believe she can. Of course, that'll be evaluated. Her left side bore the brunt of the stroke and should eventually return back to normal in a few days or so."

"Will she eventually be able to talk normal?" Marty asked.

"The slurred speech may or may not go away completely. There will certainly be some improvement, maybe not one hundred percent. Although I want to caution you, she may not regain full mobility of her limbs."

"So, she may need a wheelchair or walker?" John asked. Anguish was visible on his face like a burnt suntan.

"Possibly, it all depends on the outcome of the physical therapy."

"Based on what you're saying," Cloris asked, "she definitely can't live at home alone?"

"That's correct. I would recommend someone be with her at all times," Dr. Williams said.

Marsha sat with a dazed expression on her face, not hearing or seeing anything or anybody. She was breathing heavily and her hand fluttered to her chest. *Are my ears deceiving me? I thought I heard the doctor say that Mother isn't going to live for much longer.* Her heart rate accelerated so rapidly that she could literally feel it beating. It seemed she'd gone deaf. She could see mouths moving, but couldn't hear the words. She looked around the room at her family members one by one.

Marty seemed to be fixated on whatever Dr. Williams was saying. John looked pale, like he'd heard the same thing she did, and Howard was staring at her mutely. Cloris' face was downcast and sad. Then her sense of hearing returned and Marsha could hear Dr. Williams asking if anyone had any further questions. His voice sounded like it came from the other end of a long tunnel and she could barely hear him. She shook her head thinking, *Lord, no, not my mother.* Her ears unclogged and she could now hear Marty telling Dr. Williams that they didn't have any further questions for the time being. Both doctors stood up and took their leave, telling them to feel free to call or stop by their offices if they needed anything else.

Feeling an urge to flee the room, Marsha tried to stand up but her legs wouldn't work the way they were suppose to.

She turned toward Howard and said in a tiny voice, "Help me, my legs don't seem to want to move."

"Mom, are you okay?" Melinda asked, worriedly.

She pushed her chair back from the table and leaping from her seat, rushed over to Marsha, a concerned look on her face.

"I guess so, I'm just numb," she said. "I really didn't expect Dr. Williams to say anything like that."

Marty looked at her, eyes full of contempt. "I'm glad he told us the truth. You're always so optimistic. If he hadn't been blunt and just told us straight out what was happening, you would've had her healed and back on her feet by next week."

"That's not fair, Marty," Marsha replied, sobbing audibly. "Unlike you, I have feelings. I still can't believe Mother is going to…."

"Going to what?" Marty said, harshly. "You can't even say the words."

"Marty, that's enough!" Howard said.

John jumped up out of his seat quickly sensing things were about to get out of hand.

"This has been devastating to all of us but we have to think of what's best for Mother," he said. "She's our main concern right now."

"That's true," Cloris added, sniffling. "This has been quite a bit for us to digest. I suggest we think about what Dr. Williams has just told us and meet again in a couple of days to see where we go from here."

"I agree with Aunt Cloris," Melinda said, quietly. "Are you sure you're alright, Mom?" she asked Marsha.

"I will be, give me a few minutes to pull myself together," she said, looking forlorn.

John and Cloris rose and walked over to her, murmuring words of encouragement. Marsha put her folded arms on the table, dropped her head onto them and began wailing. Everyone tried to comfort her except Marty. They got nowhere and left the room to give Marsha, Howard and Melinda time alone. Melinda sat in the chair beside Marsha and put her arms around her as tears flowed from her eyes.

Finally, Howard told his daughter, "Just go on ahead, I'll stay here with your mother."

Marsha continued to cry, then raised her head and said, "Howard, did Dr. Williams say what I thought he said?"

"Come on," he said, pulling her up, "let's go home. We'll talk about it when we get there."

"What about Mother? I need to stay here with her," she lashed out at him.

"She's out of danger, Marsha," he said. "You can come back in the morning. Now come on, let's go home."

Marsha stood rooted to the spot, her legs still unable to move.

Melinda came back into the room. "Mom, do you want me to come home with you? I can if you want me to," she asked.

Marsha replied shakily, "I'll be okay. All of that just threw me for a loop."

Then Marty returned to the room. "Marsha, I'll talk to you tomorrow. I'm not totally heartless. The news has been upsetting to me as well. Let's meet at Mother's house tomorrow after work. I'll call everyone later on and set something up. Maybe by then we all will have settled down."

"Do whatever you want," replied Marsha, listlessly.

"That sounds like a good idea. Go ahead and do that, we'll be there," Howard replied.

Marty took her leave.

"Mom, I'm going to stop home for few minutes and then I'll come to your house," Melinda said, stroking Marsha's back.

"No, that's really not necessary," Marsha said, half-heartedly.

"I'm coming anyway. I'll see you later," Melinda said, kissing Marsha's cheek.

Howard took Marsha's hand in his. "Come on, baby, let's go."

"Howard," she said, "I need to see Mother before I leave. Give me a few minutes."

She straightened up, and with all the dignity she could muster, walked unsteadily to Mother's room. Mother was fast asleep.

"You know what, Mother?" she said, her voice hoarse and cracking. "Dr. Williams just told us the strangest thing. He said you don't want to have surgery or resuscitation if something was to happen. And I can't believe that, because I know you're not ready to leave us. Why would he tell us something like that? Mother, you never gave me a hint of how you felt. I'm having such a hard time with this. I love you and I can't even imagine life without you being here with me. You can't leave us. No, I won't let you." She took her mother's hand. "Mother, Mother," she began wailing, earnestly. Howard then walked in and led her out of the room and the hospital.

eight

During the ride home, Marsha shut down. Howard tried talking to her, but couldn't get through. She sat on the passenger side of the car slumped over and looking dejected. Her face was turned toward the window, eyes unseeing. She couldn't get the words Dr. Williams had spoken out of her mind. Howard parked the car, got out, went to the passenger side of the car and led Marsha out of the car.

As soon as they stepped into the apartment, Marsha ran to the bedroom and collapsed onto the bed. Howard followed closely behind her. He felt that maybe it was best she get it out of her system. Until she did, she wouldn't be a bit of good to herself or anyone else. Marsha sobbed endlessly as Howard rubbed her back.

"Let it out, baby, just let it go."

She cried buckets of tears it seemed. It hurt his ears to hear the sounds of anguish coming from her mouth.

"Shhh," he crooned, softly, "it's going to be okay."

"How could you dare say that?" Marsha screamed loudly. "My mother is going to die! Dr. Williams just told us that! Nothing is ever going to be okay! Just leave me alone!"

Her hair was a mess, all over her head and sticking out in different directions. Slits replaced her eyes. They were almost swollen shut. Her nose was running and the expression on her face was one of abject sorrow.

I've never seen her like this, not even when her old man passed. Howard thought worriedly.

Just then, the doorbell rang. "I'm going to get the door," he said, "I'm sure that's Melinda and Michael."

Marsha lay on the bed unresponsive to his words, keening loudly. He opened the door and Michael and Melinda stood looking bewildered. She had a horrified look on her face.

"What is that noise, Daddy? That's not Mom, is it?"

Howard seemed to shrivel right before their eyes. "I can't get through to her. Maybe you should try talking to her. She's been crying since we got home."

"Oh my God!" she said, running towards the bedroom. Marsha lay half in and out of the bed. "Come on, Mom," Melinda urged, "you've got to pull yourself together. You're scaring Daddy."

"Do you think I really care about scaring your father?" Marsha screamed. "My mother is going to die!" she shrieked louder.

Melinda, seeing the sadness on her mother's face and hearing it reflected in her voice, sat down and just held her tightly. They both cried together for a long time.

In the living room, Howard sat on the couch unmoving, and Michael sat in the chair across from him. Howard sighed loudly.

"This situation is going to be a tough one. Marsha is so close to Mother and this is tearing her up. It doesn't help matters that she and Marty are like oil and water. They do not get along at all."

"I've noticed that," Michael said, hesitantly, "I'm just not sure why."

"I don't think any of us really know why. They've been that way for years. It's the worst case of personality conflict I've ever seen. If Marsha says left, Marty will say right. If Marty says stop, Marsha will say go. Those two never agree about anything."

"I hear you," Michael said. "but will they be able to put those differences aside for Grandmother's sake?"

"That's the million-dollar question, son," Howard said. "I don't really know, that remains to be seen. I do know if they can't, they'll certainly tear open the fabric of the family relationship."

"You're right about that," Michael agreed.

Back in the bedroom, Marsha had finally stopped crying and had fallen into a restless sleep. Her body twitched and she moaned miserably.

Poor Mother, Melinda thought. *All of this has been a little bit too much for her to comprehend. I know Dr. Williams meant well, but maybe he should've talked to her alone.* She pulled the rose-colored comforter over Marsha's shoulders, pulled the door closed and walked back into the living room.

"How is she?" Howard asked anxiously, worry lines furrowed deep in his forehead.

"She cried herself to sleep. I don't know, I guess she'll be okay," Melinda answered, tiredly.

Howard sighed and said, "She just needs time to adjust to all of this."

"Maybe Dr. Williams should've talked to her one-on-one." She threw up her hands in frustration. "In all the conversations I've had with Grandmother, that's one subject we never talked about Dad. What do you think?" she asked, head tilted to her right side much like her grandmother's.

"We never talked about that much either," he admitted. "I remember her being very upset when Father Smith was sick and everyone decided he be put on life support. I had the feeling she didn't agree with that decision. That was my own feeling, so I can't really say."

"Do you think she talked to anyone else about it?" Melinda asked.

"Maybe Mother Patterson," said Howard, snapping his fingers. "Those two are like sisters."

"Dad, do you think if Mom got confirmation from someone close to Grandmother, she'd be more accepting of all this? She really doesn't want to let Grandmother go, but maybe hearing the same things Dr. Williams said from a reliable source would help her to accept what Grandmother wants."

"You may be on to something there," he said, nodding his head. "That's an idea. How are you holding up, baby girl?" he asked.

"Like everyone else, I can't believe it," she answered, sadly. "Like Mom, I can't imagine life without Grandmother. The right thing to do would be to respect her feelings though. She deserves that much, being the backbone of the family. Plus, she's been there for all of us."

"I agree with you completely," Howard said. "The hard part will be convincing your mother. I feel that if we give her time, she'll eventually come around. Meanwhile, I'm going to call Mother Patterson in the morning and see if she can attend the family meeting tomorrow. If anyone knows Mother's feelings, she'd be the one."

Marty again sat in her darkened living room in the rocking chair, facing the window. The stars seemed to mock her, twinkling brightly as if winking at her repeatedly. Her stomach knotted up with a piercing pang so sharp, it traversed the entire length of her body. Her eyes became awash with tears, but she stifled the cry attempting to burst from her mouth. As the tears trickled down her face, she impatiently brushed them away. She stood up, turned on a light and paced back and forth across the room, anger and sorrow cloaking her features. *How like Marsha to perform so badly,* she thought. *I swear that heifer stays in a constant state of denial.*

The telephone rang, startling her and halting the thoughts coursing her mind. Peering at the caller id, she saw that it was her friend Bunny.

"Hello," she said, gloomily.

"Hey, Marty, I thought I'd call and see how things went at the hospital."

"Not good," she admitted, reluctantly.

"Why, what happened?"

"Mother's in worst shape than we thought. Her heart is damaged so badly from the stroke that her health is going to deteriorate over the next year."

"What are you saying?"

"Translated, I'm saying my mother is going to die and the doctor predicated she has a year at best to live."

"Oh no, honey, I'm so sorry. Are you alright?"

"No, not really," Marty moaned.

"Give me half an hour and then I'll be there."

Marty hung up the phone, turned the light back off and sat in the dark, anxiously waiting for Bunny to arrive.

John and Cloris lay in bed.

"I'm so sorry, baby," she murmured, holding him close.

"I know, Clo. This whole thing is tearing me apart. I can't even imagine life and Mother not being a part of it. I can't even say the other word."

"Oh baby, she's tired and just ready to go home. Try to look at it like that."

"I'm trying to, but it's damn hard."

"I know," she replied, gently, "but you don't want her to suffer needlessly. We have to pull together for her. We don't want her last days to be sad and everyone engrossed in self-pity. Let's try to remain upbeat for her, she's entitled to that much."

"I know. You're right, but at this minute, I just feel so helpless. I wish there was something the doctors could do that she'd agree to."

"You shouldn't feel that way, John. Some things are beyond our control," she said. "Think of the beatitudes. There's a time for all things in life and it's almost Mother's time. We've go to let her go with dignity."

"My head knows everything you're saying is right," he sighed, ruefully, "but my heart hasn't come to accept that yet."

"Give it time, honey. All of this will work out in time. Do you think we should call Marsha?" she asked. "She looked pretty bad when we left."

"I think we should let Howard and Melinda deal with Marsha. I guess, like me, she needs time. I just don't understand Marty at all," he said, puzzled by his sister's harsh words. "I thought she was out of line talking to Marsha like that."

"Marty is grieving too. She just shows it differently than the rest of us. She loves Mother, so I know this is difficult for her as well. We'll just have to deal with her ways as best we can right about now."

"I guess so, but I'm not sure about how well Marsha will deal with her," John said, wryly.

"Don't underestimate the two of them just yet. There has never been a time when this family hasn't pulled together, at least not when it counted."

"There's a first time for everything," he predicted.

The doorbell buzzed, indicating Marty had a visitor in the lobby.

She pressed the audio button and asked, "Who is it?"

It was Bunny. Marty pressed the button, allowing her entry. When she opened the door, Bunny stood, appalled at her friend's appearance. She stepped into the apartment and Marty toppled into her arms like a baby taking its first steps.

"Oh baby, I'm so sorry," Bunny cried. "I'd give anything to spare you this."

A neighbor passed by the open door, staring at the women questioningly. Marty slammed the door shut with all her might and began sobbing earnestly. Bunny held her close. Finally, they sat down on the couch and Bunny put her arm around Marty.

"I know this has to be killing you."

"You know what?" Marty said, with tear stained eyes. "I can cope with Mother being ill, it's Marsha's attitude that's driving me crazy."

"I know you two have issues," Bunny said, warily, "but you're going to have to try and put them aside to care for your mother."

"I hear you, but you should've seen her at the hospital, she was disgusting, as usual. When it comes to big sister Marsha, it's all eyes on me."

"Don't you think you're being a little rough on her?"

"No, not at all. That's her problem, everyone has walked around her on eggshells her entire life, catering to her every whim."

"That's not true, Marty. You know she takes care of your mother most of the time. You have to realize that all this has hit her hard. You need to be patient with her. Everyone deals with grief in his or her own way, be it loudly or silently, even your big sister, whose feelings you refuse to acknowledge."

"I know you're right," Marty said, stubbornly. "Still, she just ticks me off."

"Why, baby?" asked Bunny, kindly. "Why does she tick you off?"

"I always felt she thought she was better than me."

"In what way?"

"Mostly because I'm not married and have dedicated myself to my career. I'm sure she thinks I should've followed her lead and put family before career. She's very disapproving of my choices. I sense it every time I'm around her. It's as if I don't fit the family mold because everyone else is married with children. I'm gay, how different can that be?"

"That's all well and good for you to say that, except no one in your family knows you're gay. I know where you're coming from," Bunny said, "but you can't take it out on Marsha. I told you many years ago that you should come out. In all the years we've been together, I've only met your family once. And that was when your father passed. You should've told them long ago, Marty."

"I hear you," she said, wearily, "and I know you're right. To them, I'm strange. In my family's eyesight, I'm the eccentric daughter, sister and aunt. That's exactly how Marsha would judge me and find me sorely wanting."

"You don't know that," Bunny cried. "You never gave her or anyone else in your family a chance to see how they'd feel."

"We should've been born in a different century. It's easier for the young people today, they're so vocal and not ashamed of being different."

"I don't know that I'd call it easier," Bunny remarked. "This is a different era, that's all. I'll grant you some attitudes have changed, but there are still people out there who consider us unnatural."

"You're right about everything," Marty sighed. "I'll try to do better with my sister. That's not to say I'm coming out of the closet or anything. But under the circumstances, I'll try to be more understanding with Marsha."

"That would be great," Bunny said. "This has got to be a terrible blow for you and her, as well as the rest of your family. How are you coping with everything?"

"I'm okay for the most part," she whispered. "Then it hits me like I've been struck by lightening, that Mother is going to die. If I say it aloud or think it, I feel overcome with grief. God, it hurts so badly." She began weeping.

Bunny engulfed Marty's body in her arms. "I'll stay with you tonight. You're not going through this alone, I'm here for you and I'm not going anywhere."

nine

Marsha awoke the next morning, not even remembering going to bed. Then thoughts of yesterday's discussion popped into her mind. She looked around for Howard and found a note on his pillow stating he'd gone to work and would call her later. He'd also called her job, so she had the day off. She lay lost in thought until the telephone rang, removing her from her reverie.

"Hi, Mom, it's me," Melinda chirped. "I just called to see if you're feeling better this morning and wanted company when you go to the hospital."

"Hmm, I'm okay," Marsha said, lifelessly. "I just woke up. Your dad called my job for me, so I have the day off, but I suppose you knew that."

"Yes, I was aware of that," she admitted. "I talked to Dad earlier and we put our heads together and decided a day off for you was in order."

"Did you talk to Marty?" asked Marsha, her stomach clenching.

"Yes, I did. She's gone to work. Janis went back to the hospital last night and stayed with Grandmother. Aunt Marty wants all of us to meet at Grandmother's this afternoon at five o'clock."

"Humph," Marsha snorted, in response to hearing that.

"Are you dressed, Mom?"

"I told you I just woke up," she replied, irritated.

"I'm on my way. When I get there, I'll fix you a nice breakfast. Then we can go see Grandmother."

"Fine, I'm getting up now," Marsha said, reluctantly.

Melinda arrived at Marsha's house within an hour. She let herself in and walked into her parents' bedroom. Marsha hadn't moved a muscle since they had gotten off the telephone.

"Mom, what have you been doing?" she cried. "Why aren't you up?"

"I was thinking and lost track of time."

"Why don't you hit the shower and I'll start breakfast."

"Okay, Melinda, I'm going," she said, in a grouchy tone.

Forty-five minutes later, they'd eaten, and mother and daughter were in route to the hospital. When they arrived at Mother's room, she was sitting up in the bed.

"Well, look at you," Marsha said, smiling at her half-heartedly. "This is good."

Mother attempted to speak, but her speech was still unrecognizable. She motioned to the nightstand where a pen and pad lay. She indicated through hand gestures that she wanted the items brought to her. She wrote laboriously, the tip of her tongue sticking out the side of her mouth.

She wrote, "I feel better. I got sick and fell."

"Yes, we know Mother. You're getting better," Marsha said.

"How long will I be here?" she wrote, slowly.

"Another week or so, after you're done with a few therapy sessions."

"Okay," she wrote in bold slanting letters, then dropped the pad and fell back onto the pillow.

"That's enough writing for now. Looks like they gave you real food today," Marsha remarked.

Mother frowned, lay back on her pillow and dozed off to sleep.

"I'm going to see if Dr. Williams is in the building," Marsha said, a little later. "I'd like to talk to him."

"About what, Mom?" Melinda asked.

"I just want him to explain to me again what he thinks Mother wants."

"Please give it a rest. I think maybe hearing about Grandmother the way you did yesterday was too much for you. Let's try to concentrate on her and getting her back in a state where she can come home."

"You're right," Marsha admitted meekly, glancing over at Mother. "I can't stand seeing her this way."

Melinda, noting Marsha's troubled expression, reached over and squeezed her hand. "It's going to be okay, Mom. Keep your head up, things will get better."

At five o'clock that evening, the family gathered for the second day in a row. This time the meeting was held at Mother's house. Most sat at the large oak table. Howard was not present. Cloris looked around the room, noticing he was not there and asked of his whereabouts.

"He went to pick up Mother Patterson," Melinda said. "We talked last night and thought she'd be the one person who knows best what's going on in Grandmother's head. So Daddy has gone to pick her up and bring her to the meeting."

"Good idea," said John, nodding his head in approval.

"I'd like to take this time," Marty said, squirming in her seat, her eyes downcast, "to apologize for my behavior yesterday, especially to you, Marsha. I'll try to behave better in the future," she said, huskily. "Please forgive me if I backslide."

Clearing his throat, John said, "Apology accepted. We're all going to get a little testy at times. Let's try to remember this is about Mother and not let personalities and egos get in the way of her health issues."

"I'm sorry too," said Marsha humbly, somewhat subdued by Marty's admission. "I may have come off as a drama queen yesterday. It just never occurred to me that Mother could be that ill. I guess I was in denial and selfish, I'll try to work on my attitude too." Melinda gave her a reassuring smile, nodding her head approvingly.

Howard walked in the house with Mother Patterson in tow. John got up quickly, offering her his chair. He and Howard stood along the dining room wall.

"Thank you for inviting me today," Mother Patterson said, in her dry raspy voice. "My prayers go out to all of you and my good friend, Anna. Let us pray," she commanded.

Everyone bowed his or her heads as she earnestly appealed to the Father above, and heartfelt Amen's resounded in the room when she was done.

Marty, looking about the table, cleared her throat and said, "Mother Patterson, we asked you here today to see if you had any thoughts about Mother's wishes regarding her medical care." She quickly brought her up to par about the discussion they had with Dr. Williams the day before.

"We wanted to talk to you," Melinda began, "because according to Dr. Williams, Grandmother has refused surgery and life support. She doesn't want anything done to prolong her life. We've talked many times, but I don't ever remember her saying anything like that."

"Well," Mother Patterson said loudly, taking her position as the family advisor seriously, "Anna and I have been friends for over sixty years and talked about that very subject on many occasions. In fact, we talked about it just last week."

Loud murmurs broke out among the family.

"Really?" asked Marsha in disbelief. Her eyes narrowed as she peered at Mother Patterson.

"Yes, we did," she asserted. "You children have been such a joy to Anna, she felt blessed to have such a supportive family. She was most proud of how you could discuss family issues without a lot of fighting and arguing and come together for the good of the family. So many families are unable to do that. Before your father passed, and being with him most of the time, Anna knew he was in extreme pain. Like many married couples, his pain became hers. Many times, she'd sit by his side and watch him suffer, delirious with pain. She'd tell me sadly, *'Sister, my John is suffering so.'* She felt torn as a Christian cause of her thoughts about eutha, …what's that word?"

"Euthanasia," Marty supplied.

"Yes, she felt torn about that word. We're both firm believers that our time on this earth is determined by our Father above, not man," Mother Patterson continued. "But on the other hand, she hated seeing John suffer so badly. She's been feeling poorly lately, especially these past couple of weeks. Anna told me Dr. Williams had been asking her to come into the hospital for tests and I urged her to tell you."

"Well, why didn't you say something to us?" Marty asked shrilly, her voice rising in frustration. "Mother Patterson, don't you think had you said something to us, at the very least we could've taken her to the hospital for those tests?"

"One reason I didn't is because I know you would've made her go. As far as I'm concerned, she's still capable of making decisions for herself."

"But she's now in the hospital recovering from a stroke," Marsha pointed out angrily, her nostrils flaring. "If you had said something to us, maybe it could've been prevented."

"I did what I thought was right at the time," Mother Patterson replied, her voice quivering and her eyes glistening. "The other reason is because Anna feels her time on this earth is almost up and she's ready to go to glory. I just couldn't interfere with that, especially not with Anna. She knows her body and she's ready. So, yes, I can attest to the fact that she doesn't want her life prolonged," she added.

"Thank you, Mother Patterson," said Melinda, wiping her eyes, as were most of the women in the room. "You've helped us understand her thoughts."

"All you had to do was ask her." Mother Patterson smiled through her tears. "Anna is my best friend and we've remained that way all these years because we respect each other's feelings. Even if we don't necessarily agree with each other, we still respect each other's feelings."

"Mother Paterson," Cloris said, relieved, "you've explained a lot of things about Mother that we weren't aware of, and I personally think we too have to honor her feelings in this matter."

"I agree with Cloris," said Marty. "Sometimes older people can sense those things."

"Then I guess I'm outnumbered," said Marsha, shaking her head from side to side sadly. "It's so hard and alien to me, the thought of just letting her go and not doing anything about it. I really don't know if I can go along with this."

"Marsha, honey," said Cloris soothingly, "it's not up to us to do anything. All things are in our Father's hand, he knows best. What we need to do is make an effort to spend as much time as we can with her. Make sure her last days are happy and keep her as comfortable as possible. My sisters and I wasn't as responsive to my father's needs and I regret it to this day. We had many disagreements as to his care. It was an ongoing nightmare. I would love to do anything I can to make Mother's last days peaceful."

"Amen," said Howard.

John added, "I agree with Cloris, Marty and Melinda."

Some of the tension seemed to seep from the room, except at Marsha's end of the table, the agony she felt was apparent to all.

Marty, seeing her mixed emotions, remarked, "In light of her feelings about Daddy, we really have no choice but to honor Mother's wishes. She went along with us when it came to his care. She's our mother and we owe her that much." Heads nodded in agreement, except for Marsha.

"I don't agree with you at all," Marsha said, dejectedly, "but since our family discusses, and majority rules, then I guess I'm outnumbered." She held her hands up in surrender.

"Mother Patterson, thank you so much. We're really glad that you could clear some things up for us. Would you like to stay and have dinner with us, or would you prefer that I take you back home now?" Howard asked.

Mother Patterson had been a resident of the senior citizens home for years.

"If you don't mind," she said, looking around the table, "I'd like to stay here with you all. Anna is not only my best friend, but like a sister to me. I'd really like to help in anyway I can."

"Then by all means, please stay." Cloris smiled.

"Here is where we stand," John said. "Mother will be in the hospital another week probably. Then her physical therapy outside of the hospital will begin. I suggest we set up a schedule, rotating dropping her off and bringing her home among ourselves. Since Dr. Williams has already advised us that she shouldn't be at home alone, someone will need to be with her at all times."

"Howard and I are just upstairs," Marsha cried, "we can stay with her."

Howard added, "We can move our things into the second bedroom."

"Cloris and I can stay with her on the weekends," John volunteered.

"Michael and I can do the same when needed," Melinda offered.

"Don't leave us out," cried Janis and Felicia. "We'll do whatever is needed, take her to physical therapy, the doctor or whatever."

"I think we need to get the great-grandchildren involved too. That'll give them time to spend with her," Marty suggested, glancing around the table. "Perhaps they can sit with her after school or on the weekends."

"That's a good idea," Marsha said.

"We're all going to share in her care," Howard announced. "Thank God there are enough of us to go around."

"Does anyone know if Mother made a will?" Marty asked.

"Yes, she did," Mother Patterson answered. "I witnessed it and I have a copy of it at my place."

"Now I wonder when that happened," Marty remarked.

"I didn't know anything about a will. I sure didn't take her," Marsha added.

"I'm the guilty party," Cloris stated, holding her right hand up as if she was on the witness stand and testifying in court. "She asked me to take her and I did."

"Are there any other secrets you're privy to that we aren't?" Marty asked, snidely.

"No," Cloris said defensively, her face red, "I just sat in the car and waited for her until she was finished."

"Hmm," Marty said, "Mother has been a very busy bee. I wonder what's in it."

"Me too," Marsha said, thoughtfully.

Everyone was satisfied with the outcome of the meeting, except Marsha. She still had reservations about the whole thing, but had no choice except to go along with the program.

Melinda ordered pizzas for dinner and Howard and John went to pick them up. When they returned, the warm pies emanated a warm spicy aroma. There was a mad dash to the kitchen and into the boxes. Everyone had worked up an appetite by then and dug in.

When the family had finished eating and ready to go home, Howard proclaimed, grinning broadly, "This is what family is about."

Melinda offered to setup a rotation schedule when the details were ironed out, and would e-mail everyone with their assignments. They hugged, promising to stay in touch. Marsha, Howard, Marty, John and Cloris made a quick trip back to the hospital. It was late, but they just wanted to reassure Mother they now understood what she wanted them to do.

When they walked into the room, she lay in the bed, eyes closed and the television turned low in the darkened room. She opened one eye and smiled crookedly at them as they approached the bed.

"Mother," Marsha said, struggling with her emotions, "we understand, although I don't really. We'll abide by your wishes. We talked to Mother Patterson and she cleared up some things for us."

"Goo," Mother croaked out. She picked up the pen, positioned her right hand and wrote slowly and painstakingly, "Took you long enough."

ten

Mother was released from the hospital two weeks to the day she was brought in. During the course of the physical therapy sessions, she made strides, but not as great as the family would've liked. She'd learned to use a walker to get around, but still tired easily. When she'd become impatient and felt like giving up, Dr. Williams would urge her to take a break and take it easy. Her facial contortion cleared as he said it would, and her speech would slur slightly when she became fatigued. Just like they said they would, Marsha and Howard set up camp in the second bedroom.

The women took off work the day she came home, preparing a feast of Mother's favorite dishes. Mother Patterson and Rev. Davis attended as well. After they were done eating and the dishes washed and put away, Marsha, Marty, Cloris and Melinda set up a schedule of Mother's care, dubbing themselves *"Mother's Attendees"*.

Marsha mentioned she'd talk to her boss and as the time got closer, she was going to take a leave of absence from work. Cloris added she was going to quit her job. She could always find another part-time job in retail and expressed her regret in not doing the same for her father when he'd gotten sick.

Janis suggested that they check with Mother to see if she might want to go on a trip. They ran the idea by Dr. Williams and he said it was up to Mother.

As the months passed, everyone pitched in and did their fair share of taking care of Mother. As promised, Melinda wrote a weekly schedule detailing everyone's assignment and e-mailed it to them every Friday. The great-grandchildren contributed also, stopping by the house after school or on the weekends to sit and talk with Mother. She'd recall memories from her childhood, telling them about the olden days, as she called them.

Marsha asked Mother one morning, six months after her stroke, if she felt up to taking a trip.

"I would like that," she chuckled. "I'm just not sure this old body could handle it."

"I talked to Dr. Williams and he said it was up to you."

"I sure wouldn't mind seeing the old family home one more time," she said, wistfully. "How would we get there?"

"We could drive or fly," Marsha answered.

"Let me think about it."

"Not a problem. Just let us know whatever you decide to do."

A week later, after she'd finished breakfast, Mother called Marsha into the bedroom and said, "I'd like to go home one more time."

"You're feeling okay, aren't you?" Marsha asked, fearfully.

"I'm doing tolerable this morning. I just want to see my parents' graves and walk the land one more time."

"I don't know about all of that," Marsha laughed, "walking the land, I mean." She sat perched on the chair next to the bed. "Walking may not be a good idea."

Mother grumbled crossly, "I'm not talking about a hike, Marsha, just a little walking."

"Okay," Marsha held up her hands in surrender, "give me a week to set it up."

Seven days later, Mother, Marsha, Marty and John were at Midway Airport. They booked a Friday afternoon flight, returning Monday morning. The entire clan went along to the airport to see them off. The grandchildren urged Mother to hurry back.

They landed at the Little Rock Airport three hours later, collected the luggage and rented a car. Their plan was to stay in Little Rock that night and then they would head to Woodson the following morning.

After checking into the hotel, they decided they'd stay there the rest of the evening since Mother appeared slightly fatigued from the flight. Marty gave her a dosage of her afternoon medication and settled her into bed. Afterwards, Marty and Marsha walked back into the sitting room and sat down tiredly on the couch.

"We're certainly not as young as we used to be," remarked Marty.

John had just gotten off the phone with Cloris. When he finished his call, Marsha called Howard, reporting they'd arrived safely and requested he call Melinda and let her know. She concluded the call after promising to call him tomorrow.

"Who would've thought we'd be in Arkansas, just the three of us with Mother," John observed.

"Not me," Marty said, "we haven't been down here in I don't know how long."

"I don't know about you two," John said, "but I'm hungry. Those peanuts and pop they served us on the airplane didn't do me any justice. How about ordering something from room service?"

"Count me in," they both said.

The three spent the rest of the evening reminiscing about their childhood visits to Arkansas and how nice it would be to go back to the family place. Later, John retired to his room saying he was tired and for them to be ready to head out to Woodson at nine o'clock the next morning.

Marsha and Marty sat on the couch and continued talking. Mother had awakened, complaining she was hungry and they ordered room service for her. After eating, she drifted back to sleep, saying she needed her rest for the next day.

"Marty," Marsha began, smiling brightly, "I'm so glad we called a truce. It's been really nice having you in my life again. I don't think we've been this close since we were young girls."

"Lord knows, we're not young or little anymore," Marty said, patting her hips. "This time has been nice, it's just too bad it took Mother getting sick to bring us together."

"You think John went out prowling?" Marsha asked.

"I doubt it," Marty replied. "You know he's true blue to Cloris. Although when we get to Woodson and he hooks up with the cousins, all bets are off then."

"I've been meaning to ask you, and if I'm being too nosy, just tell me to shut up." Marsha said. "Do you have a boyfriend? We haven't seen you with a man in ages."

"Actually," said Marty, taking a deep breath and praying she was making the right decision to bare all, "I have a confession to make and I don't know any other way to say it except to just come out and say it, I'm gay."

"Say what?" Marsha said, with a surprised look on her face and mouth open.

"I'm gay," Marty repeated. "You know, I think this is the first time I've said those words to anyone except Bunny."

"Wow," said Marsha, stunned, "you don't play when it comes to confessions. That's a big one. So this Bunny, is she your friend?"

"Yes, she is. We've been together for ages. She'd like us to live together when we retire."

"Didn't she come to Daddy's funeral?" asked Marsha.

"Yes, she did. I'm surprised you remember her."

"That's something. I don't know what to say behind that. I'm glad you decided to share that with me though," she said, patting Marty's hand.

"Bunny tells me all the time that I should've told the family a long time ago, but I never felt comfortable with the idea," Marty admitted. "She was married to an abusive man, whom she has since divorced, and she has two children. Before you ask, yes, her son and daughter know about us and are comfortable with us as a couple."

"That's good," Marsha said, looking at Marty with amazement. "This is so unbelievable. When did you know you were gay?"

"Probably since I was twenty years old for sure. I have another dark secret to reveal. I don't know if you were aware of it or not, but I was raped by a man in the neighborhood when I was fifteen. That kind of turned me off of men."

"That's a family secret for sure," Marsha replied. "I never heard a word about that."

"After that happened, I haven't had anything resembling lust for a man."

"What about getting counseling? Did you see someone?"

"No, not right after it happened. Later I did, while I was in college, but after a while, I stopped going. I never followed up on it, because I knew deep in my heart, even then, I was different. I met Bunny, her given name is Bernice, when I was thirty years old and we've been together since then."

"That had to be tough on you, keeping that secret for so many years," Marsha remarked.

"It has been, but that's life when one chooses that route. I guess since I'm on a roll, I might as well fess up to something else," Marty continued. "I've disliked you for most of our adult life."

"I know that," Marsha said matter-of-factly, nodding her head. "I just never understood why."

"At one point, it was because you were everything I wasn't. The dutiful daughter who did all that was expected from her and more. You married Howard and produced grandchildren for Mother and Father. Somehow, I knew I'd never have any children."

"It's too bad you felt that way, Marty and I wish we had talked about this before now. You could've adopted a child if you wanted to. I only went to a secretarial college and you graduated from the Chicago State University. You have a couple of master degrees, instead of just a certificate. I guess we both knew what we wanted even back then. That feeling you had about being gay, I always knew that I was destined to marry and have children. I have loved Howard since I first laid eyes on him. Speaking of family secrets or confessions, I bet you didn't know I was pregnant with Howard Jr. when Howard and I got married, did you?" Marsha asked, coyly.

"Not you," Marty teased, "not Miss Perfect. No, I don't believe it."

"Yes, me. Father was quite upset with me and asked me, in his dry way, why I couldn't exercise self-control."

Marty burst out laughing. "Imagine what he'd say about me."

The sisters laughed until they cried. Their father was such a stern and upright man.

"Mother took my side, in her equally dry way, and told him we'd planned to marry anyway. All we had to do was move up the wedding date. We made a pact that I'd go to secretarial school if she talked Father into letting us marry early. She felt I needed something to fall back on if things didn't work out with Howard. I didn't really want to continue going to school because I felt my role in life was to become a wife and mother. Little sister, I was so jealous of you, especially after you received your second master's degree. I don't see how you could remotely be jealous of me in any way."

Marty mused, "It appeared to me that you accomplished more from a traditional family perspective, husband, children and job, even though I knew that lifestyle wasn't for me. Shoot, everybody loves and admires you. You're the chosen golden child. Me, I'm just oddball Marty. I also have issues with the close relationship you and Mother share. I felt there wasn't love left over for Mother and me to share."

"Oh no, Marty, you're wrong. Mother loves us all the same, unconditionally," Marsha said. "I know I'm probably more possessive of her than you and John because I'm the oldest. Hey, I was jealous of you when you were born and took Mother away from me. Everyone in the family goes to you for financial advice and money."

"Trust me, Marsha," Marty chuckled, "that's one role you don't want to play."

"I don't know why not," Marsha smirked, "it's such a prestigious one. I wish Howard and I could've been more financially secure. We've had a comfortable life, but not a lot of money at times. You know that yourself from the times I've borrowed money from you. I know John's boys have talked to you about investing in the construction company. You may not actually have any children, but you've been like a fairy godmother to all of ours. You've helped with tuitions and anything else the kids needed. I've always hated I couldn't do more from that standpoint. Melinda and Howard Jr. would tell me about your sending them money from time to time when they were in college. It was a bitter pill for me to swallow, having to ask my younger sister for money when times got rough for Howard and me."

"I've never minded helping out, not in the least bit. I don't have anyone to spend my hard earned money on, except my nieces and nephews. You know Mother, buy her a new wig every few months and she's happy. She budgets her money wisely and the brownstone is paid off."

"I want to say this," Marsha said. "Because of Mother's failing health, I've had a lot of time to reflect on my life. I should've done so many things differently, including mending our relationship sooner than now. I think we've come closer to doing that tonight than we have in a long time. I'm so sorry for any pain I may have caused you in the past. I hope you can forgive me and we can move past this." Said Marsha anxiously, her eyes begging forgiveness from Marty.

"I've played my part in all this too and I'm sorry too," Marty confessed.

They hugged each other.

"This is a real Kodak moment as Melinda would say," Marsha laughed. "Now, let's go to the bed so we can push out in the morning. You know John, he hates to be kept waiting."

The beautiful lush, emerald green rolling hills of Arkansas provided a backdrop of beautiful scenery along the drive to Woodson. The mountains seemed to simmer in the bright dazzling sunlight. Mother was seated comfortably in the back seat, looking out the window, shaking her head from side to side.

"I stayed away too long, I feel a true sense of homecoming. I've really missed Arkansas." She then switched subjects, asking John playfully, "Is it my imagination, or do you detect a change of heart between your feuding sisters?"

"No, Mother, I see it too," he answered, glancing at her in the rearview mirror. "These two are definitely gentler and kinder," he laughed.

Marty and Marsha looked at each other and smiled.

"I guess you could say that," Marsha replied.

"Um, hmm," Marty seconded.

eleven

They arrived in Woodson in an hour. Marty had created a map from the Internet on her home computer, so she sat beside John in the front seat directing the way. When they pulled up in front of their cousin, Elmira's, house, John honked the horn a couple of times and she came rushing out the house, her plump face wreathed in smiles and her family closely behind her.

"Anna!" she said, hugging Mother. "I'm so glad you've come to see us. It's been a long time. Come on in," she instructed, ushering them into the house. Everyone exchanged hugs and kisses. "Why don't y'all go to the bathroom and freshen up. I'll have supper on the table by the time you finish."

After they'd eaten a hearty meal, John pushed his chair back from the table and rubbed his stomach. "Now that's what I call a spread," he said, laughing.

"That meal was simply wonderful, Elmira," Marsha said, gushingly. "I hope you'll allow me to take some of your recipes back home with me."

"Of course, you can. We're all one big happy family, sugah," Elmira replied, smiling. "Just let me know which ones you want."

Mother said, "I'd like to lie down for a while."

"Anna, I have a big ole comfortable bed with yo' name written on it," Elmira said. "Come right this way." She led her into one of the bedrooms. "You take as long as you want, we'll be in the front room when you wake up."

Marty and Marsha followed her into the room, making sure Mother was comfortable. They came back into the living room and talked with the cousins, catching up on events in their lives. Marsha and Marty brought pictures of the family with them. For a time, they exchanged photos of each other's family.

"Is Anna feelin' all right?" Elmira whispered to Marsha and Marty.

"She had a stroke earlier this year. Her health has been so-so since then," Marty answered, shrugging her shoulders. "We decided a change of scenery just might perk her up."

"It was so nice of all y'all to bring her here," Elmira drawled.

"I just love it down here," Marsha said, enthusiastically. "Do you think I could talk Howard into moving down here when we retire?" she asked Marty and John.

"Fat chance of that," John grunted. "Howard is a city boy through and through, he'll never leave Chi-town."

"You're probably right about that," Marsha sighed, then her face brightened like a light bulb had been turned on. "Maybe I can persuade him to come down here on our next vacation."

Mother awakened a short time later and announced she was ready to go to the cemetery. Elmira came along with them.

"Marty, where's the camera?" Mother asked, impatiently. "I want you to take pictures of my people's graves. I promised the greats I'd bring some back with me."

"It's right here, Mother," she replied, removing the camera out of the bag that dangled on her shoulder. "Just tell me what you want."

Once there, they didn't stay long as Mother began wiping her dripping, sweaty brow. "I'm starting to get hot, let's go back to the house," Mother said.

"Do you feel like going uptown, Anna? It's really come up a lot since the last time you were here," asked Elmira.

"If John turns up the air conditioning, I think I can do that," Mother said.

They drove through the small town, noting there had indeed been many improvements since the last time they'd visited. New factories and a movie theater had been erected. The town even boasted a McDonalds restaurant. The school had also been rebuilt. Mother requested that John drive by her family homestead on the way back to town. She seemed to be lost in thought as she sat in the back seat, her head reclining against the headrest and her eyes closed.

"Mother, do you feel okay?" Marty asked, becoming concerned.

"I feel fine," she replied, smiling. "Being home just brought back a lot of memories. This trip was the best medicine in the world for me."

When they arrived back at Elmira's house, Mother told them she felt a little hot and tired and wanted to rest for a little while. Marsha sat in the big cozy kitchen with Elmira, jotting down recipes. John was chewing the fat with several male cousins, engaged in a lively discussion about the pros and cons of city life versus country life. After sleeping a couple of hours, Mother awakened, ready to enjoy another southern home cooked meal and then head back to Little Rock. Elmira and her daughters once again provided them with an appetizing supper.

Before they could get up from the table, Elmira cried admonishingly, "Y'all can't leave here without eating some of my famous pound cake and homemade ice cream."

With that announcement, chairs were promptly pulled back up to the table. After they'd finished dessert, John said that he was so stuffed that he wasn't sure if he could drive back to Little Rock. Everyone laughed at that comment. The sisters left the table and began gathering their things together to begin the journey back. Exchanging telephone numbers and hugs, all promised to stay in touch with each other.

"Thanks for having us, Elmira," Mother said, as they embraced. "Your hospitality, as always, has been great. Being here did my soul good, even for a little while."

"You know you're welcome here anytime, sugah," Elmira laughed. "Come back anytime you want to. Our family's saying is that you can *always* come back home to Arkansas," she said, smiling brightly.

During the drive back to Little Rock, Mother asked if they could change the reservations and return to Chicago the next day.

"Are you sure you're feeling well?" Marsha asked, lightly. "You aren't holding out on us or anything, are you?"

"Actually, I feel fine. I had a secret purpose for taking this trip," Mother answered. "No, make that two. One, I wanted to see the home place one more time, and the second being, I was hoping you two would mend your differences so I could see my girls behaving like sisters, like you should've been all along."

"We're working on the sister relationship," Marsha promised, properly chastened.

Soon, they were back in the hotel. With Mother ensconced in bed and snoring, Marty called the airline and changed their return flight to the next day. John called the car rental company and told them he'd be returning the car the next morning. Marsha called Howard to inform him of the change of plans and asked him to call Melinda and have her get in touch with Dr. Williams to make an appointment for Mother on Monday. Instead of everyone meeting them at the airport as previously planned, Marsha suggested that just he and Cloris come. She gave him the flight number and arrival time. They hung up, saying they'd see each other the next day.

Marsha and Marty were in the sitting room watching television when Mother called to them from the bedroom.

"Is John with you? If not, would you please ask him to the room."

Marty dialed his room, relaying Mother's request, and he was knocking at the door in a matter of seconds.

"No, I feel fine. And no, I'm not dying, not yet anyway," Mother said teasingly, after they were all seated in the sitting room. "I wanted us to talk about what lies ahead. First, I want to say that everyone has been wonderful these past months. I know this hasn't been easy on any of you, especially Marsha Ann," she said, glancing briefly at her. "Things have progressed pretty much the way I hoped they would and now I feel I can let go. Sister Patterson has a copy of my will. In case you didn't know, Attorney Harris at church drew it up for me. Melinda is my executor. I have some money in the bank, not a lot, and some stock your father got from his job. The money and stock, I'd like split between the grandchildren. The house and insurance money, I'm leaving to all three of you to do with as you like. I'd really like to keep the house in the family though. John, your boys promised me to keep it in good condition."

Marty and Marsha's eyes shone with unshed tears. John looked down.

"Oh no," Mother said, "I won't have that, no tears for me. I know Dr. Williams has explained everything to you, as he has to me. I have no regrets about the way I've led my life. By and large, it's been wonderful. I wouldn't trade it with anyone. I'm so proud to be your mother."

John moved away from the sofa, walked over to the chair Mother was sitting in and hugged her.

"Mother," said Marty, choking up, "we're equally proud God chose you to be our mother." The women walked across the room to their mother and hugged her.

"Now, back to business," she said, after wiping her eyes on the corner of her blouse. "Cloris helped me write out my obituary, please follow it. All of you have made good choices as far as your spouses are concerned. Cloris and Howard aren't just my in-laws, they're my children. Marty, I'd like you to bring Bunny by to see me soon."

"Mother," Marty said, choking up, her face red, "what do you know about Bunny?"

"Let's say we've talked and leave it at that," Mother said, winking at her. "I also left Lillian, who you all know as Mother Patterson, a few pieces of my jewelry. She's been my sister in Christ and the best friend a person could have. Any questions?" she asked, her eyes glistening with tears, serene with herself.

"All I can say is you never cease to amaze me," John said, shaking his head. "Now why don't we order one of those room service meals?" Then he turned to Marty with a quizzical look on his face, and asked, "Who is Bunny? Why am I always the last one to find something out? Must be cause I'm the youngest child," he complained.

Marsha and Marty laughed at his grumbling, as if they'd reverted back to childhood.

The trip home was uneventful and they landed safely back at Midway Airport the following afternoon. As Marsha had requested, only Howard and Cloris awaited them when they passed through the gates. They whisked Mother home and put her to bed. As they sat at the dining room table drinking coffee, Cloris asked curiously how things had gone.

"Very well," Marty said. "Mother just laid it out in her incomparable style. She informed us how she wants things done and implied in no uncertain terms that we have no choice but to do so."

"Now that's the truth," Marsha said, smiling.

"She is truly a grand lady," John mused.

Later, the rest of the family stopped over to visit. Melinda informed Marsha that Mother had an appointment with Dr. Williams at ten o'clock in the morning.

The next day, Marty, Marsha, Melissa and Cloris accompanied her to the hospital. While Melinda helped Mother get dressed after the examination, the sisters talked to Dr. Williams.

"It won't be long now, will it?" Marsha asked, sadly.

"No," he answered, gently, "not too long. I'd say about another month or so."

"I just wish she could stay around long enough for another Christmas," she moaned.

"Don't be selfish, Marsha," Marty admonished.

"You're right," she said, putting up her hand. "It's just that I know the hardest part is yet to come."

"You'll be okay," Dr. Williams said, "because you have each other to lean on. I've never seen a family react as positively as yours has in the face of adversity. My hat goes off to you all. Your father and mother raised an exceptional family."

"That they did," Cloris seconded.

twelve

And that is where they are nine months later. After they returned from Arkansas, Mother's health began failing just as Dr. Williams predicted. Though it tore them up, the family tried to remain upbeat. Most days it was a difficult task. It felt like someone had taken scissors to their bodies, removing their hearts piece by piece.

The women had been at the hospital all the time those last days it seemed, talking to and just being close to Mother. Felicia and Janis surprised her with a new wig. She was so pleased with their choice that she asked to be buried in it.

"I want to look good," Mother joked, "when I see John Sr. again. Of course, he might not recognize me."

Rev. Davis came by to pray and visit, offering untiring support and prayers. Church members dropped in to pay their respects to the amazing woman that was Anna Smith.

Melinda, Janis or Felicia brought Mother Patterson to the hospital almost every day. She insisted on being with her *"best sister friend"* as often as she could. The grandchildren and great-grandchildren were in and out of the hospital those last days as well.

Marsha was the last one to leave that evening, kissing Mother on her forehead, telling her that she'd see her the next morning. Mother had begun her journey home, as she would call it, and her condition worsened, rendering her comatose. Marsha tried hard to be strong because she knew that's what Mother wanted, but she felt like her heart was being smashed into a million pieces and stepped on in the process. Somehow, she managed to make it through the day and back home that night. Then she received the call early the next morning. Marty, John and Cloris were already on their way to the hospital for the final time.

When they arrived, Dr. Williams explained he'd kept her on life support until they could get to the hospital and he suggested compassionately that it was time to take her off and let her go. The women began crying uncontrollably. Marsha kept repeating over and over that she wasn't ready to let her go. Marty held tightly to Mother's hand, as if she couldn't let it go, and shook her head sadly. John sat down in the chair in his usual place next to Mother, his head bowed down and tears dripping from his face. Howard kept clearing his throat as the tears fell from his eyes. Cloris stood behind John, keeping a close eye on him.

"Give us a minute to detach the equipment," Dr. Williams said, "and then you can come back in and stay with her."

They stood in the hallway outside her door, a miserable crowd. Before long, the nurse opened the door, giving them the okay to come back into the room. They all crowded around the bed, every emotion, sadness, pain, agony and anguish showing on their faces.

Mother's breathing slowed down, the inhalations and exhalations taking longer and longer to complete its cycle. All they could do was look at her and hold a hand or corner of her gown. Marsha caressed her cheek, and finally there was only silence in the room. The nurse pronounced the time of death and expressed her sympathy. Mother had left them, her family. She'd gone on to glory to be with her beloved John, her mother, father and siblings.

"Goodbye, Mother," Marsha whispered, choking up as the reality of the situation began to hit her. "You've earned your rest. We'll miss you, lady. You were truly one of a kind."

"Let's go," said Marty, her voice trembling with emotion. She brushed a tear away quickly with a shaking hand and then reached for Marsha's hand with her other. "It's time to make our calls."

Michelle Larks is a wife, mother of two beautiful daughters, and a computer programmer in the data processing industry. She is a life long resident of The Windy City and was recently named most distinguished resident in Bolingbrook, Illinois.

Her love and passion for writing prompted her to write her first book "A Myriad of Emotions" which was released in March of 2003 to critical acclaim. Michelle's other published work is a poem, "Land of the Free, Home of the Brave", a series compilation published by the International Society of Poetry. Michelle is hard at work on her next book "Peaches & Cream" which is her most creative work to date.